PRAISE FOR *THE EDI...*

'*The Edinburgh Skating Club* is an engaging read, in which discussions about art, politics, love and gender are woven deftly into the plot'
The Scotsman

'A pacy tale traversing both eighteenth-century and modern-day Edinburgh'
Dundee Courier

'In this playful and poignant offering of historical fiction, Sloan celebrates love and the unsung contributions of women to Scottish culture ... both heart-breaking and enchanting in equal measure'
Press and Journal

'Sloan incrementally builds up a plot of some complexity and provides an enjoyable symmetry between period and modern scenes'
Historical Novel Society

'History, humour, and plenty of heart, in a slice of Edinburgh heritage served up with more than one unexpected twist. Perfect for fans of Alexander McCall Smith, art lovers and anyone who loves the capital'
Highland News and Media

'As fascinating and pleasurable as I could have hoped ... Embedded in sound historical research, this is a feel-good read which tackles issues of sexism through the ages without ever taking itself too seriously'
Ali Bacon

'Most impressive and a delight to read'
University of Edinburgh Journal

A Note on the Author

Michelle Sloan trained as a primary school teacher and studied drama and arts journalism. She is the author of several books for children. Her adult fiction debut was *The Edinburgh Skating Club*, published by Polygon in 2022. Originally from Edinburgh, Michelle now lives in Broughty Ferry with her family.

MRS BURKE
&
MRS HARE

Michelle Sloan

Polygon

First published in 2025 by Polygon,
an imprint of Birlinn Ltd.

Birlinn Ltd
West Newington House
10 Newington Road
Edinburgh
EH9 1QS

www.polygonbooks.co.uk

1

Copyright © Michelle Sloan, 2025

The right of Michelle Sloan to be identified as the author of this work has been asserted in accordance with the Copyright, Designs and Patents Act 1988.

All rights reserved.

ISBN 978 1 84697 680 3
eBook ISBN 978 1 78885 718 5

LOTTERY FUNDED

The publisher acknowledges support from the National Lottery through Creative Scotland towards the publication of this title.

A catalogue record for this book is available on request from the British Library.

Typeset by Initial Typesetting Services, Edinburgh

MIX
Paper | Supporting
responsible forestry
FSC® C018072

Printed and bound in Great Britain by Clays Ltd, Elcograf S.p.A.

For Mary Paterson, Jamie Wilson, Madgy Docherty, Abigail Simpson, Joseph, Effy, Elizabeth and Margaret Haldane, Mrs Hostler, Ann M'Dougal and the many other victims of the Burkes and the Hares whose names have been lost to history.

Prologue

Cowgate, Edinburgh, 1837

The boy carefully packs seventeen tiny coffins into the basket, making sure to handle them with the reverence they deserve. Each one is the size of his own hand, intricately carved in wood with a miniature figure inside wearing hand-stitched clothes. His father had made the coffins and the clothes with scraps of wood and cloth, over many nights, his eyes straining in guttering candlelight. But the boy had helped to dress each figure; his father said his deft wee fingers would manage better than his muckle old ones. After they were clothed, he was allowed to lay them down to rest inside their boxes. Then, they said a blessing as the tiny lids were placed on top and hammered into position, ready for burial.

Now, the basket is full, and the boy watches as his father covers them with a cloth, carefully tucking in the sides to protect them from the weather, before looping the basket over his arm and swinging a shovel onto his shoulder.

The man heads out into the street, turns and looks back. 'Well, are you coming?' he shouts.

The boy doesn't wait to be asked twice. He grabs his hat and dashes out to join him.

There's a murky filth about the streets of Edinburgh's Old Town today. The rain is pelting down; everything is dark and greasy. The streets are empty, bar the usual wandering pigs and chickens, as those who can shelter inside. Father and son walk in silence, side by side, winding their way through the dripping streets until they reach the mist-shrouded outline of Arthur's Seat, the ancient volcano that looms over the city. The rain doesn't ease as they climb the steep hill, and the boy wonders how much further they must go. On and on they walk until his sodden feet ache. He wants to complain, to tell his father how much he would like to stop and go home, but he knows better than to say anything. This is too important. They have been waiting for this moment for as long as he can remember.

Finally, reaching an open stretch of grassland, the man stops. 'Here. This is a good place,' he says. 'It's peaceful, don't you think?'

'Aye, it is that,' says the boy, turning slowly to observe the bleakness of their surroundings.

It is indeed a desolate spot, far away from the noise and stench of the Old Town, which peeps through the soaking cloud that envelops them.

'You can sit a moment while I dig,' says the man.

The boy eyes the wet grass, wondering where exactly he should put himself, but he spies a craggy rock and perches on it, hunched against the weather.

His father begins to dig; it is hard work as the earth is cold and tight. The boy watches as drops of sweat form on his father's mottled brow and fall along with the rain that trickles down his hat in rivers onto the ground.

The boy puts out a hand and feels the rain pitter-patter on his palm. He looks up to the grey sky and opens his mouth, hoping to catch drops on his tongue.

'Look at me, Father, I'm having a drink,' he says, and resumes his pose, face upwards, mouth wide. But the man doesn't look up from his digging.

'Right, son. It's time. Bring us the basket, would you?'

The boy hops off the rock and carries the basket over to the fresh grave.

'You can do this bit,' says the man. 'I need a rest. That killed my back.' He looks tired now, and he plants himself on the very rock where his boy had been sitting.

The boy nods and kneels. He solemnly lifts the cloth from the basket and begins to place the coffins in the grave. 'They'll not all fit,' he says, looking up at his father.

'Two layers should be fine,' says the man, rubbing his aching sides. 'See what you can do, son.'

The boy smiles. He is pleased to have command over this important moment. He positions the coffins close together and finds that eight neatly cover the ground. He looks at his work and is satisfied. Then he continues with the next layer and places another eight exactly on top. There is just one left. He thinks about it. The one on the top should be her. But she is already in the row below. He knows which one she is, though, so he swaps them. Her coffin is a little bit smarter than the others, with special pins nailed in to make it different, so they could do something for her, even in death – even though this is just a doll version of her. Her clothes are made from the finest fabric.

The boy places her coffin on the top, across the others. 'That's your ma on the top,' he says to his father.

The man nods. 'Good lad,' he says. 'That's fitting.'

The boy tweaks the placement of the coffins, to make sure they are straight and snug. 'All done,' he says, rubbing his hands together to try to warm them. The damp air has crept into his bones.

The man hauls himself up and walks over. He crouches beside the boy.

'Do you think it will work, Father?'

'Work, son? What do you mean, work?'

'Does this mean they'll go to Heaven now? Your ma and all the others?'

'I hope so, son. Aye, I hope so,' says the man quietly.

They take off their hats. The man closes his eyes and begins to speak, and the boy copies him, dipping his chin to his chest. He tries hard to concentrate on the meaning of the words, squeezing his eyes tight so that God knows he is trying his very best.

'O God, by Whose mercy the faithful departed find rest,' says the man, 'send Your Holy Angel to watch over this grave, through Christ our Lord. Amen.'

'Amen,' echoes the boy. He looks up to his father, who meets his eyes and nods. The boy pulls something from his coat pocket – a small cloth package. He has been waiting for this moment. He unwraps the bundle, and there, tucked inside, is a tiny dried flower. He bites his lip – he has forgotten the words. The rain is now lashing down, stinging his face, and he screws up his eyes.

'We commit their bodies …' begins his father, prompting the boy to remember. He spent so long learning these lines. The boy takes a deep breath. 'We commit their bodies to the ground,' he says, 'earth to earth, ashes to ashes, dust to dust.' Then he places the flower on top of the tiny coffin. 'In sure and certain hope of the Resurrection to eternal life, through our Lord Jesus Christ.'

'The Lord bless them and keep them,' says the man, head bowed. Then he picks up some of the freshly dug earth and scatters it carefully on top of the coffins. The boy joins in, and soon a mound of sticky wet soil covers the grave. Their hands are as filthy as the ground itself.

'There's no gravestone, Father,' says the boy.

'No matter,' says the man. 'God won't notice. He'll just be glad they're finally at peace.'

The boy presses a handful of small stones into the soft dirt in the shape of a cross. 'That's better,' he says. 'They need a cross at least.'

The man nods and rests back on his heels. 'It's done, lad. We can't undo the terrible things that happened in the past,' he murmurs, 'but we can help to smooth the path onwards for these unfortunate souls. And we'll never forget.'

The boy looks at his father. His head is lowered and his eyes are wet – with tears or rain, or both, he doesn't know. He puts a hand on his father's arm. 'No, Father, I will never forget,' he says quietly.

'Never forget,' repeats the man solemnly, wrapping an arm around the boy's shoulder. 'Remember always.'

PART I
Edinburgh, 1827

Chapter 1

There's an artery that clings to the side of the skull, and when anger rages within, it pulsates like a snake. For Margaret Laird, it is a recurring feature on her waspish face. She feels anger and rage at the slightest provocation, and with it comes violent retribution, a reaction to her as natural as blinking.

Margaret's provocateur this time is a fellow navvy on the Union Canal, a man she doesn't know, who is faceless and nameless to her, who has muttered something scurrilous. Likely a trivial remark – something or nothing, but it's the *way* he said it. And she won't have it. She immediately shifts the grip on her shovel and with an almighty whack knocks the man across the back of his legs. The force is enough to slam him to the ground, where he shrieks like a suffering animal. Margaret remains silent; her face is expressionless apart from the steady thrum of blood pulsing through that artery. The man, shocked, scrabbles and slithers in the mud, twisting his head upward to see his attacker. Margaret raises her shovel above her head as though she is about to decapitate the poor fellow. But before she can strike, two hands the size of spades themselves wrestle her arms down to her sides. Her shovel falls to the ground and her cap is dislodged, revealing long, crow-black, tangled hair. Only now does her face reveal her rage. Her green eyes bulge with fury, and she spits like a cat, lashing wildly as another man steps in to help restrain her. The two men struggle to drag her away as she thrusts her neck and torso forward in an attempt to break free. The other labourers stand and gawp; a kind of fascinated silence hangs in the air. They are used to fights; they are a welcome distraction from the drudgery of their days. But a *woman* in their midst, here in plain sight, attacking a *man*? That wasn't such a pretty sight. They shake their heads, but some are impressed, awestruck even, by the gall of the woman.

The victim on the ground, still writhing in agony, suddenly lets forth a stream of obscenities. Margaret lets out a vicious laugh; she is enjoying this too much. With a sudden violent twist, she breaks free from the men's grip, runs forward and boots the man with all her might below the ribs, right in his kidney before launching a neat ball of spittle into his wretched face.

'You should watch your mouth,' she sneers.

'Get that woman out of here,' bellows the foreman, storming over. 'If she is one. No women are allowed here – certainly not a savage creature like her.'

The two men reach forward and grab Margaret once more, struggling to restrain her.

'Let me go,' she snarls. 'I'm done.'

They pull her back to where they deem it is safe, and when they sense that the wrath that had engulfed her has now passed, they release her. She stumbles and quickly straightens herself, then puts her hands on her hips and glares at the man she has attacked. She spits on the ground this time, as if expelling the last of the venom, then drags the back of her hand across her mouth.

Her victim, still rolling in the dirt, wails and clasps his mangled legs. No one attends him. The foreman peers down at him and gives him another kick as if that will snap him out of it.

'Are you fit to work, man?' he shouts.

The reply is more wailing.

'Get him out of here.' The foreman snaps his fingers at two navvies standing like ghouls nearby. They haul the fellow up, but it's obvious he can't use his legs. They manoeuvre him to the edge of the pit they've been digging and shove him up the bank.

'Back to work, all of you,' hollers the foreman. 'If you want paid, that is.'

The men slowly return to shovelling the dense soil, the sound of their labours drowning out the pitiful sobs from the injured man. The foreman shoots a glance towards Margaret and the two men who have restrained her. 'Make sure that witch is well away from here before you return to work.'

The taller of the two men attempts to pull her by the arm, but she shakes him off.

'Don't touch me,' she snarls.

'Now, now. None of that. You're a lady, remember,' he says with a wag of his finger. 'And you're a lucky lady too – lucky we held you back. You might have killed the poor bastard, and then where would you be?'

'Lucky for him, not me; he's lucky I didn't leave him cold,' she says, her eyes narrowing at the memory of the insult.

'Then you'd have swung for it. Not so lucky, then,' says the other, stocky man. 'Now move.'

They set off towards town, the clanging of tools fading behind them, the fug and noise of Edinburgh ahead.

'And just how long have you been working there?' says the tall man, eyeing her carefully. 'Had us all fooled. You must have some strength to you, digging like a man.'

'And fighting like one too,' adds the other.

Margaret shrugs. 'You take the work where you can

get it.' She eyes her minders for the first time. The stockier man has weather-worn skin, a deeply lined face and thin, curved lips. He looks as strong as an ox. 'Come have a drink with me,' she says. 'I need one.'

'You buying, are you?' says the tall man.

'Aye,' says Margaret. 'I suppose I owe you.'

'Must be our lucky day,' he replies, pushing back his hat to scratch his head. 'Lucky.' He smiles warily. 'Suits you.'

'If you say so,' says Margaret. 'So, if I'm Lucky, who are you? Peter and Paul, sent to save my soul?'

'I'm Hare,' says the tall man. 'William Hare.'

'Burke,' says the other, touching his hat. 'Also William.'

'Burke and Hare,' says Lucky. 'A fine pair of gents, so you are.'

Chapter 2

Helen McDougal tiptoes down the steep slope of the Vennel. She likes trying to avoid the cracks between the cobbles, her heels never touching the ground. The walk up is one she would rarely attempt; it is such a sharp climb that the effort makes her whole body ache, particularly with a basketful of tatties on her back, but coming down is a different story. She has been hawking her wares at every street corner up and down the Cowgate, up Candlemaker Row, and now with her last potato sold, she is winding her way home. She has deliberately chosen a longer route, so that she can enjoy the thrill of the descent. Above her stands the mighty castle – the silent, all-seeing eye that observes the ants scurrying up and down each close and wynd: the vendors and the whores, the barefoot children and the fishwives all going about their lives in the wretched slums of old Edinburgh. Helen doesn't notice the castle any more. She has become used to its omnipresence and instead concentrates on the careful placing of her downward steps. With her basket now empty, there is nothing to anchor her thin, birdlike body, and she looks as though the wind which swirls wildly in the narrow passageway might lift her skirts and toss her upwards like a rag doll, to wave and swing with the washing strung out above her head.

At the very bottom of the hill, the Grassmarket opens out in front of her. Still busy with sellers trying to rid themselves of the last of their wares, their calls and shouts are interrupted by the lowing cattle waiting to be slaughtered for the morning's market. Helen is about to head left towards the West Port and her lodgings when she sees her man across the street. William Burke is coming out of the White Hart Inn, and another woman, a tall young woman, is at his side. Helen stands frozen to the spot. She is confused. He shouldn't be here; he should be at work at the canal. And Helen has never seen this woman before. She watches them as they laugh and chat – there is an easy familiarity between them. The young woman leans close to William's ear, whispering something, and then touches him lightly on the arm. Helen bites her lip hard. She won't stand for it! She strides across the Grassmarket, no longer on tiptoe, until William is directly in front of her. She says nothing but punches him hard on the arm. He swings around, startled, a fist clenched, but then his eyes soften and a smile stretches across his red face.

'Nelly!' he says, his eyes dancing and swirling. His breath reeks.

'Who's she?' snaps Helen, now glaring up at the woman, who folds her arms. Helen sees that the stranger's face is sharp-boned, pretty even, but her eyes are hard and cold, a single eyebrow raised.

'Now, now, this is my new friend, Lucky,' says Burke with a tipsy drawl. 'Lucky, this is my Nelly.' He puts a protective arm around her.

'I'm his wife,' says Helen. 'Sort of,' she adds quietly.

'Is that right?' Lucky replies with a smirk. 'Well, let me tell you, we've all got one of those. A *sort-of-husband*.' Then she laughs loudly.

Burke joins in, chuckling along with her.

Helen feels herself stiffen. She wants to meet Lucky's stare, but this woman scares her, and she looks away.

Another man staggers out of the inn to join them. He comes to a stop beside Lucky but struggles to steady himself. Helen frowns and then softens a little. Perhaps, she thinks to herself, this is Lucky's man. Perhaps she was wrong to think badly of her William.

'Who's she?' asks the man, jabbing a wavering finger in Helen's direction.

'His wife,' says Lucky, still staring at Helen. 'She's mighty quick to tell you, too. A right little firecracker, that one.'

'Why aren't you at the canal, William?' stammers Helen.

'Oh-ho,' scoffs Lucky. 'Watch out, Burke. You're in trouble now with your sort-of-wife.'

'Well, now, Nelly, Hare and I had a little bit of trouble we had to sort out, with Lucky here,' says Burke, patting Helen's hand, but she sees him give Lucky a tiny wink and she feels heat rising in her face. As if sensing this, Burke quickly snatches up her hand and squeezes it. 'Nothing for you to worry about, sweetheart. Now, then, did you sell all those tatties?' He glances towards the basket.

'Aye,' says Helen. She is wary. She knows where this is headed.

'Good lass,' he says. 'Well, now, let's go and have a drink to celebrate.' He leers down at her. 'What you got there in your pocket?'

'Oh, William, are you sure?' says Helen. 'Don't we need to keep it back?' She reluctantly puts her hand in her pocket and fishes out the pennies she has collected.

Burke, Hare and Lucky all peer at the meagre number of coins in Helen's grimy palm.

'That should do it,' says Hare.

'Come on, little Nelly,' says Burke, planting a kiss on

her cheek. 'Just the one, now. It's good to share our fortune, be it a small one, with good friends.'

She looks up at him suspiciously. These people are not good friends – she's never seen them before, and there's something about them that troubles her – but surely William must know best. She gazes at him and wishes she could lift her hand to trace her fingers over his cheeks and rough beard. 'If you say so, William.'

'That's my Nelly. After all, what use is tomorrow if we can't enjoy today?' Burke grins.

'Yes, of course, you're right, William,' she says, 'and besides, there's more tatties to be sold tomorrow, I'm sure of that.'

'My, my, how touching.' Lucky rolls her eyes. She links her arm through Hare's and sets off down the street. 'Now that everything's settled, come back to my house. I'm just down on Tanner's Close,' she shouts back. 'She can buy a bottle on the way.'

Chapter 3

Warmed and cheered by whisky, the merry group sit by the glow of a meagre fire in the lowly lodging house owned by Lucky and her husband, John. Burke, perched on a low stool, plays a joyful tune on a flute as shadows dance on the walls like puppets. Helen dances, all twirling skirts, spins and curtseys, with Donald, an old soldier, who throws his feet in a merry jig and then doffs his hat, sweeping it down to the floor in an exaggerated bow. The others clap and throw their heads back in laughter; they stamp their feet and punch the air. There is much clinking of cups, drinking toasts to this and that, whatever they can think of to keep the merriment alive lest the chill of the night creep into their bones and their souls. The flickering light of the cruisie oil lamps, reeking with acrid fumes, distorts their shining faces into grotesque masks that grin and gurn as they consume more and more of the fiery spirit, easier to procure than water.

Burke finishes the melody with a long flourish and, putting the flute down, reaches for a dram.

'Again, again, William!' cries Helen, her eyes bright, sweat gleaming on her brow. She lands heavily on his lap and curls her bony body to nuzzle her face into his neck. He places his cup on the table and wraps his arms around her.

'Oh, but now I've stopped,' she murmurs, 'I don't think I can get up again.' She says this in a childlike voice and then lifts her eyes to look at Burke. He strokes her hair, wrapping sweaty ringlets in his fingers, and smiles drowsily.

The sound of coughing and a painful, dry wheezing comes from the corner. 'I can dance no more. I'm done for,' wails Helen's dance partner. He collapses on the mucky straw bed in the corner of the room and places his hat over his face. It's not long before he is snoring loudly.

'Aye, Donald is very nearly done for, that's for sure,' mutters Lucky, reaching over to pour herself another drink. She sits back and puffs on her pipe. 'Don't die before you've paid your rent, mind,' she shouts over, smoke curling from her lips. Then she takes a gulp from her cup and swallows slowly, eyeing Helen sitting on Burke's lap. She sucks on her pipe and watches as

Helen and William giggle conspiratorially, their heads pressed together, almost as one.

'And where do you lay your weary head at night, Mr Burke?' Lucky enquires.

'We stay at Mickey Culzean's place,' says Helen.

Lucky lets out a mocking laugh. 'The Beggars' Hotel? That hellhole! You sleep well with the rats and the whores, do you? They say the walls are crawling with bugs and lice.'

'No,' retorts Helen. 'It's not like that, is it, William? It's a clean place for decent folk. Isn't it, William?'

She pokes him, and he sleepily scratches his head under his hat. 'It's not the finest,' he concedes. 'But it's not the worst either. And it's cheap.'

'Is that so? How many folk in your room?' asks Lucky.

'Not many,' says Helen. 'Is there, William?'

Burke sits up and, as if suddenly bored, pushes her off his knee. She slithers to the floor beside him but still gazes upwards, gripping his arm.

'I've got a room you can have here,' says Lucky. 'All to yourself, through the way.' She waves a vague hand. 'It's small, but it'll be cheaper than whatever Mickey's charging you.'

Burke rubs his rough chin. 'Is that right?'

Helen frowns. She doesn't know if Lucky is including her in this offer or not. 'William, we don't need to move, do we?' Helen makes a feeble attempt to clamber back onto his lap, but he pushes her aside. 'We're fine at Mickey's.'

Burke leans forward and swills the whisky in his cup. He stares at Lucky, with watery eyes that seem to glow in the candlelight. 'All to myself, you say?'

'Ourselves,' prods Helen, now standing beside him, her hand on his shoulder.

'Well, now, that is something to think about,' says Burke. 'I might have space to mend shoes, and you could hawk them, Nelly?' At this, he places a protective hand over hers. She likes his touch but not his words.

'But why?' Helen says sharply. 'You have a good job at the canal. I don't want to live here, William' – she bends down to loudly whisper – 'with *her*. Why would you want to live here with her? Why, William, why? Tell me.'

Lucky shakes her head. She enjoys watching this stupid, indiscreet woman squirm and plead like a pathetic child, gesticulating and pulling at Burke's arm until, like an angry bear prodded to the limit, he can take no more. He roars at her, and they fall into a loud and bitter squabble.

Lucky puffs on her pipe and turns her gaze towards Hare. He is slumped over the table, his head tucked into his folded arms. His shoulders are wide and muscular. She wants to run her fingers along his naked skin, to feel his warm body under his ragged clothes. She takes a swift gulp of whisky and then stands up.

She walks behind him and begins to rub his shoulders. He moans softly.

'And what about you? You looking for a bed for the night?' she says soothingly.

Blearily, Hare raises his head and looks at Lucky. She grabs at his hair, pulling his head back, so his neck stretches long and exposed. Her finger circles his Adam's apple.

'I'll make you comfortable,' she says and then leans down and kisses his mouth. He grins and licks the whisky from his lips.

'Oh, Mags could make you comfortable all right,' says a voice. 'But it'll cost you.'

John Logue, Lucky's husband, stands in the doorway, his eyes burning with rage. Then, in an instant, all hell breaks loose. He springs forward and kicks the leg of the chair on which Hare is still sitting. Like everything else in their house, the chair is rotten and so it collapses immediately, taking Hare with it, who lands on the floor with a grunt. Logue grabs his wife by the hair and yanks it hard, so she gasps in pain and falls to her knees. He leans down, still gripping her hair until it stretches tight from her scalp, and whispers in her ear, 'Stop your whoring around, woman. It does you no favours.'

Lucky says nothing. John releases her with a flourish and she falls forward onto all fours where, like a dog, she remains, panting heavily. Eventually, she sits back on her heels and then stands and brushes down her clothes. The room is quiet. Burke and Helen have stopped shouting, spectators of this dismal scene. Hare is sprawled on the floor, too drunk to retaliate or even get up, and John Logue now takes a seat by the fire, glaring at his wife. He grabs the bottle of whisky and drains it into a chipped cup, taking an angry swig.

Lucky calmly walks to the table and picks up her pipe. She sits down and quietly, methodically, empties out the ash, and next refills it from a rusty tin, pressing the wisps of tobacco into the clay bowl. Then, she takes a taper and lights it from the candle, transferring the flame to the pipe which she now grips in her teeth. She puffs and inhales as the tobacco catches. John and Burke begin to talk, and Lucky wanders over to the far wall, as if to smoke her pipe in private. But rather than smoke it, unseen she holds the bowl of the pipe over the flame of an oil lamp until it burns red-hot. Then, silently, she walks over to where John sits, now chatting animatedly with Burke. From behind, she wraps an arm tightly around his neck, as though to kiss him, but instead swiftly presses the scalding pipe bowl against his cheek. Her husband shrieks as his skin melts. He waves his arms wildly, flapping like a helpless bird, trying to stop her, desperate to stop the pain. But Lucky only smiles and grips him tighter.

'Stop squealing like a pig, John,' she sneers. 'It does you no favours.'

Chapter 4

Lucky does not grieve for her husband; his death was a blessed relief when it came. The wound on his face from the pipe burn became a festering sore, and then inevitably infection crept in and raged like wildfire through his body. She enlisted the help of Hare to shift her ailing husband to the cellar lest his ruined features be misread by the tenants as a sign of pestilence in the house. Feverish, writhing and calling out in agony, John Logue lay in the dark in his own sweat and reek, for days. Lucky had ignored his cries. She cared not. Finally, John succumbed, and the suffering for all was over.

No, grieve she does not. But, for the sake of propriety, Lucky does mourn, loudly and publicly. Now, on the morning of the burial, a frigid, dreich November day when the sun barely rises, she dresses as carefully as she can with the little clothing she owns and makes sure to clutch a handkerchief in her hand, ready to dab her dry eyes. She arranges her face in such a way as to appear sorrowful then joins a handful of mourners, some supplied for a small fee by the church, to walk behind the cart through the grubby West Port streets, circumnavigating the Castle Rock to St Cuthbert's churchyard. With the elegant, clean streets of the New Town only spitting distance away, she is pleased that she paid the extra required to ensure a better quality of mortcloth was draped over the cheap coffin; the shoddy palls were reserved only for paupers.

She has not been to St Cuthbert's for some years. Deaths in the lodging house, when they occurred, were usually of little interest to her as most of the tenants were drifters, moving in accordance with their labour being needed. As long as tenants paid up, they could live or die as far as she was concerned; if they did happen to die under her roof, their families or the church took care of the rest. But now, standing in this cold, damp place amongst the skeletal trees, with the dead under her feet, she considers, for the first time in a long while, her Maker. She had little time for Him. After all, despite her baptism and her fervent belief as a child, He had had little time for her. When had God ever answered *her* prayers? Standing here with the slums of the Old Town to her right and the opulence of the New Town on her left, it occurs to her that all folk end up in the same small patch of ground in death. The Holy Trinity didn't alter the hard scrabble of her life. Praying as hard as you could was a waste of time: it brought you neither food nor clothes. It didn't bring you the warmth and solace that a bottle of liquor could. The only thing that had the almighty power to make your life better was money.

She has rarely considered her own death, or indeed what lies beyond. If in life there was such a divide between the rich and the poor, then who was to say it wouldn't be the same in death? Like mortcloths, you would only get as close to Heaven as your status allowed. And status was determined by money: no amount of pitiful supplication to God was going to change that. If money bought you a place in Heaven, then Lucky knew she was already on her way to Hell.

Staring at the gaping hole in the ground before her, she knows how it ends – as food for the worms, and fresher bodies piled on top.

With the coffin now interred, two gravediggers, one old, the other a young lad, perhaps his son, begin to dig in a steady rhythm from a mound of earth, flinging soil over John Logue's flimsy box and many others in the same grave, ready for the next layer. Lucky finds herself standing alone now, watching, as if overseeing that it is done properly. Her expression appears to be one of quiet contemplation, as if wistfully reflecting on her husband's life, their time together, but in fact she is wondering now of the risk to his body in death. She has heard that the resurrectionists are busy on dark Edinburgh nights, supplying fresh bodies to those men at the medical school. The anatomists, they were called.

'Have there been bodysnatchers here recently?' she asks the diggers.

'Two nights ago,' says the old man, not even raising his head to look at Lucky. 'Tried to dig up a grave of a young boy. Imagine that.'

'How many of them?' she asks.

'It was a gang,' he continues, happy to stop and rest. He thrusts his spade into the earth beside him and rests his arm on the handle. His face is creased and haggard, and a drip hangs from the end of his nose. He rubs his brow with a grimy hand.

'And? Did they succeed?' pushes Lucky.

He shakes his head. 'The family gave chase. They were keeping vigil, over there in the watchtower.' He points to the far corner of the churchyard to a circular structure, almost obscured by some trees. 'They'll not be back,' he says. 'With all the dead coming in every day and so many families keeping watch, it's not worth the risk. There's other graveyards to try. Other places too. I hear they'll go as far as Dundee for a body.' He returns to his digging.

She is about to leave the graveside when a thought

enters her head. 'How much money do they get?' she asks. 'Must be a considerable amount for them to even try.'

'They say those men pay eight pounds a body,' he says. He shakes his head in something like horror, or envy, perhaps both.

Lucky's eyes widen. 'Eight pounds, you say?' She considers this. This is more than she earns in a month. A fleeting image of herself leaping into the hole and hauling out her husband's coffin to take the body to be sold flits across her mind. Or, better still, getting someone else to do it. But then there was the question of that hideous burn on his face. Would 'those men' know what had caused it? Would there be too many questions? Perhaps, like her, they wouldn't care.

She turns to leave the churchyard.

'What do they do?' she overhears the young boy say, his voice full of wonder. 'With the bodies?'

Lucky pauses, listening intently to his reply, although she knows the answer.

'What do they do? Hack them to pieces, that's what they do,' says the old man with a cackle. 'Like butchers, they are. While the young students watch.' He says this as though taking great pleasure from it. His voice is loud, and she realises he is well aware that she is within earshot. He wants her to hear.

'They peel back the skin and pull everything out,' he bellows with glee.

There is no reply, and she can imagine the young lad's face. She hears them settling once more into the steady rhythm of digging the soil into the grave.

'It's the Devil's work,' the lad finally says. 'All of it.'

Ah, but working for the Devil brings its rewards, thinks Lucky with a smile as she heads homeward.

Chapter 5

'Will you read to me, William?' Helen whispers.

They lie together on a threadbare blanket that covers their straw mattress. The room is dark, lit only by a cruisie lamp on the wall that intermittently hisses and spits and a spindly candle on a low table beside them. They are not alone in the room; other lodgers, maybe five or six of them, shift and snore in their miserable rags. Over time, living this way, Helen and Burke have learned to ignore the strangers they are forced to share their life with, and make their own little world together.

'Which book shall we read from tonight, then, Nelly?' asks Burke.

They own four, including a Bible. Helen, who can't read, found herself in possession of the books when her first man died. She sits up and reaches for them beside her on the floor. Although she cannot decipher the strange shapes of the words on the spines, she knows each book by the colour of its thick cover and the patterns or engravings in gold. She likes to run her fingers over the bindings, and sometimes she inhales the scent from the pages; they are dusty and comforting. She has been told they are all books about Jesus and God; her most favourite of them is a story called *The Pilgrim's Progress* – and it is the one she reaches for the most. This is the book she passes to William. Its pictures entrance her. She likes to gaze at the image of Christian with the great weight on his back. During her long working days, she thinks of this as she hauls her huge basket of potatoes or whatever she is hawking. Perhaps, she wonders, she is like Christian, carrying the burden of the 'knowledge of her sin'. She isn't sure exactly what sins she is carrying but she's sure she has many. God hadn't ever really been part of her life, not until she met William. He speaks of God being with them, and the Virgin Mary too, watching over them. They pray together and ask for guidance. William, she had learned, was a Catholic. But then his priest told him to leave Helen and go back to his wife and children in Ireland. He refused. He said he loved Helen too much and so the priest told him he wasn't Catholic any more. This caused him great distress, but Helen said he didn't need a priest to speak to God for him: he could read the Bible and all the other books about God and Jesus by himself. She was pleased she said this because it made him smile and he kissed her and thanked her. Sometimes, though, she does wonder about the wife he left behind. And a fierce jealousy creeps over her body like a prickly rash. She imagines them together, her an Irish beauty with red hair and a passionate temper, and Burke kissing her, loving her, their bodies entwined. She wonders if he thinks of her too. And when she feels like this she becomes quite weak and sick to the stomach. But then she reminds herself that he left Ireland and refused to return because of his love for her. They may not be married in God's eyes, but in her heart at least, they are husband and wife.

She focuses on the books in front of her, and even though they are her books, she knows that William treasures them, pores over the words that he says are precious and divine. So she listens to him read to her, trying to understand what these sacred words actually mean.

'Which part do you want me to read?' says Burke. He shuffles up to a sitting position, closer to the candle flame.

'The bit about the – what do they call it? – the slough,' says Helen. 'That's what it's called, isn't it?'

He nods and with his rough fingers begins to thumb

the pages until he finds the place. '*And he said unto me,*' Burke reads slowly, straining his eyes in the poor light. '*This miry slough is such a place as cannot be mended: it is the descent whither the scum and filth that attends conviction for sin doth continually run, and therefore it is called the Slough of Despond; for still, as the sinner is awakened about his lost condition, there ariseth in his soul many fears, and doubts, and discouraging apprehensions, which all of them get together, and settle in this place. And this is the reason of the badness of this ground.*'

'Like a bog?'

'Yes, or a swamp.'

'Is it real, William? This place? And you sink into it, until you cannot breathe?'

'No, Nelly. It's just a story to make us think, but you could say that sin and the guilt of our sin pulls us down. But once we know and accept our sins, we're able to get out of the mire.'

'What if we can't? What if we don't know if we're sinners?' Helen imagines herself forever stuck in that pit of despair, her hand reaching upwards for someone, anyone to pull her out. She imagines the wet mud filling her mouth and her throat and then her nostrils so that all hope of breath is gone. She gasps in horror and puts her hands over her face.

Burke places a comforting arm around her waist. He shakes his head. 'It's not real, Nelly.'

'But Hell is. Maybe that's where you sink down to?' she says through her fingers.

William sighs and continues reading: *'It is not the pleasure of the King that this place should remain so bad . . .'* He stops suddenly. He sniffs and then looks around, and inhales again, longer and slower.

'What is it?' says Helen.

'I can smell burning. Can you smell it?'

Helen sniffs and then jumps up.

'Yes,' she says quietly.

Burke stands up, grabs the candle and instinctively goes to open the door. Malevolent black smoke roils and billows along the corridor.

'Fire!' he shouts.

'Fire?' says Helen. Then panic sets in. 'Fire, fire!' she screams, and the others in the room are snapped out of their dreams. They immediately begin bundling up their rags, screaming and shoving to get out of the room. But as every overcrowded room begins to empty, there is terrifying chaos. The corridors are crammed with desperate souls forcing and shoving their way through the dense blackness like rats swarming from a sinking ship.

'Nelly, stay with me!' yells Burke. He pulls her to him, and together they push their way out and down the curving tenement stairs in total darkness. There are children bawling, men shouting and women wailing. It is wild and petrifying, and as the smoke burns her eyes and throat, Nelly grips Burke's hand, and she feels him grip hers tight in return for if she were to let go, she would fall and be trampled upon and lost forever.

They continue to battle downwards, stumbling blind, until somehow they make it outside, and pushing through the hordes of people they get to safety and fall to the ground, into the squalor of the street, coughing and wheezing. Burke holds Nelly close to him. They have made it.

'I couldn't breathe,' sobs Helen. She is shaking and coughing and rubbing her blackened hands and face. 'That smoke filling my lungs . . . it was like Hell itself.'

William holds her close. 'You're safe now, Nelly. We both are.'

Up above they hear the building collapsing in on itself, beams and slates, walls and floorboards, already rotten and worn, tumbling, crashing, surrendering to the blaze. And now, somewhere in amongst it all, lie Helen and Burke's books: their precious words alight, the pages curling, consumed by the inferno.

Chapter 6

Some days after the funeral of her husband, Lucky walks the streets of the Old Town alone in her thoughts. She has shed the mask of grief but still has death on her mind, or rather raising the dead. This is not an enterprise she can consider running alone, but with John Logue now gone, Hare is fit and strong and waiting in the wings, ready to slide into the marital bed and eager to make money. For him, running the lodging house is a better wage and easier life than working on the canals or hawking fish. She acknowledges to herself that he is young and lacks the wit of her former husband, and he can be lairy and fiery with drink. But she is used to such behaviour, and, unlike John, Hare is submissive and allows her to have the final word without giving her black eyes. As she heads back to Tanner's Close the sun is setting and the silhouette of a man meets her at the top of the wynd. It is Burke.

As he sees her, he removes his hat. 'Condolences to you,' he says. 'I hear you buried your old man the other day.'

'Aye, I did. Are you stopping in for a drink?' she says. She notices the soot smeared over his face; it has settled into the lines and crevices on his skin.

'Well, now, that would be pleasant,' he says, following her to the lodging house. 'I was going to ask if your offer still stands. Nelly and I need a place to stay. You'll have heard about the fire at Mickey's last night?'

'I did,' she says. 'I'm not surprised. But razing the place to the ground was the best thing for it. Anyone dead?' She asks this with a touch of hope.

'Not as far as I know,' says Burke. 'Everyone managed to get out, which was a mercy.'

'A mercy? Death would've been a kindness to some of the poor souls who inhabit that place.'

They walk into the house, straight into the kitchen. There is no fire burning in the grate as there is nothing to burn, but there is a lamp flickering on the wall, and as daylight is now fading, Lucky lights a candle and places it on the table. She goes to a corner of the room, listens to make sure there's no one else around, and lifts a loose floorboard. Reaching in, she retrieves a bottle. She pulls out the stopper and fills two chipped cups which are sitting on a shelf. She takes a swig, tops it up again and passes Burke the other cup.

'To your dearly departed, may God rest his soul,' says Burke, raising his glass.

'He was a treacherous bastard,' says Lucky. 'Hell mend him.' She knocks back her whisky and refills her cup. She picks up her tobacco tin and sits opposite Burke. She begins filling her pipe but looks up from time to time to see Burke watching her. He has a slight smile on his lips. Then he looks away, shyly almost, and swills the contents of his cup.

'Where's Helen?' asks Lucky.

'Out hawking,' says Burke. 'We lost everything we had in the fire. Apart from my tools which I managed to grab. But everything else, what little we had, is gone. Burnt to cinders like the rest of that tenement.'

'You can stay in that room I told you about. Perhaps it's providence.'

'What? That we nearly died?' Burke smiles incredulously.

Lucky takes a sip of her whisky and savours the fiery burn. A long silence passes between them. 'Somehow, I don't think your sort-of-wife will want to stay here,' she says.

'Well, unless she wants to sleep on the streets with the beggars, we have no choice.'

'What do you think to making eight pounds?' says

Lucky suddenly, watching for his reaction.

Burke frowns. She raises her eyebrows. He laughs. He is handsome when he smiles, she thinks. The slight indent of a dimple appears beneath the soot and stubble on his cheek, and there is a hint of devilry in those blue eyes.

'What about it? That's a tidy sum,' he says.

'That medical school is paying up to eight pounds for dead bodies,' her voice is quiet, steady. 'I heard the gravediggers talking about it. They say that's where the bodysnatchers take their booty.'

Burke sits back and rubs his brow. 'That's a dark way to earn your keep, Lucky. And that amount of money sounds like a tall tale to me.'

Lucky leans forward. 'It's true, William. Eight pounds. Think of that. How long would it take for the likes of you and me to earn that kind of money? You, hacking at frozen earth with a pick for three months. Three months of hard labour? Me, taking in all the waifs and strays, cleaning out their muck like it's a cow shed. Or one body delivered to those men. Eight pounds. Why shouldn't we get our hands on it?'

Burke shifts in his seat. 'Do you really want to go digging up graves? That's dreadful low work, so it is. Heaving the dead from their resting place in the middle of night?'

Lucky rolls her eyes. 'What? Don't tell me you're scared of ghosties and ghouls?'

Burke shakes his head. 'It's not that,' he says. 'Not that at all. They're at *rest*.'

'I don't care about their "resting" place,' she scoffs. Her eyes bulge. 'They're dead! And I'll tell you, William, it's the living you should be worried about. Not the dead. What do they need their bodies for? They're just empty vessels – flesh and bones. They're only going to rot away, become worm food.'

Burke sighs. 'These words, Lucky, should not be spoken.'

Lucky sits back in her seat and puffs on her pipe. 'Shocked you, have I?'

'What about their immortal souls?' he says quietly, rubbing his rough beard.

'What about them?' snaps Lucky. 'Do you think they're attached? The soul and the body? If there even is a soul, it's long gone. Upwards or more likely downwards.'

'Have you been visited by the Devil? Did he come whispering to you in that graveyard? You've just buried your husband and you're talking like this?'

'I see your fear,' says Lucky. 'It's written all over your face. But, no matter, I'll get Hare and someone else.' She waves her hand dismissively.

'If you rip these bodies from the place that's been blessed as their final place of peace, where families have watched them being lowered into the ground,' he falters, 'you are disturbing the dead, interrupting the natural order. Not only is it wrong, Lucky, it's an abomination. I'll not have anything to do with this business – eight pounds or not.' He stands as though he's about to leave. 'But I will take that room. Mending shoes will be my business, Lucky, not robbing graves.'

Lucky tuts. 'I thought there was more to you. You disappoint me.'

Burke is about to reply when Hare wanders into the room. He acknowledges Burke with a nod. 'And what might you two be talking about?' he asks, placing his hands on Lucky's shoulders.

Burke stares at them. And then his face cracks into a knowing smile. 'Ah, I see. You two are together now! Before the bed's even cold, Lucky?' He laughs. 'Needs must, I suppose.'

'It's all above board, Burke,' says Hare smoothly. 'Margaret's going to be my wife. When the time is right.'

'We'll run this place together,' says Lucky, placing a hand over Hare's. 'Burke and his lady companion are going to move into the back room ... to mend shoes,' she adds, with a curl of her lip.

Hare nods and then goes to the shelf to take a cup for himself and fills it from the bottle. 'Take a drink with us,' he says. He refills Lucky's cup and then Burke's.

'Old Donald is dead,' Hare says. 'His heart must've given up in the night. He was as lifeless as a stone this morning. The joiner came when you were out, so he's in his box in the cellar until they come for him in a day or two. The old wretch died owing us four pounds. Died before he claimed his pension.'

'And?' asks Burke.

Hare looks up, wicked mischief on his face. He raises his eyebrows and looks between Lucky and Burke.

'Providence indeed,' says Lucky, her eyes glittering. 'I know exactly what we can do with him.' She leans back in her chair and stares directly at Burke. 'What about snatching a body *before* it's been buried, eh? How does that sit with your precious morals?'

Chapter 7

Three figures, holding candles, silently enter the inky black underworld of the cellar beneath the lodging house, closing the door behind them in case they should be disturbed. The old soldier's corpse lies on the floor, boxed up in his coffin, ready to be collected by the parish for a burial at St Cuthbert's.

'Take the lid off,' says Lucky, holding her candle aloft. Her breath is white in the cold, fetid air. She points to a pile of tools by the wall.

Hare fetches a chisel, slips its smooth edge under the wooden lid and prises it open with little effort. Sliding the lid onto the ground, he pulls back the blanket to reveal Donald's dead dry eyes open, staring. There is a moment of silence. Then Burke takes a long, slow intake of breath. Lucky feels nothing as she gazes upon the dead man. Life has so clearly departed this body;

under the dim candlelight his skin has a yellow waxy sheen and his matted grey hair loops in greasy coils around his sunken cheeks. His mouth has dropped open; his thick, dark tongue rests on toothless gums. A white foam has encrusted the corners of his mouth. His bloated, swollen legs stretch out from under his nightshirt. Burke reaches in and tries to close his eyelids, but it takes too much effort and he gives up.

'Just think of the money,' whispers Lucky. 'Not the person he was or the body he inhabited. Dumping this carcass in a hole in the ground is a waste of what it can do for the living, for those left behind.' She stares at Burke, hoping he sees the sense in this. She needs his aid. 'Eight pounds,' she whispers, gazing at Burke's profile silhouetted and shimmering in the candlelight.

'It makes no difference to old Donald now. But think what it can do for us,' she adds.

Burke's jaw is clenched tight.

'I'm thinking of the money all right,' says Hare. 'The money he owes us, dead or not.'

Burke nods as though resigned to it, puts his candle down and, without saying a word, reaches his hands under the old man's shoulders as Hare moves to grab his feet. They lift with some effort the stiffening body, and as they do so there is an exhalation from Donald, a long moan as though they have disturbed him from a deep sleep.

Lucky steps back in alarm. Hare drops the old man's feet as though they're burning hot. 'What in God's name? Is he still alive?' he gasps.

Burke calmly rests the shoulders and head down on the ground. 'It's just the air coming out. You never seen a dead body?' he says. 'You're a bit jumpy there.'

'Oh, I've seen death aplenty,' says Hare quickly. 'But I've not lingered around to witness what happens afterwards.'

'We need to fill the box with something, so that the weight feels the same,' says Lucky. 'Once the lid is back on and nailed shut, they'll never open it.'

'I'll go and see what I can find in the yard,' says Hare. He picks up his candle and wanders outside.

'Something that won't shift around,' says Lucky after Hare, 'or make a noise.' She grabs an old piece of sacking she has brought from the house and hands it to Burke. 'We'll need to take the body up to the doctors,' she says. 'Tonight. I don't want it lying around here.'

'And where might the doctors be?' says Burke. He lays the sacking on the ground ready to roll the body up.

'It's called Surgeons' Square,' says Lucky. She helps Burke shift Donald into position, and they roll him up in a tight bind of fabric.

'I know where it is, it's not far. I can take you up there. But that's all I know. We need to know *who* we're taking it to,' Lucky says. 'We can't be knocking at doors with a dead body in tow.'

'Now, I might just have the answer to that one,' says Burke. He reaches into his pocket and pulls out a piece of paper. It is a broadside, bought for a penny on the streets. He unfolds it and holds the candle close to the tiny writing on the page.

'Dr Monro,' he says, looking up at Lucky.

'How do you know?' she says.

Burke jabs with a finger at the article. 'It's about a hanging.' But Lucky can't read. She shrugs. 'Monro is the butcher who picks apart the criminals' bodies once they're cut down. I've seen his name there many times,' he explains. 'It's always him.' He folds the paper back up and stuffs it in his pocket. 'He's our man. We just need to be sure of ourselves,' he adds, more to himself.

Hare bursts back into the room, kicking the door open. He is bent low with a sack on his back, which he swings forward over his shoulder and onto the ground. 'Tanner's bark,' he says. 'I found it in the yard. It should be heavy enough, but there's more we can shovel in.'

They tip the sackful of crushed bark into the coffin, spreading the powdered shards evenly into the corners. Then Hare goes back to fill another. Once finished, they try out the weight of the coffin. It is suitably heavy. They cover the bark with the old blanket as though Donald lies beneath, and then Burke hammers the lid back on. Lucky stands at the door, looking out in case they should be disturbed. But no one comes.

'It's done,' says Hare with a smile.

'The tanner's bark will rest in peace,' says Lucky with a smile.

'Now to sell the body,' says Burke. Using the empty sack from the bark, they bundle Donald inside and tie it up tightly with string.

Hare hauls it up and over his shoulder and lets out a groan. 'The weight of him,' he complains.

'Shouldn't we put it in a box or a cart?' says Lucky. 'It looks like what it is. Like you're carrying a body in a sack.'

'I'm just delivering a dead pig, if anyone asks,' says Hare. 'And why would anyone ask?'

They stand and consider this for a moment.

'We have to walk with purpose,' says Lucky. 'Eyebrows will only be raised if we look unsure.'

Burke nods. 'No one will ask,' he decides.

They climb the steps up from the cellar into the backyard and then round the house and up the narrow close. As they emerge onto the street, they see a figure looming out of the darkness, coming towards them. It is Helen.

'William!' she says. 'I've been looking all over for you. Where have you been?'

'Nelly, sweetheart,' he says. 'I'm sorry, I've been

involved in doing a small job for Lucky and William, here. But I've got good news: we're moving into Lucky's place. She's letting us take that room. So I can start mending shoes tomorrow.'

'What? But . . .'

'We've got to go,' interrupts Lucky.

Helen frowns and looks between Lucky and Burke.

'There's no time to talk about this now,' says Burke, stroking her face. 'We've got a delivery to make.'

She looks at the sack on Hare's shoulder. 'What's that?' she says.

Hare chews his lip but says nothing.

Burke places both of his hands on Helen's shoulders and stares into her face. 'Just a pig. We're doing a job for the abattoir, making a delivery. We'll be back in no time.'

'I could come too,' she says.

'Oh, now,' says Lucky, mustering up as much kindness in her voice as she can. 'You must be tired. You've had a hard day pounding the streets. Go inside and rest. We'll be back soon.' She puts her arm around Helen and draws her towards the lodging house. Then, leaving her at the door, she turns and walks back to join Burke and Hare. They set off once more, leaving Helen in the street looking pensively after them.

Chapter 8

The anatomist Dr Robert Knox is enjoying an excellent performance by the Edinburgh Professional Musical Society beneath the glittering chandeliers of the Music Hall in the Assembly Rooms. Amongst the pieces played so far, he has enjoyed Rossini's overture to *Il barbiere di Siviglia*, and Beethoven's grand Symphony No. 5 in C minor. But now, his personal favourite, and one he can play himself, it is Bach's melodious Violin Concerto in E major. He scans the rapt faces of Edinburgh's finest. Many of his medical colleagues are amongst the small but distinguished audience, including Dr Alexander Monro, whose face is sporadically hidden by the enthusiastic bowing of a cellist. Knox regards the man: he is expressionless and emotionless, devoid of any colour, passion or ambition, like a walking cadaver. Knox smiles to himself, enjoying his observations. Here, he reflects, sits the bored third generation of the respected family of anatomists: his grandfather, Dr Alexander Monro *primus*, set the lofty standards of excellence; his father, Dr Alexander Monro *secundus*, maintained and extended the family name; but now Dr Monro *tertius*, like a bitter, grumpily played diminuendo, reduces the fine work and reputation of his family, an imposter trading on name alone. Lazy and entitled, his dissections are few and far between, his lectures dry and lifeless like the skeletons that hang in his dusty office. Knox reflects with pleasure that, on the contrary, he himself is on course for high eminence; his stimulating, theatrical classes inspire and educate the next generation, eclipsing the moribund Monro. He knows what the students say about Monro, that they mock and deride him. In fact, he often joins in. On occasion he has even incorporated mimicry into his own lectures, to the delight of the students.

As if aware of being watched, Monro turns his head slightly to meet Knox's eye. Knox smiles and bows his head in acknowledgement, then looks away, the trace of a sneer still on his lips. He feels Monro's bitter stare boring into him, and he enjoys it. Suddenly, he feels a light tap on his shoulder; standing there in the aisle, flushed and bright-eyed, is his assistant Thomas Fergusson. He beckons for Knox to follow him. Knox whispers to his wife and heads down the aisle out of the room.

'Apologies for interrupting you, sir,' says Thomas once they are on the other side of the door. 'But,' he leans in, his voice barely audible, 'you did say I must come to find you day or night, particularly if there are new suppliers.'

'What is it, man?' says Knox.

'A body has been delivered to your rooms, in Surgeons' Square,' says Thomas. 'I thought you might wish to see it.'

'Is it fresh?' Knox murmurs, one ear on the sound of a solo violin soaring through the closed doors.

Thomas nods enthusiastically. 'Oh, very much so,' he whispers. 'So very fresh, or I wouldn't have thought to trouble you. I'd say within the last day. You see,' he leans in closer, 'it's not been buried, sir.'

Knox raises his eyebrows and folds his arms. No maggots, no decay, no decomposition. This was indeed a gift to anatomy, and would be a tremendous draw for students to his classes.

'Two men we have not seen before brought it in,' adds Thomas. 'I did not ask how they came to have possession of it. I suspect they found it on the backstreets.'

'Its final resting place is not our concern,' says Knox, patting Thomas on the back. 'Let us go immediately. We need to retain these men. They could be useful.'

'I took the liberty of fetching your coat and hat, sir,'

says Thomas, snapping his fingers at a footman who brings them over.

Knox leaves word to make his excuses to his wife, and then the two men head out into the cold Edinburgh night.

Thomas has a coach waiting, and soon they are driving at speed across the North Bridge and up to Surgeons' Square.

'They were trying to take it to Monro,' says Thomas.

'Ah!' says Knox with a broad smile. 'You intervened and diverted them?'

'I did, sir. I told them not to bother with Monro as he's never there after dark.'

'Quite right, Thomas, well done,' says Knox. 'The man is a sham and deserves no advantage.'

Before long they are pulling into Surgeons' Square, the neat quadrangle of buildings which forms the beating heart of the city's prestigious medical establishment, and here they alight the carriage and stride towards Knox's rooms at number 10. It is deathly quiet at this time of night, but Knox notices under a fingernail moon the outline of a woman standing nearby. She is alone. Even in the poor light, he can see her clothes are shabby, her frame thin and tall. She wears a hat, but long wisps of unkempt hair lie over her shoulders. She doesn't look at them directly, so he cannot see her face, but he already knows that she has something to do with the delivery. Her appearance does not fit this setting; she is no whore touting for business here at this hour with so few students around, and why else would a woman of her lowly class be here?

Inside the main dissecting room they find the two men, one short and stocky, the other much taller but younger by many years. Knox pays them no heed; his eyes are fixed on the body stretched out on the table. He removes his hat and steps closer to observe the corpse; he can see instantly that it is remarkably fresh.

'Remove his shirt,' says Knox. He throws the men a glance. 'Get rid of it. We only purchase the naked corpse.'

The younger man looks at his companion, who steps forward without waiting to be asked again and begins to pull off the shirt. It is heavily soiled and still wet from excretions.

'Older than perhaps is ideal,' Knox observes, 'but an interesting subject, nonetheless.' He prods the swollen limbs with a finger. 'Pay them seven pounds and ten shillings,' he says to Thomas without looking at the men. 'And, Thomas' – he beckons to the young man to follow him out of the room into the hallway – 'you might suggest to the two fellows that we would be glad to see them again. That is, if they come across any further bodies as fresh as this one. Unburied.'

He pats Thomas on the back and then turns to head out once more into the night, an animated spring in his gait. He is just placing his hat on his head, taking a lusty lungful of the clear night air, when the woman steps out in front of him, blocking his path. She has a ghastly expression that makes him recoil in disgust.

'Like what you see in there, did you?' she says.

'Madam?' says Knox.

'The body.'

'Indeed.' Knox nods. He does not want to linger with this unkempt creature, but she blocks his path.

'Do you want more?' she says. 'We can bring you more, if the price is right.'

He takes out a glove from his pocket and begins to put it on, slowly and carefully pushing his fingers in one by one. He watches her as he does this, regarding her from the top of her head to her feet. She is a vile specimen. He despises her impertinence.

'Well?' she snaps.

He doesn't put the second glove on; instead, he leans into her and grabs her arm, tight, above the elbow. She gasps in pain. They stand like that for a brief moment, her in shocked silence. He squeezes her bony flesh tightly. Through her thin, ragged clothing, he can feel the brachial artery pulsate quickly under his thumb. He is hurting her, but she does not struggle.

'Oh, yes,' he says slowly. 'Don't take them to anyone else but me, do you hear? The younger, the fresher, the better. And just like the one they brought, no marks.

Those men, tell them to keep their dirty great hands away. I'll not ask any questions. And you shall forget this conversation.' He grips her tighter for good measure. 'Don't come anywhere near me again. I don't associate with your kind unless stretched out dead on the table. What a fine cadaver you would make, my dear. With so little flesh we could get to the bones in no time.'

He releases his grip but slowly traces his thumb down the contours of her arm to her hand. Then, as though at risk of contagion, he quickly steps to the side, away from her, and walks off into the night, now slipping his hand into his other glove. He leaps back into the waiting carriage to return to the concert, smiling to himself. The fools, he thinks, the poor desperate fools, happy to do his bidding. What depths people will sink to for money. But that was not his preoccupation. With the help of these hapless idiots, and a steady supply of fresh bodies, he would eclipse Alexander Monro *tertius* to become the most distinguished anatomist in the city.

Chapter 9

For the Burkes and the Hares, where there is money, there is whisky. What they earned from the cadaver is divided between Burke, Hare and Lucky, and now the men are blind drunk. They shout and dance and make no sense in their gibbering. They stumble and fall and grab onto each other as they try to stay on their feet. They laugh uproariously at nothing, finding each other hilarious without understanding a word the other says. Helen is passed out on a straw bed in the corner of the room, unable to keep up with the men. She began the evening revelling in Burke's happiness, but then the drink made her weep at everything; she kept grabbing Burke's face and pleading if he loved her, how much he loved her and did he love her as much as she did him? Unsatisfied and downcast, she collapsed in a whimpering heap and then, mercifully, fell asleep.

In amongst the chaos, sober despite the quantity of drink she has consumed, Lucky sits and broods. She watches the men wrestle, tumble on top of each other before staggering back to their stools, where they sit with their heads tipped back so they can see each other through leaden eyelids.

Hare looks over. 'Where is my wife?' he hollers, trying to focus on Lucky. 'I want my wife on my lap.' He attempts to pat his knee, but his hand misses and he almost loses his balance. Lucky doesn't oblige. Burke begins to sing raucously so that Hare, forgetting what he has just said, joins in.

Lucky coolly regards this spectacle of debauchery from her position by the fire, but her mind is elsewhere. Her finger circles the rim of her cup, catching the chip on every rotation, and she presses deeper as she recalls her encounter with Knox, replaying that brief moment with him. Over and over, she sees his pock-marked face in the shadows, and feels his hand squeezing her arm. She cringes at the memory. He had eyed her like meat as a butcher might stroke the flesh on a carcass before making his first incision. She pulls up the thin sleeve of her dress, and sure enough there are dark red welts. He has left his mark on her. She wonders why she did not retaliate as she had with so many others. She is disgusted with her own weakness.

She places her finger back on the cup and begins circling once more, digging repeatedly at the sharp chip. All the ways she has been touched, handled, beaten, kicked, grabbed and thrown by men cloud her thoughts until her anger, like toxic poison, floods through her veins.

She knows, if she wishes to make money, good money, then a doctor, even a vile character like Knox, is the key. Perhaps that was why she hadn't fought back. Holding a knife to his throat and making one quick slash would have been satisfying in the moment, but stupid. She needs him to buy their wares, and, besides, his mutilated naked body sprawled on his own dissection table will remain an intoxicating dream.

Suddenly, her finger ceases its rotation. She replays the moment he grabbed her once more, but this time she tries to recall his words. What was it he said? At the time, she was so focused on his grip and the heat of his breath on her face, that she hadn't fully listened.

No marks . . . Tell those men to keep their dirty great hands away.

She frowns. What had he meant? She pulls up her sleeve once more and examines the fingerprints on her arm. Then Lucky understands. Knox wants more, dead like old Donald but with nothing visible on the skin – killing without a mark on them. She thinks about how that might be possible: stopping the breath, that is.

And then swift transportation: so simple. Much cleaner then digging up graves.

She shifts her gaze to Helen, curled in a ball on the floor. She is rendered unconscious by drink, so much so that she appears dead. Lucky reaches out her foot and nudges her. Helen doesn't respond. She pushes a little harder, but still Helen lies unresponsive. Lucky can see a faint twitch of her mouth. It wouldn't take much. With someone as incapacitated as Helen, it would be easy, thinks Lucky. A pillow on the face and some force to hold them down. Then the body would be clean: no marks on the neck from strangulation, no blood, no injury, no obvious 'method'. Just death that could be explained away by an unknown illness, perhaps.

And, of course, who to do away with? Tempted as she is to practise on Helen, Burke might disagree. She stands and, taking a candle, walks through into one of the lodging-house rooms. There are seven beds but only three sleeping tenants. The place was quiet at this time of year. She slowly walks between the straw beds and considers. She remembers Knox's words: *the younger, the fresher, the better*. But, thinks Lucky, too many too young and questions might be asked; too old, and the price would be lower. A hacking cough interrupts her thoughts. Joseph. Joseph, who had been with them for some time and who had an unrelenting chest ailment that sometimes consumed him, occasionally raising fears of the fever. No one would suspect foul play, thinks Lucky. She goes closer and looms over him, candle in hand. He is fast asleep but coughs all the same. He was young enough and would surely get them a good price. If they just restricted what little breath he had, for a short time, he would slip away. Hare would do it. Burke with his superstitious mind might take more convincing, but for £7 or so she was sure he could be persuaded. It was, she considered, *how* she suggested it. Not murder: no, that was too strong; they would just be helping a dying man on his way. Like you might put a dog out of its misery. Death would be better for this man. She could make Burke see that. Joseph convulses violently once more and wakens with a start, shocked at the sight of Lucky by his bedside.

'Ah, you poor thing, Joseph, God bless you,' she says in a consoling voice. 'You sound terrible, so you do. Let me get you something to drink to ease your throat. Come through to the kitchen, and I'll sort you out.'

'You're too kind,' wheezes Joseph, staggering after her.

Chapter 10

In a corner of the Hares' squalid kitchen, Helen McDougal comes to her senses. Her bones ache, and she is shivering. As her eyes adjust to the darkness, she can see candlelight at the far end, and the shapes of people huddled together. She raises her head too quickly and is gripped instantly with the need to vomit. The room is spinning, and there is a clammy sweat on her brow. She needs water. She closes her eyes and waits for the sensation to pass. Then, opening her eyes once more, she tries to focus on what is happening in the room. She wonders if perhaps she is dreaming. She can hear whispering, and although she can't make out what is being said, there is a sense of urgency, of purpose. Someone is telling someone else what to do, and she knows that voice: it is Lucky.

'William?' she calls out weakly. 'Are you there?'

The whispering stops and the candle is abruptly extinguished. The room is now pitch-black.

'Who's there?' she says. 'William? I'm cold. I don't feel well.'

'Go back to sleep, Helen.' Burke's voice sounds strange, as though he is lying down, or his voice is restricted somehow.

'What's going on?' she cries. 'What are you doing?' She begins to shuffle forward on all fours, the icy roughness of the stone floor grazing her hands. She has a creeping sense of unease and suspicion. 'Are you with her?' Her mind is galloping, nausea and jealousy are raging within, competing for dominance.

'No!' says Burke, his voice rough.

'Don't let go,' says Lucky. 'It's almost done.'

Helen is confused. Let go of what? What is she talking about? She crawls faster, towards the voice and the blackest of outlines. A tiny sliver of moonlight is shining now through the window, and Helen can see two bodies, one on top of the other. Burke is on top. But it isn't Lucky beneath him, for she is crouched on the floor beside Hare.

'What are you doing?' she says.

'Shut up,' snaps Lucky.

Helen now sees that Burke is lying across a man who is flat on the floor. Hare has a hand near the man's nose, and Lucky is pressing what looks like a pillow on his mouth.

Helen can barely believe what she is seeing, let alone say it aloud. 'Are you . . . ? William, what are you doing to that man? Are you hurting him?'

She reaches Burke and begins to pull at his jacket sleeve, at his shoulders, desperately trying to heave him off the body.

'Stop it, William!' she shrieks. 'Are you killing him? You mustn't. It's murder, it's murder!'

Burke bats her away with his arm. 'Get off me, Nelly,' he says, 'or, God help me, I'll kill you too.'

'I'll cover his nose,' says Lucky to Hare, calmly readjusting her hands so she can pinch his nostrils tightly with one hand, the pillow still pressing down with the other. 'Just shut her up.'

Hare grabs Helen and clamps his hand over her mouth. She struggles violently, attempting to scream, but instead she tastes the foul, salty skin of Hare's palm. She tries to bite him, but his hand is too tight on her mouth. She panics, struggling to get air through her nostrils, and tears begin to stream down her face. It is like the swamp; the slough of despond flashes before her eyes, and now she has fallen in and she cannot find air. Hare holds her tight and spins her round so she cannot see Burke and Lucky. She feels blackness creeping over her eyes.

'Is that it?' she hears Burke murmur. 'Is it over?'

'Yes,' confirms Lucky. 'No thanks to your woman.'

Helen hears movement, a shifting of bodies and a sigh of relief from Burke.

Hare releases Helen, who gasps for air and then flings herself in a tirade of punches on her captor. He doesn't flinch. He barely notices, and she feels like a child attacking him with tiny, beating fists. She is throwing herself at him, shouting and screaming, then she turns around, the full extent of what they have done consuming her in a fiery rage.

'What have you done, William? This is *murder*. *You're* a murderer.' She points a trembling finger at him. She has become something other than Helen McDougal; she is wild and desperate and has lost all sense of what is real and what is right.

Burke grasps her by the shoulders and shakes her violently. 'Stop it, Nelly, stop it,' he growls. 'You don't understand. It was better for him, for everyone.'

But she doesn't stop it. She lashes out at him, throwing punches and slaps at his head and his body, until with one swift movement, Burke strikes her so hard with the back of his hand that she is thrown to the floor. She lies stunned, her head swimming, her sight blurred. Then, slowly dragging her herself up to a sitting position, she vomits, groaning and retching like an animal.

Lucky calmly lights a candle, illuminating the aftermath of the chaos. 'Never mind her,' she says. 'Take the body to the cellar and cover it with straw. You can carry it to Knox tomorrow evening.'

Without a word, the two men do as they are told and, taking an end each, they stumble out of the room, manoeuvring Joseph's lifeless body.

Helen, deep in shock, rocks and shakes on the floor.

'Go to bed, Helen. It'll be sunrise soon and you need to sleep,' says Lucky.

Helen rubs her face where Burke slapped her. She can feel her cheek beginning to swell. 'I'm not staying here,' she mumbles. 'Not with you, you murdering witch.'

'Is that right?' sneers Lucky. 'And where exactly would you go? Back to Mickey's place?'

'Why did you kill that man?' Helen says. 'What did he ever do to you?'

'Joseph had the fever,' says Lucky smoothly. 'He was dying anyway, and he might have infected all of us. We were helping him by putting him out of his misery and stopping the spread. You should be grateful. You could've caught it too.'

'Lies,' whispers Helen. Then she looks up at Lucky, her eyes blazing. 'All lies. You've bewitched my William with your lies!'

Lucky just laughs and shakes her head. Burke and

Hare wander back into the room. The drink still has a hold of their senses, and they appear befuddled as they sit down.

'No one heard?' asks Burke.

'No,' says Lucky. 'And if they did, they would think it was a drunken squabble.'

'I've got to get out,' says Helen, her eyes wide, her face now red and puffy.

'You can't leave,' says Lucky. 'She can't leave, Burke. She knows too much now.'

Burke eyes Lucky carefully and then nods. 'Now then, Nelly,' he says. His voice is soft and consoling. He kneels beside her on the floor. 'Come here, my sweet one.' He strokes her hair. 'There, there. I'm sorry about all this. But it's over now. I had to calm you down, you see that, don't you? You made me do it, with all that daft screaming.' He traces a large finger down her bruised, tear-stained face. One eye is now closing over with the swelling, and he pulls her head into his chest. 'Yes, it's all over now.'

Helen lifts her head and gazes at him imploringly.

'And it was for the best. That poor fellow needed our help. It was all for the best, my love.' He takes her face in his hands. 'I need you, Nelly.' He smiles. 'I love you – and I promise you'll never see anything like that again.' He kisses her gently on the forehead.

Helen's anguished expression softens. She grips his

hands, holding them around her cheeks, now wet with tears. 'I love you more than anything in the whole world, William,' she whispers. 'But don't fall into the mire – and don't pull me in with you. I don't know if I have the strength to pull us both out.' She shakes her head, imagining the picture from the book and that swamp, so very thick and so very deep, and the weight of their sins sucking them down. 'I'm just so, so weak, William.'

Burke reaches down, scoops her up like a child and carries her to their room.

Chapter 11

Their pockets jangle with the money earned from selling Joseph. Ten pounds this time, and the anatomy students made it clear on behalf of Knox that they want more. Knox, it would seem, wants their business. A woman next time would be pleasing to him, they are told, should they happen to come across a dead woman, of course.

'Just one more,' lies Lucky. 'Come on, Burke.'

It is late in the day, and they are sitting in a dank corner of a drinking den in the malodorous bowels of the Cowgate, drinking beer and supping a fatty broth with thin slices of stale bread. Their heads are bowed close together.

'It's too dangerous,' says Burke. 'There's too much risk, and I don't want Nelly involved.'

'None of us want her involved,' says Lucky, rolling

her eyes. 'She doesn't have to be. But how else are you going to earn money?'

'Just shoes, Lucky.' Burke sighs and dips his bread into the broth. 'The simple, honest trade of buying and mending shoes, and Nelly can sell them'.

Lucky smiles. 'What's that in your pocket?' She jabs a finger. 'How much money have you made?'

'A lot of money,' admits Burke.

Lucky leans in closer. 'People like us can't get our hands on money like this doing anything else. It'd take weeks of you trailing around selling old boots to make anywhere near what we've made carting a couple of tired old bodies up to Knox. At least those bodies have some worth. I've said it before: this way, they're being *used* for something, not just rotting in the ground. Which is where they would be now, then dug up and sold to line someone else's pockets – not yours.'

'Besides,' adds Hare, soup dripping down his chin, 'you can't stop now. We're all in this enterprise together.'

Burke stares hard at Hare. 'If I didn't know better, I'd say that sounded like a threat.'

Hare raises an eyebrow and then takes a bite of his bread and swigs his beer, without taking his eyes off Burke's face. Then he grins. 'You need to calm down, fella.'

Burke lunges for him. He knocks the table, spilling beer as he clamps a beefy hand around Hare's throat.

Hare raises his hands in mock surrender. Lucky pushes the men apart, aware of nervous glances from those nearby.

'*Enough,*' she hisses.

The men sit back down. Burke takes a breath and composes himself. 'Fine. Just one more,' he says. 'The last one, mind. Who will it be, though? We can't just despatch one of your tenants.'

'One more?' Hare shakes his head. 'We could make this our business, William – don't you see that?'

'Meaning?' says Burke, narrowing his eyes.

Hare wipes his mouth with the back of his hand. 'We just "remove" people. People who don't matter, people who won't be missed. Edinburgh's swarming with them. Vagrants. Folk who come and go and are never seen. We pluck them off the street one at a time – or at the boarding house. It's like this: someone arrives who no one knows, no one will care if they suddenly disappear. They were never there in the first place: they're invisible people.'

All three consider this for a second.

'As to the how: whisky is the key,' says Lucky. 'And plenty of it. It lures them in. Then we ply them with it until they're insensible. It means they can't call out or fight back.'

'Whisky doesn't come that cheap,' says Burke, frowning.

'The sale of the body covers it, now we're making ten pounds a shot,' says Lucky with a wave of her hand. 'And maybe more if we push our luck.'

'What if Knox catches on? Then what?' says Burke, pushing his bowl away and picking his teeth with a fingernail.

'He won't ask,' says Lucky. 'Trust me.' She doesn't tell her accomplices of her encounter with Knox outside his dissection rooms. She sees no reason to share their conversation.

'How can you be sure?' asks Burke.

'He doesn't want to know,' replies Lucky. 'If he knows, then he can't take them. And he wants to take them. More than that, he needs them.' She remembers his words: *Don't take them to anyone else but me.* There is competition at play here. Competition for bodies. And she considers there's an equity in their power; Knox needs them as much as they need him. 'I think younger bodies would be preferable to him, though,' she adds, glancing at Burke and Hare. They both nod. 'I imagine they will make more money too.'

'What makes you say that?' says Hare.

'Consider what they're using them for,' she says. 'They aren't just cutting them up for entertainment. They're learning from them. They will tire of the clapped-out corpses of the old and infirm. Younger, fresher flesh will yield more than shrivelled old husks.'

'You seem to know a lot about this, Lucky.' Burke is staring at her.

'We must be awake to opportunities,' she says.

They make to leave, placing coins on the table to pay the reckoning. But as they are about to depart, Hare appears to think twice and, not so surreptitiously, scoops the money into his pocket and makes for the door.

'Hey, you!' roars the irate publican who has witnessed the theft. 'What's this? Trying to leave without paying? Not on my watch.'

Burke and Lucky turn round to see Hare shrug, his face a picture of innocence.

Burke shakes his head and puts his hand in his pocket to retrieve some coins and puts them on the table. 'We're sorry about that,' he says calmly.

'Thieving Irish bastard,' mutters the publican, turning back to his work, but this time it is Hare whose temper ignites. He spins round, grabs the man and yanks him out into the close. It is a grossly uneven fight: the man's scant frame is no match for the tall, powerful Hare. Hare throws him to the ground and kicks him in the head repeatedly. The man groans and pleads, blood sprays on the cobbles, and still Hare will not cease. His steel-capped boots reduce the man to a mass of fleshy pulp.

'Call me that again, and I'll drag your filthy corpse up to the butchers at the medical school,' hollers Hare, unrelenting.

Burke yells at him and drags him away, bundling Hare down the close onto the Cowgate and then into the side gate of Greyfriars' graveyard, into a dark corner. Burke pushes him onto the ground beside the dead.

'Has the Devil himself taken a hold of you?' says Burke. 'Calm yourself!'

Hare spits and rubs his face. 'I'm alright now.'

'*You're* alright?' Burke says in disbelief. 'And what about the other fella? One more kick, and not even Knox would take him.'

Hare bursts out laughing. 'Oh, I see, only pleasant killings allowed? Did you hear what he called me? What he called us?' He shakes his head. 'I'll not have it.'

Lucky kneels beside Hare. 'Do you think this is some sort of game, you fool? Draw attention to us like that again, and we're doomed. We will kill with quiet purpose. But to the people of this town, we run a respectable business.' She stands up, 'Make no mistake, William Hare. I'll not linger if you're caught. I know how to play the suffering wife. And I'll make sure it's *you*, not me, who faces the gallows. And when you swing, my eyes will be dry, and I'll take the child growing in my belly to watch them dissect your body.'

Lucky stands, then she and Burke walk out of the graveyard, leaving Hare to sulk.

Chapter 12

Some weeks later, on a raw December evening, Abigail Simpson stops to rest in the Grassmarket. She leans a shoulder against a wall, reaching down to rub her aching calves. The basket strapped to her back, now empty of the salt she has been selling, still digs into her flesh. She eases it off her shoulders and enjoys the sensation of lightness, arching her spine like a cat and then pushing her shoulders back. It has been a long day. She lowers herself to the ground and rests, closing her eyes for a second. She had left her village of Gilmerton in the cold dark of early morning and walked the four miles into the town – as she did every day and as she had done for years – watching for the sun to rise over the contours of Salisbury Crags and Arthur's Seat. She had waved and nodded to the usual, familiar faces as she made her way through the streets to meet Geordie, who delivered the salt from Joppa. Then she had loaded her basket and headed for the New Town, calling out, filling her lungs with the bitterly icy air, selling her salt to the cooks and housemaids of Edinburgh's most affluent neighbourhood, so they can season their fine foods.

Abigail is one of a dying breed – there aren't many saltwives like her left, and soon they will disappear, as salt is being sold in the shops. She doesn't worry about such things, though. She takes each day as it comes; she lives in the present and never looks forward or back. God has looked after her and given her a good life. She pulls her plaid shawl tighter and looks up at the castle. The light is fading, and the sky is a murky grey. Snowflakes, fat and feathery, begin to fall; she knows she'll need to set off home soon before the snow gets any heavier. She glances over to the other side of the street and the welcome glow from the White Hart Inn. She puts her hand into her pocket and feels for the pennies she has earned. Just a nip of whisky, she thinks, just the one will warm her and help her on her way.

Abigail hauls herself to her feet and sets off, carrying the basket in her arms. Out of nowhere a gang of wild lads chasing something or someone crash into her, spinning her round and knocking her off her feet, so that she falls heavily onto the cobbles. She is winded for a moment, disorientated, and then there is a shooting pain in her right arm from wrist to elbow. She lets out an anguished cry.

'Are you alright there?' a kind voice speaks to her from up above.

'Ach, don't mind me,' she says, without looking up. She attempts to get to her feet, but she is dizzy. Her cheek caught on the basket edge, and blood appears on her fingers when she touches her face. The shock at the sight of her own blood and the pain in her arm overwhelms her, and she crumples.

'Ah, bless you,' the voice says again. 'That was terrible, so it was. Those boys should be strung up.' It is a woman's voice, and now she is kneeling down beside Abigail, her face all concern and kindness.

'Here, let us help you up – that was a nasty fall,' she says. A man's hand then appears, and when she grasps it, she is hoisted up as though she were as light as one of the snowflakes landing all around.

'I'm sure I've seen you before,' says the man. 'Oh, yes, I'm sure I have.'

Abigail rubs her wrist. 'You surely have,' she says. 'I'm here most days.'

'You've hurt yourself?' says the woman.

'I've had worse,' says Abigail. 'Crying like a bairn won't help things.'

'You poor thing,' says the woman, looking intensely at Abigail's face. 'Heavens, I see blood there on your cheek.

What a terrible shame.' The woman reaches for a corner of Abigail's shawl and mops her tears and slips an arm around her shoulders. 'Don't cry, dear, you'll be all right now. You've been out selling all day, I expect. You must be exhausted. Why don't you let us buy you a nice fortifying drink? You've had a shock, and you need to sit down somewhere warm for a moment to gather your wits.'

'You're so kind,' says Abigail. 'I was just heading for the inn there. Thought I'd have a wee dram to warm up before the walk home.'

'And so were we, so let's go together,' says the man. 'We have to look out for each other in this world.' And now, the woman and the man usher Abigail towards the White Hart Inn, the man carrying her basket for her. He opens the door. 'After you, ladies,' he says, and a blast of warmth from a cheering fire welcomes them as they step inside. The woman fusses round Abigail, taking her to a seat near the hearth, making sure she's comfortable, and the man brings them all a small glass of whisky. Abigail tries to flex and swivel her right hand. It is swollen and hard to move.

'You'll need to rest that arm,' says the woman.

'You'll have to use your other hand to drink,' says the man with a twinkle in his eye.

'Now, then, a toast to you, my dear,' says the woman, lifting her glass. 'You deserve it after the shock you've had.'

'Sláinte!' says the man with a nod to Abigail.

Abigail feels lucky to have met them; their sympathy and benevolence make them feel like family. She lifts the glass to her mouth using her left hand and takes a drink. It slips down her throat with a familiar soothing burn. She is feeling much better. Her arm is painful, perhaps even broken, but the whisky takes off the edge.

'You'll have another?' says the man.

Abigail hesitates as she puts her glass back on the table. 'Oh, that's kind of you, but I'll need to be on my way. And you've been so generous to me already. I really haven't got much money.'

The man waves away her protests.

'Have you far to go, to get home?' asks the woman.

'Gilmerton village, a few miles out of town,' says Abigail.

'You can't be walking home in that,' says the man, gesturing to the window. The snow is falling thick and fast.

'I run a boarding house just around the corner,' says the woman. 'Why don't you stay with me tonight? Then you'll be up and hawking tomorrow without the long walk in.'

'Well . . . I don't think I've enough money for that,' says Abigail. 'Besides, my daughter's at home, and she'll be expecting me.'

'I'm sure your daughter will assume you've found a

place to stay and be glad of it. And don't you even think about paying a thing,' says the woman. She pats Abigail's hand.

'She won't hear of it,' agrees the man, 'not after the shock you've had.'

'Let us look after you,' says the woman. 'You remind me of my mammy, back in Ireland. I can't do much for her, so my helping you will make me feel better.'

Abigail smiles. 'Ach, you're a good sort,' she says, taking the woman's hand in her own and squeezing it. 'You're so kind – like my own daughter.'

'Ah, if she's anything like you, I bet she's a bonny lass,' says the man. 'I should marry her and then we'd be family.'

This makes Abigail laugh, and she adds shyly, 'I'd be fair happy if she married a handsome man like you.'

'We've got whisky at home, so let's get you settled there. You can make yourself comfortable and give that arm some rest,' says the woman. 'Drink up now.'

Abigail tips the last drops of the whisky down and nods. They all stand and make their way to the door. The man insists on carrying her basket again.

'You two are like angels,' says Abigail. 'I don't know where you came from, but the Lord must be smiling on me today. What are your names? I'm Abigail.'

'I'm Margaret,' says the woman, 'but everyone calls me Lucky.'

'You're certainly lucky for me,' says Abigail, looping her good arm through Lucky's.

'William Burke at your service,' says the man with a bow, 'but you can call me Handsome.'

At this, they all laugh, and they are a merry party as they head out of the inn and through the snow to Tanner's Close.

Chapter 13

His face is very close to hers, so close that she can feel the roughness of his chin on her cheek. William is lying on top of her, his whole weight bearing down on her. At first, she is comforted by this intimate contact, as though they are in the throes of love, but then she looks upwards and her eyes widen in horror as she sees her – a grotesque image of Lucky holding a pillow, moving towards her face, and Hare behind her. Lucky presses the pillow down hard on her mouth, the cloth pushing against her tongue and teeth. She tries to scream, but no sound comes, and then strong fingers pinch her nostrils so tightly that pain shoots through her skull. She tries to thrash her body, but her arms are pinned down by the crushing weight of William. No matter how hard she fights, she cannot get air into her lungs. Her eyes swim, she squeezes them shut, so she cannot see their faces, finding comfort in the black.

Helen shudders and shakes her head; she has pulled herself out of this fever dream, but her face is wet with tears. She looks around, and it is over, but these nightmarish images have haunted her every day since Joseph's murder at the hands of her husband and the Hares. Even now, standing on a busy street on a bright, fair winter's morning, she feels shaken. Although William had reassured her that she is mistaken, that all they were doing was helping Joseph by easing him on his way, Helen knows something is wrong. His insistence makes her wonder if something is amiss with her, if she is ill and has imagined the whole thing. But then there was the old saltwife who died. One minute she was there, laughing and drinking with them all in the kitchen, and then, the next morning, she was dead and Lucky was wearing the old woman's shawl. William had blamed an illness, said she had simply died in her sleep. Maybe that was true, but deep down Helen knows it is more likely that they killed her when she was full of drink. She sighs and tries to focus on her surroundings.

They are on the High Street near the Canongate and William is cobbling by the roadside. Helen is hawking for him but now takes a moment to cross the road to gaze into a shop window while Burke mends a pair of shoes for a passing gentleman. It is a clear day, and from here she can see all the way down the Royal Mile to the rippled blue sea and green fields beyond. She closes her eyes and takes a long, deep breath, enjoying the sensation of filling her chest. The air is clearer and fresher here than in the Grassmarket and by their lodging house where the malodorous fumes from the tannery are a constant presence, hanging over them like a poisonous cloud. All around her the street is alive with hawkers crying their wares and barefoot children laughing and playing in the filth. Heavily loaded carts trundle up and down the cobbles, pulled by exhausted little ponies. Bright stalls stud the pavements where finely dressed gentlemen and ladies walk amongst the melee. Mangy dogs bark and chase each other, getting under the feet of the women queuing at the water well to fill their pails.

But Helen's attention is drawn elsewhere; she is gazing at her man as he works swiftly and efficiently, chatting and smiling with the gentleman who is waiting for his heels to be repaired. He has an easy charm that is, for Helen, not just a comfort, but her lifeblood. William is as essential to her existence as the air she breathes; he is her saviour, her redeemer and protector.

She is distracted by two women who appear behind William, dancing and spinning out of a whisky shop, clutching a bottle. They are young and giddy. One is tall and willowy with twists of long, thick auburn hair that catch the sunlight. Her friend is small and curvaceous, and she twirls the redhead around, shrieking. Helen has seen them before on the streets; they are fallen women who sell their bodies. At this moment they have the eyes of every man on them, including William. Helen stays where she is and observes. William smiles, and the two women spot him. They dance over, and William finishes his work, then stands up to talk to them. The redhead puts a hand on one hip, tosses her hair back and touches his arm, laughing at everything he says. She swigs from the bottle, allowing it to dribble out the sides of her mouth, and then passes it to William who takes a drink. Helen watches as he reaches out and tenderly wipes a droplet of whisky from the woman's chin with his thumb, which he then licks, all the while laughing and joking. He is never like this with her. Helen squirms in her own jealousy. She swallows the bile rising in her throat and lifts a hand to rub the prickle that burns on the back of her neck. She feels dizzy now and places her hand on the wall beside her to steady herself. An image is creeping into her mind, an image that brings her great pleasure: William is lying on top of a body, with Hare and Lucky ready with a pillow. The body is not Joseph, or the saltwife, or her own; this time, the body is the redhead. A mist descends and she marches across the road.

'Hello,' she says interrupting the tableau.

The two women look from Helen to William and then to each other and burst out laughing. William smiles awkwardly. The redhead whispers something in his ear and he laughs, then the two women walk away. Still smirking, he watches them go. They look back from time to time and wave and simper. When they have disappeared into a nearby tavern, he turns to look at Helen and sees her face.

'I was just exchanging pleasantries,' he says too quickly.

'You're different with those women,' says Helen quietly, '*that* woman, than you are with me.'

'What? Now, don't say these daft things,' says William, turning to return to his work, but Helen grabs his arm.

'Her, the one with the red hair,' says Helen quietly. 'I saw how you looked at her. Did she remind you of someone?' She means his wife. His wife still in Ireland.

'Nelly! You sound like a fool,' he says, shaking her off. 'She's a street woman, that's all. A nobody. A nothing.'

'Well, why don't you do to her what you did to Joseph?' she says.

William glares at her. He is irritated now.

'And the old saltwife. You did for her too,' says Helen.

'Keep your voice down, woman,' he snarls.

'You and Lucky and Hare. I know you're up to something. Well, then, make her next,' says Helen defiantly. 'Do it for me. Get rid of her like you did them.'

He looks at Helen in horror. 'Stop this nonsense, Nelly,' he snaps. 'You don't know what you're saying – it's all in your head.'

'What deal have you made with the Devil, William? Am I next?' she says defiantly, her voice becoming shrill. 'Is that what you're all planning? You want rid of me. Maybe I'll just throw myself off the North Bridge before you have the chance to stifle me.'

William shakes his head. He grabs Helen by both arms as though he might shake the life out of her right here in the middle of the High Street. 'Stop it. Stop this right now or God help me–' he pleads.

'Kill her,' says Helen. She is standing quite rigid, her eyes fixed and determined. She sees everything clearly now. It is as though by his doing this, she will be forever sure of his love. It seems so terribly simple, it makes her laugh.

'I want her dead, William,' she says matter-of-factly. 'Do it. Prove you love me. Or I'll walk up to the bridge this instant.'

William is astonished. But then something shifts in his expression. A realisation? Or a decision perhaps. He looks down the hill to the tavern where the women have gone.

'Go and get Hare,' he says.

Chapter 14

'Remove her clothes, gentlemen,' says Dr Knox. 'You should know the rules by now.'

He watches as Burke and Hare clumsily roll the body of Mary Paterson to and fro, yanking off her shabby garments. Hare stuffs her skirt and petticoat under his arm as he helps pull off her shift. She is now quite naked, with pale, luminous skin and full breasts, flat out on the dissecting table, her red hair cascading off the edge and almost touching the floor.

Knox takes off his gloves and runs a finger along one leg, stopping at her thigh. 'Beautiful symmetry to the body, pleasingly proportioned,' he murmurs, tapping the flesh. 'Unusually handsome. And fresh, very fresh – cold but not yet rigid. Thomas, get a messenger to the painter,' he says without looking up. 'I rather think I would like some sketches done.'

There is no reply. Thomas, ashen-faced, is standing perfectly still, staring at the cadaver in front of him.

'Thomas? Did you hear me?'

'Sorry, sir,' says Thomas, snapping out of his thoughts. 'Dr Knox, sir, I wonder, might I have a quick word?' There is a deep crease across his brow.

'If you must,' says Knox, unable to tear his eyes away from Mary.

Thomas walks quickly out of the dissecting room to the corridor. Knox follows and looks at him expectantly, but Thomas hesitates to speak, waiting until the door is shut firmly behind them both.

'Spit it out,' says Knox.

'That girl,' says Thomas, scratching at one ear. 'I think I recognise her.'

'So?' says Knox quickly. 'What of it?'

'I saw her yesterday. Alive, so very much alive. I have ...' He is wrestling with something, something too terrible to comprehend, let alone utter. He looks directly at Knox. 'This girl is well known on the streets of Edinburgh. I have been in her company.'

'Again, I say, what of it?' replies Knox.

'Sir, she was in rude health only yesterday and yet here she lies dead, reeking of whisky, on the dissecting table.'

'Where did the men say they acquired the body?'

'They said they bought her from an old woman in

the Canongate. They were told she had killed herself with liquor.'

'Well, there we have it. An untimely end, but hardly anything we need concern ourselves with. Why should it matter?'

'Why should she kill herself with drink today when yesterday she was full of joy?' says Thomas. 'I don't believe it.'

Knox shrugs. 'We cannot know what was in her mind. She clearly led an immodest and reckless life and died in the same manner. Let God be her judge, not us.'

'No, I mean her death seems unfeasible to me,' says Thomas. 'I fear there is more to it.'

'Nonsense, man,' says Knox, patting Thomas on the shoulder. 'Licentious women like this, they live short, brutish lives and then they die. Their lives are inconsequential. It is all part of the natural order of things. Besides, perhaps it wasn't the girl you knew. They are as one pea is like another around the Canongate, no? The woman who sold them the body was no doubt running a house of ill-repute.'

Thomas is not convinced. 'It's the hair, sir. It's so distinctive. Not something I would forget.'

Knox considers this for a minute. Then he opens the door, and they step back into the room once more. Knox looks at Mary, then at Burke and Hare, who are standing awkwardly waiting for their payment.

'You, sir,' he points at Burke. 'Cut off her hair.' He reaches for a pair of scissors and hands them to Burke.

Burke hesitates.

'Thomas here will settle up once you're done. We shall say eight pounds,' says Knox.

'Is that all?' says Burke. 'She's so very young. A girl in fact – surely she's worth more?'

'You want *more* money?' says Thomas. He glances at Knox. Knox shakes his head. 'Eight pounds,' repeats Thomas firmly.

'There is an additional expense,' says Knox, 'because I want to preserve her. But bring me another and we'll see what we can do.'

Burke nods his agreement and tentatively begins to cut her hair.

Knox pats his assistant on the shoulder again. 'You see, Thomas?' he says. 'All is well. Immerse her in whisky and we will spread word that we have quite the most exquisite subject for dissection. She will draw quite a crowd – perhaps we should increase the ticket price?'

'Yes, sir, she will be of great interest,' Thomas says quietly.

Knox heads briskly for the door. 'It is ironic, is it not, that this creature is worth more to the world in death than she ever was in life?' He smiles with amusement as Burke continues to hack at her hair. Long red tresses slip and coil onto the floor.

Chapter 15

Helen can't sleep. It is raining heavily outside, and she stares up at the ceiling, listening to it battering against the window. She knows that William is awake too; she can hear him breathing and muttering beside her. She used to like the sound of the rain when she was warm and cosy with William in bed. But misery clouds her thoughts, and she can find no joy in the simple pleasures of her worthless life.

Slumber, which once used to come so easily to them both after long days trudging around the town hawking their wares is now a distant memory. When they do sleep, it is shallow and fitful, accompanied by nightmarish visions that exhaust the body and mind. A guttering candle beside William's head throws sinister shapes around the room. He insists on it now, burning one steadily through the night until by morning it is just a pool of wax. She has noticed that he keeps a bottle of whisky by the bed too, reaching over to swig from it repeatedly as the hours pass. He shuffles and tosses and turns and sometimes calls out. Nothing he says makes sense, but there is always distress in his voice. Helen stays silent. She has stopped trying to soothe him as he won't listen or take comfort from her words. He flinches at her touch. He changed that day, she thinks; the twinkle in his eye has been replaced with a haunted melancholy. There are no stories or jokes, no songs to sing; his flute stays firmly in his pocket. But more than that, he doesn't pay attention to anything around him. He has become something brooding and frightening since her – since the woman with the red hair.

It is several days now since Helen left William at the Canongate. He had returned to Tanner's Close late at night, in body but not in mind. He had walked into the kitchen alongside Hare and placed a small sack on the table in front of her. He had not waited for her to look inside but had swiftly left the room. Hare had given Lucky a petticoat, a skirt and a striped shawl, so Helen too had thought that perhaps Burke had brought her a gift. She had poked at the bundle, and it seemed soft and weightless. For a foolish, fleeting moment, she even wondered if it was a kitten. She loved kittens. She would often stop to play with them if she saw them on the street. But when she had opened the bag and plunged her hand inside, she quickly knew it wasn't anything alive. It was indeed soft, but it wasn't fur. Confused, she had tipped the contents onto the kitchen table. A mass of long red curls tumbled out. She knew instantly it was the girl's hair. Horrified, Helen had stumbled backwards and slapped a hand over her mouth to quell a scream.

'We should sell that,' Lucky had casually remarked between puffs on her pipe. 'Some fine lady in the New Town would pay a tidy sum for a wig made of that lustrous hair.'

Hare had snatched up the gruesome pile of hair and put it on his own head, mimicking a woman's voice. 'My name is Mary Paterson, and you can have my body for eight pounds.'

This had made Lucky shriek with laughter. Helen had run from the room, their cackles ringing in her ears, and hurled herself at William. He hadn't fought back. He had sat there, wordless, his head in his hands. Humiliated and confused, she had become hysterical, pleading with him to explain his macabre gift. And then, desperate for his attention, for something, anything, she had used her full force to punch and kick him. She had known full well that she had gone too far, that it would end badly, but his reaction this time had been unlike anything she had known previously. He had pounced with a savage fury, grabbing her by the throat and slamming her with his full force against the wall. Pain had exploded from the back of her skull with shocking intensity.

'I did it for *you*,' he had snarled, inches from her face, a froth of spit on his lips, his eyes bloodshot, his breath reeking of whisky. 'I killed her for you. What more do you want? She was so young. Barely a woman, and I killed her like you asked me to. And then *he* made me cut off her hair before he would give me the money. I brought you the hair so *you* would know the deed was done and we would never, ever, need to speak of this again.'

Then he had released his grip and she had crumpled to the floor, gasping for breath. He had turned away from her and collapsed on the bed, leaving her there to cry herself to sleep.

Now, as Helen lies awake reliving that terrible night, she feels an overwhelming sense of loneliness. Although she lies beside him, the William she loves is not there any more.

When she closes her eyes, the girl with the red hair comes to her in her dreams; playful and childlike, she spins and twirls, laughing, gazing at Helen with teasing eyes. Helen puts out her hand to try to grasp hers, perhaps to tell her she is sorry, but she is always just out of reach. She wonders if William sees her too. Only yesterday, Helen convinced herself that she caught glimpses of Mary in the busy Edinburgh streets, her glossy red hair, gleaming in the sunlight. Helen had followed but couldn't catch up; the girl was like the end of the rainbow, like a will-o'-the-wisp that dances in the moonlight but can never be caught.

Tears spill out of her eyes as guilt and shame press like a great weight on her heart. She knows she is in the mire now, and no one can pull her out. No one cares enough to even try.

'William?' she whispers between muffled sobs.

He doesn't reply. She knows he has heard her, but he has nothing to say. His misery must be heavier than hers. There is no comfort in thinking about the stories William used to tell her from *The Pilgrim's Progress* or the Bible; they only make her feel worse. No prayer or confession will right her transgression. Jealousy seized her that day, hot, burning jealousy. And, in its grip, she became a sinner.

It had changed everything.

Chapter 16

The next morning, alone in the kitchen, Lucky smokes her pipe beside the cold fireplace. The sun is slowly rising, but Burke and Helen left hours ago. She had heard them shuffling around, gathering their meagre possessions. Given their shared misery since Mary Paterson's murder, Lucky isn't surprised. She doubts they will return; they will take their wretchedness elsewhere, probably to Mickey Culzean's latest rat-infested hovel in the Grassmarket. Lucky cares not, for Helen's presence is more than mere irritation: she is a bleating lamb amongst wolves and cannot be trusted. If Lucky had her way, they would finish her off and cart her body in a tea chest up to Knox. It would be quick and easy, like it had been for all the others. Helen didn't need much whisky to slip into oblivion, and Lucky would be only too willing to place a pillow over that jabbering mouth.

As she takes long draws of the tobacco, she considers that something is troubling her. It is not Burke and Helen, and it is not the murder of Mary Paterson. She delves further into her agitated disposition to examine its cause; it concerns Knox and the money.

Hare had crowed that Mary Paterson's body, despite its allure and quality, was only worth £8 to Knox. Lucky resents this. She resents Knox deciding the price on a whim, without prior agreement. She resents the power he yields and, most of all, she resents that a body so admired by men when alive – and indeed as a corpse – is so undervalued.

Burke and Hare should have bargained for more. But they had slithered away into the dark with their pockets a little too light, relieved no doubt to be rid of the body. If Lucky had been there, she would have had something to say about that. But then she remembers her encounter with Knox and she feels her skin crawl with anger. Her lack of control over him gnaws at her with a persistence she cannot shake off.

Mary's hair still sits in a fiery bundle on the floor, where Helen left it. Lucky wanders over. She fingers the soft lustrous curls, remembering Hare describing the girl's beauty and how she had bewitched Burke in life, and Knox in death. And how Burke's young assistant, known only as Thomas, had become quite pale at the sight of her. Hare had overheard his conversation with Knox, and Thomas had known her, no doubt in every sense of the word.

Curious, Lucky raises the pile to her own head, covering her own thin greasy strands. She walks over to gaze at her reflection in the grimy windowpane. Framed by Mary's hair, her pale skin gleams in the lamplight. She slowly shifts her head from side to side, admiring the curls that cascade down her shoulders. She wonders how she might look naked, with this hair against the curve of her breasts, or down the length of her spine, and whether she too might be as alluring as Mary Paterson lying on the dissecting table. She leans closer to the window and bites her lips to redden them. She strokes the curls; yes, this hair would make a wig for a fine lady.

Suddenly, there is a face on the other side of the windowpane, gazing back with an expression of utter horror. It is Burke, frozen to the spot. Lucky doesn't move either, and they stare at each other. She is intrigued by his reaction; it is as though he really believes he is seeing the woman he has murdered. She enjoys seeing his fear. He steps back, and she hears him enter the house, and then he is behind her in the kitchen. She spins. His expression is now one of revulsion. He says nothing but picks up his tool bag, slings it over his shoulder and walks out. Lucky watches him go, then bundles Mary Paterson's hair back into the sack. She sits back down by the fireplace; an idea is forming of how this dead girl's hair might prove to be useful.

As a new life grows inside her belly, so too does her enthusiasm for wealth. Money buys her freedom from the deplorable existence to which she has no intention of returning; it affords her new clothes, better food and copious amounts of whisky. At first, this alone had been thrilling, but now there is more to this venture than the money. She likes the ease of the transaction, the simple process of supplying a product, and she wants more: more power and more influence. Burke and Hare simply work to order and live day by day. They don't look forward and they don't look back. Hare spends his money on pigs, which he keeps in the yard, but much of his cash is squandered at the cockfights, and so he frequently finds his pockets are empty.

The money will never be enough to buy them out of their lowly position in life. And the continued acquisition of new, finer clothes only raises eyebrows around the slums. This scrutiny means there must be care in her spending. But she has no intention of stopping.

This dead girl has changed things; indeed, she has helped them. For, now, they don't have to limit their killing to the old or infirm. There is money to be made across all the ages of anyone who happens to cross their paths, anyone they can find. Lucky must now roam the streets and observe the people around her with a keen eye for death. She feels intoxicated at the prospect. Yes, yes, the sick and the elderly would always be there. But there were many youngsters who lived on the streets or slept in the muck with the animals in the Grassmarket, pathetic paupers who drank themselves into insensibility at every opportunity, who could be lured back to the lodging house for some warmth and hospitality. There were other dubious characters too: those fallen women who lingered on the streets or committed petty crimes. The girls who left the prison or the Magdalene Asylums in the morning with nowhere else to go but the spirit shop, and there Lucky would be, close at hand with her gentle words and convivial cheer. She presses her hand to her growing belly and considers it a most opportune prop to her strategy, for who doesn't trust a kindly woman who is with child? Then, once the whisky has done its work, the killing now perfected by Burke and Hare is easy. The transportation of the body across town had initially been done surreptitiously under the cover of darkness, but now they simply bundle it into a box or a sack and stroll through the town to Dr Knox's dissection rooms without a care. Nobody so much as raises an eyebrow as long as they appear to have purpose and a destination. Lucky considers that, in fact, they are doing the town a service, clearing the streets of those blighted individuals who plague the wynds and the closes and are nothing more than a scourge on the neighbourhood. But Knox is a problem: that needs attention, reflects Lucky. The bodies are worth more than he will pay. If she can get the young man Thomas on side, she might be able to put a strategy in place. For if Lucky is to have agency in this endeavour, then she must have power over Knox and his cronies. And the only way she knows how is through tyranny.

She swings the sackful of hair over her shoulder and heads outside. As the sun rises with a red glow silhouetting the mighty castle, she steps into the streets of the West Port with a spring in her step, her eyes keen and alive.

Chapter 17

Mr Dickie's (Barber, Perruquiers and Ornamental Hair Specialists) stands at the far end of the Grassmarket at the West Bow. It is an establishment quite alien to Lucky. Never before has she given much thought to such finery and the idea of having hair that is in some way decorative is strange and somehow ridiculous. She stares momentarily at the wigs and pictures in the shop window.

The second that Lucky enters the establishment and the tinkling bell on the door rings, Mr Dickie, standing at a polished wooden counter, eyes her over his spectacles with an air of curiosity. He has a powdered face and wig, in a style long since passed.

'Can I help you?' he enquires with some scepticism.

Lucky says nothing but walks over to the counter and opens the sack to show him the mop of russet hair.

'Can you make me a wig?' she says directly.

Mr Dickie frowns and peers inside. There is a trace of something across his raddled face, recognition perhaps. Does he suspect foul play? Or is he doubtful that she can afford his services?

'I can pay,' she says, slapping some coins on the table beside the sack.

Mr Dickie looks hungrily at the money and something in his countenance shifts. 'Well, now, let us take a closer look, madam,' he says. He tips the hair onto the counter and paws at it tentatively, at first with a long hair pin but then with his slender fingers. 'Remarkable quality,' he murmurs. He lays it out flat in front of him, deftly teasing and arranging it into a long, sweeping mane.

'Forgive me for asking, madam. I wonder how, or indeed where, might you have procured this?' He smiles broadly, his cherry lips revealing a hideous mouthful of brown and missing teeth. He whispers conspiratorially, 'Red hair is so very *intriguing* on a woman, don't you think?'

'From my dear beloved sister,' Lucky replies. 'She passed over two weeks ago, and the last thing she said was that she wanted me to have her hair. It was the only possession she had to give me to remember her by.' She looks directly at Mr Dickie, never breaking his gaze and speaking without hesitation or guile.

'Oh, my dear,' Mr Dickie replies, placing a hand on his heart. Lucky knows that, despite her story, he is quite unconvinced. Or indifferent. 'What a touching tale, eh, Mrs–?'

'Hare,' replies Lucky curtly. 'Mrs Hare.' She dislikes this man, but she needs his services so restrains the urge to throttle him then and there.

Mr Dickie observes her closely and strokes his chin. 'Mrs Hare,' he repeats slowly. 'Well, this might take several days, but it is a task I shall take great pleasure from.'

'Fine,' says Lucky.

'And when you return for your fitting, Mrs Hare, would you like the wig dressed and styled? Perhaps into braids or swept up in a chignon,' he says with a dramatic sweep of his hand, 'like the ladies of the New Town?'

'No,' Lucky replies firmly. 'I want it long and loose.'

There is a lengthy pause while Mr Dickie absorbs this information. He is still fingering the hair. Lucky realises he is quite desperate for every scrap of information he can pounce on. He is nothing more than a bawdy old gossip.

'I see.' Mr Dickie narrows his eyes, then purses his lips and cocks his head to one side. 'For a performance, is it?'

'Of sorts,' Lucky says.

'You do know I supply all the wigs for the local

theatres?' Mr Dickie continues. 'And for ladies who like to "dress" for their men. I stock stage make-up too.' He studies Lucky's face more closely. 'A little rouge would do wonders for those cheeks, and you can dab some on your lips to make them cherry red,' he says. 'Like mine,' he adds with a puckering of his mouth.

Lucky is about to dismiss his suggestion when she stops. 'Might you have something to make my skin appear paler? I have always longed to have a fair complexion.'

'Oh, of course, my dear. And something a little more favourable than a handful of flour, eh? Face paint perhaps?'

He pulls out a drawer from under the counter, and Lucky sees a row of tiny tins. He runs his finger along them and then lifts one out. He removes the lid to reveal a smooth paste, so white that, even in the dull light of the shop, it gleams with a pearlescent glow.

'Try some,' he urges.

She scrapes a fingertip over the top and then smears it over her hand. She examines it closely; it is pale, deathly so. 'I'll take it,' she says.

'Very good, madam, very good,' he says approvingly. 'And will there be anything else, Mrs Hare? For your *performance*?'

'Could you write me something?' she says, ignoring his irksome tone.

'Write you something, Mrs Hare? Whatever do you mean?'

'Can you write me a note? For my husband?' She raises a coquettish eyebrow. 'I cannot write, you see, but it's for a game.'

Mr Dickie frowns, but then a knowing smile plays on his lips. 'Of course. I do so like a *game*. And what would you like the note to say, madam?'

'I would like it to say, "I was worth ten pounds".'

Chapter 18

There is a heightening of the senses in the dissection room. Every sound, smell and texture brings an energy and vigour to the air, despite the presence of death. Thomas and his fellow teaching assistant, Victor, are accustomed to the slice of scalpel into flesh and fat, sinew and muscle, right down to the bone, and it garners no horrors for them now. Or at least it didn't for Thomas – until Mary Paterson. The days since her naked body was folded and submerged in a whisky-filled cask have been shrouded in a gnawing inner turmoil that he has attempted to keep at bay by consuming more and more ale. And now, in the early spring afternoon, as the light is beginning to fade and lamps and lanterns are lit, he and Victor portion a cadaver, mutilated and exhausted beyond its own purpose by eager students now entering preparation for its final stage, as a skeleton.

Thomas bends over what is left of the corpse, carefully dividing the flesh into the six sections. He is sweating profusely, nausea rising in his gullet. The scraping, the slicing, the cracking has become too loud and overwhelming; it is insufferable. The sour smell of putrid flesh catches in the back of his throat. He swallows the bile down and waits for the urge to vomit to pass. He wipes cold sweat from his brow.

Victor looks up from his butchering and stares at Thomas. 'Too much ale last night, man?' he says with a chuckle. He barely lifts his head; he is too busy scraping flesh from bone.

Thomas takes in a long breath and tries to gather some strength. He has barely slept in days. His mind is haunted by Mary. He cannot get the girl out of his mind. They had shared a night together days before she had appeared in Knox's dissection rooms. He'd met her as he'd walked home from a drinking session with his fellow students. They had been carousing in the Canongate, racing and leapfrogging, and she had come to join in. She had jumped on his back, her friend on Victor's, and they had charged up the street, laughing and shouting, Mary kicking him with her feet as though he were a horse. Then, leaving the others, they had tottered all the way back to his lodging house on Lady Stair's Close where they had spent the night together. She was a free spirit, wild and beautiful. And yet, days later, her corpse was stretched out on a slab. And now he saw her everywhere. He was convinced he had seen her in the Grassmarket. It was as though she were following him, or was close by, watching him.

'I'm going to have a go at that little dollymop again tonight,' Victor breaks Thomas's imaginings.

Thomas gazes at the carcass in front of him and swallows the sea of saliva that seems to be forming in his mouth.

'Thomas?'

He looks up at Victor and tries to focus on him. 'Sorry, what did you say?'

'The girl I had last night. Quite delightful,' continues Victor. 'And reasonably priced too. Pretty little thing. Works at the dressmaker on Cockburn Street. I saw her in the window and next thing I know, well, I'd bought her.' He laughs. 'We went to that circus show on the Mound, I bought her a plate of oysters and that was it. It took little persuasion for her to come to bed. And she was fresh. Goodness, she was fresh!' He winks at Thomas and smacks his lips. 'Fresh meat, you might say!'

'That is no way to talk,' snaps Thomas.

'What do you mean?' says Victor.

'I said don't talk of women as meat.'

Victor frowns. 'I merely meant that she was a virgin. The fresher, the better, I say.'

It happens so suddenly: Thomas lunges at Victor, grabbing a handful of his soiled apron at the chest, scalpel still in hand.

'I said, don't talk that way. She is alive. She is a human being. She is not meat.' His mind is racing, and then, as though at once self-conscious of his violent reaction, he pushes Victor away. '*Yet*,' he adds with a wag of his finger, 'She isn't meat *yet*.'

Victor staggers back. 'Have you lost your mind?' he splutters.

Thomas rubs his hand across his face. 'Perhaps,' he says. He goes to the basin, pours water from a jug and splashes his face. 'Did you study the classics, Victor?' he asks as he rubs his face with a cloth.

'Of course,' says Victor, his tone a little sulky.

'Homer? The *Iliad*?'

'Yes. What of it?'

'The ghost of Patroclus pleads with Achilles. He pleads with him to give him a proper burial, otherwise he cannot pass through the gates of Hades. He warns Achilles that if he doesn't, he will be left to wander. That if he gives him his due rites, he'll not visit him again, because he will have passed over.'

Victor frowns. 'I remember that. But what do you mean?'

'Look around you, Victor. Look at the fragments of human life lying scattered, spilled, torn and butchered on these tables, which we will then macerate until all that remains is bone. In the next room we have a cask with a woman submerged in whisky until such time as Dr Knox sees fit to cut her up.' Thomas can hear his voice becoming louder, angrier, as sweat begins to trickle down his forehead. 'And I objected – no, wait, I *baulked* – at the idea of paying more money for her. I bargained over that woman's body. A transaction for the dead. And there will be no burial, no rites, no remembrance.' He stares at Victor. 'Will they visit us too? I'm beginning to wonder if it isn't already happening. For I keep seeing *her*.' He turns away so that Victor will not see the tears that are now spilling down his cheeks.

Victor shakes his head. 'You're wallowing in self-pity, man,' he says. 'I have no belief in phantoms or in visitations. Stories made up in antiquity! Look at us!' He pulls Thomas to face him and puts his hands on Thomas's shoulders. 'We are on the cusp of medical greatness. Our knowledge and understanding will inform and shape the future.' He gestures at the bodies and sliced pieces of flesh. 'Think not of these slabs of meat as people, think of them as specimens. This is modern science, Thomas. What we glean from the dead will help the living, now and in the future. The dead owe it to us. Who cares how much you paid for the flesh and bones, the subjects of our learning. The soul has gone. The body is a mere shell.'

Thomas sits down heavily on a stool, his head in his hands.

'Now pull yourself out of this depressing mood and come and dine with me tonight. I shall find you a girl and we can drink and be merry!'

Thomas pushes his shoulders back and looks at Victor. 'Yes, you're right,' he says with mock fervour. 'Distraction!'

'Absolutely!' says Victor. He roars with laughter.

They finish the preparation of the body for skeletonisation, plunging each section into casks of water to macerate until flesh departs from bone. Thomas feels lighter in his spirits. Victor has renewed his focus and reminded him of their purpose. He must shake off his macabre attachment to Mary. Perhaps it wasn't her in the cask anyway; perhaps he had been quite mistaken, and she was alive and well! Maybe the girl he had seen on the streets of the Old Town in the last few days had been not a phantom, but a real, living, breathing girl.

They are about to leave when a messenger boy stops him at the door.

'Excuse me, sirs, I've got a message for the assistant to Dr Knox, a Master Thomas.' He thrusts a grubby hand out.

Thomas takes the envelope. There is no name on it. He flips it over, but there is no indication of its sender.

'Who gave you this?' says Thomas.

'A lady outside, sir,' says the boy.

'An admirer?' chuckles Victor.

'She looked peculiar,' says the boy.

'How so?' says Thomas.

'She was as white as death, with long red hair, and she said she was called Mary.'

Thomas frowns at the boy and slips his finger inside. He touches something soft. He pulls out a lock of red hair. He recoils, an icy chill coursing through his veins. A message is scrawled on the card: *I was worth £10.*

'Who gave you this?' he shouts at the boy, grabbing him by his threadbare jerkin.

'I told you, sir. A lady,' says the boy with an innocent expression on his freckled face. 'She was outside a moment ago.'

Thomas pushes past the messenger boy and runs outside, but the square is deserted apart from one or two students walking with purpose. The sun is setting. From the corner of his eye he sees the boy run off across the cobbles and out of sight.

Chapter 19

'Well?' says Lucky, taking the pipe from her mouth.

'Ten pounds,' says Hare, walking into the kitchen with a beaming smile, raindrops glittering like diamonds on his hat and coat. 'Again! No discussion, no bargaining. That fellow who works for Knox, Thomas, well, he just slapped it into my hand without me even having to ask. Couldn't wait to pay me. It's been like that for the last few bodies now, eh?'

Lucky nods and takes a long draw. 'Good boy,' she murmurs to herself. 'Let's hope it stays that way.'

She had kept her performances as Mary Paterson to herself and had enjoyed the secret. For now, at least, she could put the disguise away.

'And where's the money?' she asks.

'I bought a horse,' announces Hare.

'You did what? A horse? What need have we of a horse?'

'Think of it as an investment,' says Hare. He beckons to her, and she follows him out of the house and into the backyard where, standing in the lashing rain tied to a post, is a small, miserable-looking beast.

Lucky folds her arms. 'It's not much of a horse. How much did you pay for that?'

'Never mind the cost,' says Hare, patting its bony rump. 'Why shouldn't I have a horse? A man like me should have one.'

'Oh, is that what this is about? *A man like you?*' scoffs Lucky. 'And what would that be? A fine gentleman?'

'It's good for business,' he retorts. 'It will pull my cart, and we can load any deliveries to Surgeons' Square on it rather than walking the streets with a sack over my shoulder. You've no idea how heavy a corpse can be. It hurts my shoulder.'

Lucky rolls her eyes. 'Well, we can't have that now, can we? Who did you buy it from?'

'The same person who sold me this,' says Hare, moving closer to Lucky and opening his coat. Resting in the belt of his breeches is a pistol.

'You bought a gun?' seethes Lucky. 'For what?'

Hare smiles. 'I think it might have its uses.'

Lucky shakes her head. 'For a highwayman, perhaps. You are a halfwit, William Hare. Don't you realise that spending money like this makes people talk? And we don't want talk, do we?'

'Well, well, well,' says a voice behind them. It is Burke. They turn to look at him. 'Is that your horse, Mr Hare? Are you lord of the manor now?'

'It is indeed my horse,' says Hare, closing his coat quickly.

As Burke stands beside them, Lucky notices that he is a changed man. He is dishevelled, a heavy growth of beard on his face, and his clothes, while new, are dirty and hanging loose from his depleted frame. A bottle of whisky sticks out of his coat pocket. He is deathly pale, and heavy bags hang under his red-rimmed eyes.

'And you being without money all the time? Strange, that,' says Burke.

'And how was your wee trip away to Falkirk? You and the wife well rested in your snug little abode just along the way there, neighbour?' says Hare.

'I'd say we're back just in time. So do tell: where did you get enough money to buy a horse? Eh?'

'I've been doing just fine,' says Hare with a grin. 'Got some work. A little bit here, a little bit there.'

'Business continues to prosper here at the lodging house,' Lucky interjects. 'The springtime always brings new bodies looking for a place to rest their weary heads.'

'Is that right?' says Burke. He moves closer to Hare until he is inches from his face.

'You seem a little angry, William. Not good for the blood, that,' taunts Hare.

'I think you and your missus have been busy without me,' says Burke. 'Am I right?'

'Ah, we're always busy, my wife and I,' says Hare with a wink. 'Just take a look at her belly.'

'If I find you you've been taking little trips up to Knox without me . . .'

'You'll do what exactly? Stick a pillow over my face while I sleep?'

'Oh, I think that was your plan, was it not, if Helen and I hadn't moved out?' snarls Burke. 'Now, let's just straighten things out. What have you two been up to?'

Hare sighs. 'The truth is, you were away, and I didn't know if you were coming back. I needed money, and I happened upon a drunken old woman who was begging to be finished off. So I did. Well, we did.' He glances over to Lucky.

Burke grabs Hare by the lapels of his coat. 'How many more? Tell me. How many?'

'Easy, now, easy. It was just the one. Honest,' he adds with a defiant twinkle in his eye. 'To be fair, I didn't think you were up for it any more, after that last one. The divine Mary Paterson. She really got under your skin, didn't she? Were you a little soft on her, William? She smelled good, didn't she? I bet she doesn't smell so good now.'

Burke's face contorts with rage. He shifts his grasp so that his fists clamp around coat, neck and skin, his knuckles white. He presses and twists so that now there is fear in Hare's eyes.

'Let him go,' says Lucky, her voice steady. 'This gets us nowhere. It's done and over, and the money's spent. There's more to be made.'

'We don't need him,' Hare strains to talk, his throat restricted by Burke's iron grasp.

'Oh, I think we do,' says Lucky. 'We need him to collect the money and bring it back – not throw it away on needless trinkets and clapped-out old nags. Whether we like it or not, we three are bound together in this enterprise. Till death us do part.'

Burke releases his grip but doesn't take his eyes from Hare.

'Mrs Hare? Mrs Hare?' The croaky voice of an elderly woman is calling from the front door.

Lucky snaps out of the intensity of the moment and plasters a bright smile on her face. 'Yes, yes! I am here,' she calls, bustling away to the door. An old woman and a young lad stand, huddled in the rain, waiting. Despite being the same height or perhaps even a whisper taller than his grandmother, the lad holds her hand tightly.

'Excuse me, Mrs Hare, might my grandson and I stay here?' says the woman. 'We've come a long way, from Glasgow, and the boy is tired and needs to rest. You were recommended to us, Mrs Hare. We were told you were a most kindly hostess.'

'Of course,' says Lucky with a warm smile. 'Let's get you in and out of the rain. You look exhausted, so you do. Come in and we'll light a fire. Are you hungry, laddie?' she asks of the boy. 'Would you take some porridge?'

'He'll not talk to you,' says the woman. 'He's deaf. And he can't speak a word.'

'Ach, the wee soul,' says Lucky, ruffling the boy's hair. 'Perhaps you might like a wee splash of whisky to warm you?'

'Oh, you're so kind,' says the woman. 'I do enjoy a dram on occasion.'

***

Hours later, Burke stands in the same doorway, a dead boy in his arms. The child looks as though he could be sleeping. But like his grandmother, he has been extinguished, suffocated like all the others before. It is the dead of night, but in these early summer months there is always a faint light, and so they need no lantern as Lucky checks the close is empty before they head round to the yard where Hare is waiting with the body of the boy's grandmother. Silently, they strip them and then tip them into two waiting herring barrels. The barrels are then rolled into the stable beside Hare's new horse.

'Come and sit by the fire until it's time to visit Dr Knox,' suggests Lucky. 'I'll make you some breakfast.'

'No,' says Burke, pulling a bottle out of his pocket and taking a swig. 'Nelly will wonder where I am.'

Lucky bites her lip. 'Suit yourself. William will call for you when it's time.'

'Make sure he does,' says Burke, turning to leave.

'Oh, he will,' says Lucky. 'You have my word on that.'

Chapter 20

Helen holds William's shoulders as he vomits into a bucket. She strokes the back of his head, his neck, and whispers to him how much she loves him, that he will be all right, that it's surely not the fever and just a passing sickness. Perhaps it was something he ate, she suggests. He sits back and wipes his mouth with the back of his hand. He has beads of sweat across his brow, and every line and crease in his haggard face seems etched deeper, like slashes in his flesh.

'I deserve all the ills,' he whispers.

Helen holds him closer, 'You are a good man.'

Burke begins to chuckle, but it quickly turns into loud, maniacal laughter. Tears are streaming down his face. Helen is unsure what to think. What to do.

'Why do you think I cannot rest, Nelly?' he says

eventually. 'I have become the Devil himself. I have just killed an old woman and a child. A child who gazed at me with innocent, pleading eyes before I finished him off. And I felt no urge within me to stop. Nothing. Each of the seven deadly sins consumes me.'

'Don't say that, William,' says Helen.

'Pride, greed, gluttony, lust, wrath, sloth and envy,' he muses quietly. 'Each one is in me now, festering and devouring me.'

'Maybe you've just lost your way. We can both make it stop. That boy could be your last. Remember in *The Pilgrim's Progress*? *Get thyself rid of thy burden, for thou wilt never be settled in thy mind till then: nor canst thou enjoy the benefits of the blessings which God hath bestowed upon thee until then.* You can stop!' she cries, as if his life depends upon it.

Burke turns to look into Helen's eyes and shakes his head. 'No, Nelly. I can't stop. You see, I don't want to stop. I feel this hellish lust for killing, I am greedy for it and greedy for the money it brings. I want to gorge on it. I have a rage inside me – a rage against those who have money without needing to kill and a rage against those who have no money but are lost souls, who don't deserve to live. Oh, sure, they inhabit a body, but they don't *live* a life. I envy those who have money and I envy those poor souls who are content without it. And pride – I am killing because I can, and it gives me power above all others. I can end life, and this nourishes me, and so I lust for it, and so it goes on and on.'

Helen searches William's face. He doesn't meet her eyes but reaches for the bottle once more.

'You scare me, William,' she whispers.

'I scare myself,' he murmurs, wiping his lips. 'Because I can kill and no one is stopping me. No one. No god, no heavenly power, has struck me down. So on I go. And on I shall go until *something* stops me.'

Helen stares at him in horror, recoiling at his words, pulling her body away from his. She can offer no further words of comfort and he doesn't want them. And so they sit like this for some time with silence between them until suddenly there is a knock at the door.

'Burke,' shouts a voice from outside. 'It's time.'

'Don't go,' says Helen, placing a hand on his arm. 'Let us pray to God for guidance.'

But Burke shrugs her off and staggers out of the house and down the wet street to Tanner's Close with Helen at his heels.

At the top of the close, they walk round the house to the yard where Lucky is leading the horse out of the stable. Helen leans against the wall, watching as the cart is wheeled out and the horse harnessed into it. Then the two barrels are rolled out of the stable and Burke heaves them onto the cart.

Helen knows what is inside each barrel, but she says nothing.

Lucky stays behind in the yard as they leave. She calls after them, something about getting a good price. Hare walks at the front, leading the horse, and Burke and Helen follow. Helen wants to be at Burke's side. She feels sure that if she stays close to him, she can help him and, besides, she has no intention of being left alone with Lucky.

They set off down the back of the tannery and the slaughterhouse onto King's Stables Road. It is raining, and mist hangs low over the craggy castle rock. They walk steadily through the Grassmarket, the horse's hooves clopping on the cobbles. The streets seem quiet, and no one gives them a second glance.

But on Candlemaker Row the horse suddenly stops.

'Get on with you,' says Hare. He pulls the horse's bridle. But the horse won't move. It jerks and tosses its head, refusing to be dragged. It is as though an invisible barrier stops it from proceeding any further.

'What's wrong with it?' says Burke, coming up to join Hare. He snatches the bridle from Hare and tugs hard.

But the horse will not budge. They all stand staring at it, bewildered. Burke slaps its rump and attempts to push it from behind, but, like a dead weight, it will not shift.

'Bastard horse,' snaps Hare. 'The beast is bewitched.'

'You try, Nelly,' says Burke. 'Some horses respond better to a woman.'

Helen walks nervously forward, patting the horse on its neck as she gets closer. Its large glassy eye watches her warily, and its nostrils flare.

'Come on, boy,' she whispers. 'Let's go.' She takes the bridle and pulls gently. Once again it lifts its head and stubbornly refuses to move. Helen waves her hand to show the horse the way, but it pulls its head up and steps backwards, bumping its legs against the cart. This spooks it further, and it begins to struggle, fighting against its harness. Helen jumps out of its way. It is now causing a scene, with people stopping to watch. Some folk laugh as they witness the horse's refusal to move.

'Stubborn old nag, eh?' laughs a toothless drunk propped up against a nearby wall.

'This horse is a bloody waste of money,' complains Hare bitterly.

'What's stopping it?' says Helen, looking around. 'Is it injured?' She looks down at its spindly legs. She doesn't dare go too near in case it should kick her.

'I know what it is. It's the bodies in the barrels,' says Burke under his breath. *'It knows.* It's telling us something.' His face is blanched of colour.

Hare sighs. 'Superstitious nonsense. But if the horse will not move, then we can't get these barrels up the hill. Oi! You, boy,' he shouts to a passing child. 'Go up to Surgeons' Square, find a porter and tell them we have a delivery for Dr Knox.' He hands the boy a penny. The boy stares at Hare warily, 'Get on with you!' he snaps. The boy snatches the coin and tears off.

Burke and Hare heave the barrels from the cart and place them on the ground.

'Take the horse and cart back,' Hare says to Helen.

'I don't want to,' she says nervously. 'What if it bolts or does something? I don't like it. I'm scared of the thing.'

'Do it, Nelly,' barks Burke, his face livid. He turns away, arms tightly folded across his chest. 'Now! Get it away from here.'

Helen realises she has never seen him show any kind of fear until now. She feels protective of him – like a mother removing a spider from the bed of a terrified child. She takes a deep breath, musters her courage and steps forward to take the horse's bridle, and then, slowly, gently, coaxes the horse up and around to face the other direction. As if the spell has been broken, the horse is perfectly biddable and settled.

'There now, everything's fine,' she says soothingly, both to the horse and to William. She pats the horse's neck, and now, effortlessly and obediently, woman and beast walk back across the Grassmarket, leaving Burke and Hare waiting with the barrels for the porter.

Chapter 21

'Ah, Nelly! It's yourself! Come join me for a drink,' says Lucky to Helen who has returned with the horse and cart. She has tied it up in the yard, relieved to be free of the whole business, and had hoped to creep past the lodging-house entrance without being seen, but just as she walks by, Lucky calls to her. She turns to see Lucky sitting on the doorstep, smoking her pipe, a bottle beside her.

'Just a drink,' Lucky says with a mocking tone. She picks up the bottle and offers it to Helen, who shakes her head. 'You don't need to look so scared, woman. I'm not going to kill you.'

'I'm not so sure about that, Lucky.'

Lucky lets out a snort. She takes a swig herself, looks up at the sky and then back at Helen. 'You know, you and I, we have to look out for each other,' she says wistfully.

'What do you mean?'

'We women have to stick together. We're a lot alike, you and me. We should be like sisters.'

'You're not my sister,' says Helen quickly. 'And you're nothing like me.'

'That's right, my dear,' says Lucky, leaning back on one elbow. She seems not to notice the pelting rain. 'You're all sweetness and innocence, aren't you?'

Helen turns to leave.

'But wait a minute now, is that a new bit of lace on your bonnet? And that dress, is that new too?'

Helen stops and turns round once more. 'William bought them for me,' she says with a tinge of pride in her voice. 'He likes buying me things. He says I deserve them.'

Lucky smiles. 'So you wear the clothes that he buys for you. And I'm guessing you drink the whisky he buys for you, and maybe eat the food too?'

'Yes,' says Helen. 'Of course. What of it? He loves me. He treats me well.'

'The money for all these things doesn't come just from cobbling. You do know that, don't you, Helen?' Lucky stares at Helen.

Helen shifts uneasily and folds her arms. She can feel herself blushing. 'I don't ask my husband how he gets his money,' she says defiantly. 'It's not my place to ask.'

Lucky lets out a harsh cackle. 'Don't fool yourself, Helen. You know fine well where your *husband* gets his money. There's no shame in it, my dear. You're just like me. You want a better life, and what's wrong with that? You don't get your hands dirty, but you enjoy the rich pickings that come with selling the dead.'

Helen's eyes widen. 'I don't know what you mean, Lucky.'

'Oh, but you do, dear,' says Lucky, her pipe clamped between her teeth. 'You tell yourself you've only got this life, so why not enjoy the good things when they come your way. I mean nobody cares about us, not those rich bastards in the New Town. We don't want to sell our bodies like the fallen women. And we shouldn't have to. So why not just allow the men to do what they do and we'll not ask too many questions. We look after their needs, and we'll enjoy the comforts they bring us? Yes?'

Helen shakes her head. 'No, I don't see it like that.'

Lucky stands up and moves closer to Helen. Helen doesn't move. She wants to hold her ground, but Lucky moves so close to her, she can feel her breath on her cheek.

'So how exactly do you see it? Oh, sweet Nelly. You don't kill but you turn a blind eye. That makes you up to your neck in the whole business, in the eyes of the law.' She reaches out and encircles Helen's throat with her right hand. 'And if you're caught, you'll swing like the rest of us.'

Helen feels tears welling in her eyes. Lucky presses her fingers harder. 'Ah, poor thing. You don't like admitting you're more like wicked Lucky than you realise.'

Just at that moment, they hear voices in the yard. 'Do it and I'll pay you my share,' Hare is saying.

Helen moves away from Lucky and walks around the back, quickly wiping her eyes. She sees Burke and Hare standing by the stable. They have taken the harness off the horse and are stowing the cart. The horse stands tethered to a post.

'I'm not doing it,' says Burke.

Hare takes the pistol from inside his coat. 'Just one shot and it's over.'

'Why wouldn't you do it yourself?' asks Lucky.

'I can't shoot a horse,' says Hare, shaking his head.

'Why do you have to kill it?' Helen blurts out.

'I'm not paying good money to feed a horse that's useless,' says Hare. 'It's better off dead.'

'William, don't let him kill it,' says Helen.

'Do it yourself – I'm not harming that woeful creature,' says Burke.

'No,' says Helen, tears welling again. 'Please don't – it's done nothing wrong.'

Hare pulls a paper twist of gunpowder out of his

pocket and loads the pistol. 'I can't kill animals,' he says, now ramrodding a ball into place. 'They look so pitiful. It would break my heart.' He holds out the pistol to Burke.

'Please don't do this,' pleads Helen, looking between Burke and Hare.

'I said no. That horse is cursed or something.'

'Away with your nonsense, Burke, just do it,' says Hare. 'I'll make it worth your while.'

And then it happens so quickly that there is no time for protestations or final words. Lucky grabs the pistol from Hare's outstretched hand and fires it at the horse's head. Smoke rises from the gun and the horse buckles heavily to the ground. Helen lets out a scream and kneels beside it, in utter dismay.

'Take it round to the tanners and be done with it,' says Lucky, handing the gun back to Hare. 'You kill humans without remorse, but not an animal?' She shakes her head and walks away, leaving Helen weeping, the horse's blood soaking her dress.

Chapter 22

The top of Lucky's head is pressing against the wall. Sweat drips from every pore so that her hair clings like coiled black snakes to her clammy skin. She feels cold, so very cold. Somewhere outside a dog is barking incessantly. The room is inky black, and she has a vague idea that it must be the middle of the night. She feels herself drift in and out of consciousness. The barking fades. A noise in the room forces her to open her eyes again, but everything is blurred. There is the soft glow of a lantern, someone is in the room with her, and she flinches as she feels rough hands pressing on her stomach. She tries to shift her body, but she is sluggish and heavy. She blinks, desperately trying to make out who is there. She cries out in dread. The figure becomes clearer: is it a man? At first, she thinks it is Hare, then Burke, until finally it morphs into Dr Knox: the sweep of his hair, the sharp features, a white collar, stiff and tight around his throat, and on his forefinger a glittering diamond ring. Pain sears like a hot poker through her back, radiating round her stomach like a tight band; it is a sickening sensation that spreads and burns, and now she sees Knox holding aloft a small, sharp knife. She watches in silent horror as he sweeps it downwards, slashing with a single movement into her body from breast to womb. Someone somewhere shrieks. Perhaps it came from her own mouth, she cannot tell. Knox is slowly, carefully peeling back her skin. And now she rises up and out of her own body, to float somewhere above. She looks down at herself on the bed. She is sprawled below, sliced open, a red mass of bloody meat, and she can make out something squirming in her gaping womb. She shuts her eyes in horror and disbelief. When she opens them again, she is lying once more on the bed, looking up at Knox and several golden-haired, hearty young men who gawp at her body. She is a living cadaver. Knox is staring at her open womb, a smile on his blood-spattered face. He reaches in, and she can feel him pulling and tearing. And then the men begin clapping and cheering as Knox lifts his arms up to the heavens; they are blood-soaked, dripping, and in his hands is something wrapped in swaddling. Slowly, reverentially, he lowers his arms once more, and what Lucky had thought was swaddling is in fact a covering of thick black hair, sticky with blood and excretions; it is not a baby, but something monstrous, goatlike, cloven-hoofed; instead of the gentle mews of a newborn baby, it is bleating furiously. The cheering from the men becomes a wild cacophony, and in the centre of it, Knox gazes at the hideous creature like a proud father, until he turns to pass it to her, and she hears herself screaming in utter terror.

'Lucky?' shouts Dr Knox. But it's not Dr Knox's voice any more. It is a woman's voice, sharp and commanding. Lucky feels her hand being lifted and then slapped. 'Lucky. Come now. Enough of this. We need to get this baby out.'

Lucky stares hard, concentrating, focusing as sweat drips into her eyes, and she sees it is not Knox but a ruddy-faced woman who is standing over her, her face framed with a white bonnet. Lucky tries to speak, but her words are slow to form.

'Who are you?'

'I'm Jean, the howdie,' she says. 'The handywoman,' she clarifies. 'That bairn is stuck. You're away with laudanum and goodness knows what else you've taken, but we need to get it out or you'll not survive this.'

Lucky moans incoherently.

'Your man sent word,' says Jean impatiently. 'Now, let's get you sitting up.' She hauls Lucky upwards and places a pillow behind her head.

Fragments of the day before now swim in Lucky's mind. She had been fetching water from the well when she had felt a gushing from within. At first, she had thought the water from the bucket had spilled, but then she saw the pink-tinged bloom on her skirts. She had managed to get back to the house, where she was gripped by a spasm of such overwhelming agony that she had vomited violently. She had tried to carry on, sweeping the floor and attending to the chores of the day, swigging whisky and laudanum too, to ease the pain, until it had all become unbearable, the spasms becoming more intense and more frequent, and she had crawled through to her bed.

The woman stays with her now, for what feels like eternity, talking, encouraging and attempting to pull the baby out. This wasn't like the last time; then, the baby had slipped out of her small swollen belly, tiny and shrivelled, dead on arrival. Now, through the relentless agony, Lucky begins to panic. In a moment of despair, she reaches out and grips the woman's arm. 'Don't let them take me to *him*,' she urges.

'What's all this?' says Jean.

'If I die,' says Lucky, with all the strength she can muster, 'don't let them sell my body to Dr Knox.'

Chapter 23

Lucky's child finally arrives, and as Jean helps to heave him out into the world, the room is quickly filled with the sound of his angry shrieking. He is a hefty, healthy boy with a mass of black hair and mottled red skin. Lucky decides to call him Jack, and with his voracious appetite and tenacious grip on life – the way he fought his way, ripping and tearing himself out of her womb – she knows he will survive. With her son's birth, Lucky feels the dawning of a renewed sense of purpose. By rights, she should have died. Her son too. Jean praised God for her survival, but Lucky's not so sure it is God they should be thanking. After all, why would God spare her? No transformation of her soul has taken place; she has not been blinded by a holy light of hope and goodness. Instead, her continued survival, and that of her son, will depend upon their arrangement with Dr Knox: her laudanum-induced vision had taught her that. Lucky recognises the worth of her son, and as he feeds lustily from her breast, she sees a path for them: they will thrive in spite of this miserable life, together. He will help her.

Lucky's respite is short-lived for she cannot rest. There is no gentle confinement, no time to lie and heal. There is work to be done, and without her the momentum of their business will fade. Since the day she shot the horse, William has been distracted, intent on spending rather than earning, and Burke has become distant. Yes, Burke and Hare have managed a few killings over the last couple of months that brought in some money, but they were just meagre pickings: a drunk woman Burke extricated from the police, a washerwoman, and an old hag and her daughter who infested the Grassmarket. The pace has slowed. Now with another mouth to feed, and this refilling of her cup, Lucky must set the wheels in motion once more. So, over the coming weeks, as summer slips into autumn, Lucky carries Jack everywhere she goes, and quickly sees how people are drawn to a woman holding a new baby, even more so than a woman with a baby in her womb. Women coo round Jack to catch a glimpse of his cherubic features and ruddy complexion. Such a healthy boy, they say. God bless him, they whisper, some making the sign of the cross. Many remark on his impressive size, his chubby wrists and mighty grip. He's going to be tall and sturdy like his father. And Lucky nods and smiles and comments about him being a good baby, easy to placate, a hungry eater, and, God willing, a healthy child. As if already understanding his role, Jack charms and bewitches with gurgles and bright, knowing eyes, watching, taking it all in.

It is on one of these outings to the Grassmarket that she notices Helen, out hawking but resting idly, chatting to the lad, Daft Jamie. A stupid creature, thinks Lucky, a child in a man's body. He is seen all the time in the Old Town, pacing barefoot up and down the High Street in his tattered clothes, visiting the same closes and wynds in a daily pattern that never alters. The townsfolk are used to him; he is part of their daily life. He has a special trick that he uses to garner pennies, whereby he can name the day of the week for any date or year: a pointless sideshow of little use to anyone. He has a glaikit expression and eyes that never meet your own; if for a fleeting second they do, they roll around like marbles. Helen is sitting on the steps outside a house and Jamie is beside her, head down, smiling with wet lips. The fact that Helen has befriended the simpleton fills Lucky with disgust. Lucky considers him as another unfortunate who must be removed, along with the paupers and beggars.

'Well, hello, there,' says Lucky with a breezy air.

Helen snaps her head up, her eyes wide like a frightened animal. 'Hello,' she says quietly. She stands up and immediately hoists her basket onto her back as if to leave.

Lucky turns her attention to the boy. 'Jamie, and how are you today?'

Jamie doesn't look up, but shifts awkwardly, wiping his large, dirty feet one after the other on his shins. One foot is grotesque and misshapen. Lucky is repulsed at the sight of it. She reaches out and lifts his chin, so that he is forced to look at her. She smiles at him, but he shrugs her off, refusing to meet her gaze.

'Jamie's having a bad day,' says Helen, laying a kindly hand on his shoulder.

'Oh, how so?' asks Lucky, feigning concern. She lifts Jack up onto her shoulder and pats his back.

'I've run away,' he says with a giggle. 'I pulled down a cupboard. Everything went smash!' he says, his hands flying out wide. 'And my mother boxed my ears. So I'm not going back there.'

As if remembering this moment of violence, he rubs his ears, then tucks his fingers into his waistcoat pocket.

'Have *you* seen her?' he says to Lucky. 'My mother, is she looking for me?' He stands and gazes up and down the street.

'No, dear,' says Lucky. 'I've not seen her. But where

will you go, Jamie? It's a cold day, and tonight will be bitter.'

It is at this moment that Helen takes notice of Lucky, as if grasping where the conversation might be headed. She scowls at Lucky, her brows in a tight frown.

'I wonder, would you like to come and stay with me, at my lodging house,' continues Lucky. 'You don't even need to pay a penny.'

As Jamie absorbs this offer, Helen gives Lucky a nudge and shakes her head. 'Oh, I don't think you'll need to do that,' says Helen. 'Your mother will soon forgive you, Jamie. She always does.'

'Well, here's an idea,' says Lucky smoothly. 'You could just come and wait at ours for a wee while, have some porridge, maybe a dram too and warm yourself by the fire until your mother has calmed down. And if you need to stay longer with us, well, you are most welcome. Wee Jack here would love the company.' At this, she turns the baby round and shows him to Jamie.

Jamie grins at the baby. 'Hmm, all right,' he says slowly. 'Just for a bit, mind. I like porridge. Nice and hot. I don't like the fiery stuff, though; it burns my throat. I like snuff. I like the way it tickles. D'you have any?'

'Of course,' says Lucky with a broad smile. 'Helen, go and tell Burke, would you? I'm sure he'd like to join us.'

Helen looks panicked. 'I don't know where he is,' she lies, her voice a little shrill.

'Sure you do,' says Lucky.

'Well, I can't join you,' she mutters. 'I've got work to do.'

'No matter,' says Lucky calmly. 'I think I saw him head into Rymer's. He's often in there, these days, is he not? That is if he's not in the White Hart. I'll call in myself on the way past.

'Come along, Jamie, there's a good lad,' she says, taking the boy's hand.

Rymer's grocery sits in the Portsburgh, just a stone's throw from Tanner's Close, and when they reach the door, Lucky steps inside, telling Jamie to wait for her. Burke stands at the far end of the counter, an empty glass in front of him. He is slouched against the wall, staring at the floor, and there is something lost in his countenance. He no longer appears robust in body or in mind; he seems defeated. As she approaches, she sees he is talking to himself. So as not to arouse suspicion, and with Jack still in her arms, Lucky purchases a pennyworth of butter and a dram from the shopkeeper and moves closer to Burke, boldly tapping his outstretched foot with her toe. He looks up with surprise and stares at her, his eyes red and watery. His face is thin now; so different to his old self that he looks almost wild. Lucky notices spots of vomit on the front of his jacket. She flicks a glance to the window, where Jamie stands outside, his arms wrapped around his body against the cold.

'Who's that?' slurs Burke, straining to see through the glass. 'Is that Jamie?'

'Aye,' says Lucky, checking to make sure the shopkeeper isn't in earshot.

'He's well known,' says Burke, eyeing the boy. 'Just a boy, Lucky. Someone's baby.'

Burke is gazing at Jack in Lucky's arms. The baby coos and gurgles.

But Lucky is unmoved. She glances over to the window. Jamie's forehead and nose appear, pressed hard on the glass as he tries to peer inside, making his face look distorted.

'He's a daft lad,' murmurs Lucky. She shifts Jack into a different position on her hip and then knocks back the whisky in one gulp. 'An easy end,' she mutters through the fire in her throat. She places the glass down on the counter.

Burke considers. There would be no resistance, no fight. 'A lamb to the slaughter,' he drawls.

'Get some whisky on the way, although I'm not sure he'll take any,' Lucky instructs.

'Whatever you say,' says Burke.

She is not used to such obedience. She can operate him like a puppet, she thinks with a sense of triumph. Finally.

'Some snuff too,' she adds. 'He says he likes it. And find Hare. He'll be around somewhere, spending any money he has ... Burke?' she says impatiently. 'Do you hear me?'

His blank eyes swivel to hers, but the man behind them is long gone. For the first time, Lucky imagines placing a pillow over his mouth and pinching his nostrils tight. Hare lying on his chest. If he sinks much further into this mouldering self-indulgence and is no longer fit for purpose, his body will be of use in other ways.

'Don't linger,' Lucky snaps. 'There's work to be done.'

'Aye,' sighs Burke. 'I'll be right along.' He fumbles for his hat and, with some effort, places it on his head.

Chapter 24

'The foot, gentlemen, is composed of twenty-six bones and is divided into three regions: the tarsal, metatarsal and phalangeal regions.'

Thomas leans forward on the front row of the steep lecture theatre, his chin resting on his hand. He is looking down at Dr Knox as he struts and performs beside his anatomical specimen: Jamie Wilson's right foot. Behind him hangs a complete skeleton.

'This foot, from our subject here, is a fascinating example. However, it is important we remind ourselves that the tarsus in the human subject is composed of seven bones. Their arrangement when well formed, unlike this one' – here he nods to the malformed pale foot lying in front of him before turning to an exquisite skeleton hanging beside him and lifting the foot, stroking the tiny white bones with his bejewelled forefinger – 'when well formed, like this, it yields an exquisite beauty and perfection comparable to no other part of the human body.' He holds it aloft so that the foot falls downwards like a dancer's, as though outstretched and pointed, and his gaze lingers on its structure. 'This part of the skeleton seems indeed perfected in man. Or indeed in the case of this skeleton, in *woman*.' There is a ripple of laughter at this comment.

Thomas shudders; he visualises flesh once more on the bones of Mary Paterson, for this is her skeleton that Knox fingers with such delight. Looking at what remains of her now, Thomas once more sees that flowing, wild red hair and imagines her looking up at him, not with the hollow sockets of this empty skull, but with her living eyes, mischievous and seductive, her delicious full lips wide in a laughing smile. Now, her face is preserved forever in a perpetual ghastly grin. He considers that since his more generous payments to the two men who supply the bodies, his sightings of Mary have ceased. It is as though she has simply melted away, like the flesh on her pulverised bones.

All that remains of her has been painstakingly connected with wire and hangs suspended on a frame beside Knox as he delivers his lecture. Perhaps it had all been just a terrible nightmare or hallucination brought on by nerves. He had been quite alone in that hell; no one else had even considered the sudden, unexplained fate of Mary Paterson, let alone tortured themselves over it as he had. And just as the worry of it all had begun to fade with the new academic term, now he is confronted with Jamie Wilson's right foot, and facing once more the terrible realisation that something insidious is at work.

The minute he had seen the body stretched out on the table, he had known it was Jamie. There was no lingering doubt, no margin for debate. He had mechanically paid the two men £10, they had vanished into the shadows, and he had remained rooted to the spot until Victor had burst into the room, his usual effervescent self.

'That's Daft Jamie!' he had announced boldly – innocently even, as if he was delighted to see him, pleased with this recognition. But then his face had dropped. 'But, hang it all, I just saw him the other day. Hale and hearty!'

Knox had instantly and vehemently denied that it could be anyone they knew, dismissing it as merely a 'striking likeness', and ordered the subject to be immediately prepared for dissection, with the peculiar request that his feet be removed. He had muttered something about using one or both of his feet for a lecture.

Remembering this remark now, Thomas begins to bite his fingernails. Trying to think rationally, he considers that perhaps Knox didn't know Jamie like the students did, for he was a frequent presence in the vicinity of the university buildings, asking for snuff or money. He wasn't much younger than they were, and he was a lad they all teased, but not in a cruel way, for they understood he was different. They tried to make him drink spirits, thinking it would be amusing to see Daft Jamie stagger and carouse with them. But he wouldn't. He didn't like the taste. He liked to impress them with his memory and his knowledge of dates; he could be funny too, and the students would gather round him to ask all kinds of questions in the hope of a witty retort.

'Here, Jamie,' someone had asked. 'In what month of the year do ladies talk least?'

'February,' replied Jamie with a grin, 'because there's least days in it.' And so they would laugh and pat him on the back and give him a penny. Tiny boys would run up to him with tight little fists challenging him to a fight, but Jamie was too soft-hearted and wouldn't think to hurt a flea. The good folks of Edinburgh looked out for him, giving him their old clothes, like his green waistcoat and the spotted kerchief round his neck. Sometimes he would refuse, explaining that if he dressed *too* well, nobody would give him money or snuff any more. Many tried to give him hats or shoes, but he refused. Even on the coldest day, Jamie would walk barefoot, his mousy hair flapping in the raw, icy winds that swirled up and down the High Street. Thus Jamie's feet were distinctive; thick and gnarled, they clearly belonged to someone who regularly pounded the cobbled streets. His toes were unusually widely spaced, and his right foot was twisted and diseased – a fascinating subject for anatomists.

Obediently, silently, Thomas and Victor prepared the body. But as they looked closer, they observed marks on his skin and knew without doubt there had been foul play. This was something they had never seen before. Victor had gone quite pale as he had traced the scratches and bruises found all over his body.

'Oh, Jamie,' he had murmured sadly, looking up at Thomas. 'Somebody has attacked him, hurt him. Do you think he was . . .?'

Thomas had swallowed hard and nodded.

As if unwilling to accept what had happened, to say the unthinkable, they had said no more and gone their separate ways.

But Thomas knew there was more to this. Jamie had clearly been assaulted, and this was itself surely evidence of murder. That was shocking enough, but the question remained: why? Jamie was gentle, kind and honest. He was well loved by the folks of the Old Town. He would never choose to get into a fight. And there was something else gnawing away at the back of his mind. That the two men who brought the bodies in were untrustworthy was undeniable. When questions were asked about the cadavers they delivered, the provenance was always placed elsewhere. They said they had purchased them from someone else or been given them to dispose of. Or they had found them, already dead, in some backstreet. And this had been enough to satisfy them all, Knox possibly the most. But Jamie's body was different to all the others. There had been no markings of any kind on any of the other bodies brought in by those men. No visible cause of death. No evidence of a struggle or a fight. He thinks back and allows his brain to skim over as many of them as he can remember. His recollections are hazy, but there is something they all had in common apart from Jamie and perhaps the young child in the barrel: the others all stank of whisky. The child was very young, just a small boy, so he wouldn't have partaken in drinking. And Jamie, they all knew, didn't like liquor. Jamie was young, but he was a stout, healthy lad. Jamie, he now realised, had bruises and scratches because he had fought back. Jamie hadn't wanted to die; he had been sober enough to know his assailants were intent on murder. And those others who had died were either weak and infirm, or elderly – or had been so drunk that they had been easy to subdue. They had been incapable of fighting back. Were those men *killing* rather than *procuring*? Had they been lying from the outset? Thomas mentally counts the bodies he can remember purchasing from them, adding them on his fingers. At least fifteen or sixteen. Possibly more. Suddenly, he feels clammy. Thomas now thinks he knows what the two men have done – what they are doing. Mary Paterson didn't die naturally ... neither did Jamie, the old women or the sick aging men. Or the old woman and child crushed into herring barrels. It was obvious, really, hidden in plain sight. Those men – Burke and Hare, was it? They were murderers: killing for profit. And if he, Thomas understands this, then Knox with all his anatomical expertise *must* know too.

Thomas snaps his mind back to the present. Knox has finished his lecture and is gathering his notes; the students have left. They are alone.

'Dr Knox, sir,' he says, standing.

'Ah, Thomas,' says Knox, glancing upwards. 'And what did you make of today's lecture? Isn't the foot an astounding piece of engineering?'

'I wonder if we might talk in private?' Thomas sidesteps along the row in a clumsy fashion and then walks down the steps to the front. 'I have something of the utmost urgency I need to discuss with you, regarding the two gentlemen supplying the cadavers. I'm afraid it might be a matter for the police.'

Knox is unfazed. 'No, Thomas, that won't be possible,' he says quietly as he places his papers into his briefcase and swiftly fastens the two buckles. 'My timetable is full, and I'm sure I have no interest in those men. People like that are of no consequence to me, nor should they be to you.'

'But, sir!' Thomas struggles to articulate the words to explain.

Dr Knox raises a hand. 'There is no need to trouble the police, Thomas,' he says, with a quick smile, 'for no crime has taken place. And if you were to involve the police, it might harm your prospects.' He looks up. 'I'll entrust you to return the specimen to its bucket of spirits. Good day.'

With this, he turns and walks out the door, humming a jaunty melody, his heels clicking on the polished floor.

Chapter 25

Raised voices carrying on the wind catch Helen's attention as she meanders down the winding street on her way home from hawking. She picks up her pace, straining to see what is going on. She assumes it is a thief caught red-handed, a pie or a pocket watch in his sticky hand. But then her blood runs cold, and she stops. Daft Jamie's green waistcoat stands out, bright and vivid against the dullness of the late October day. She tries to make sense of what she is seeing. As she approaches, she quickly realises this is no ghostly apparition but a familiar face. The scrawny lad wearing the green waistcoat and spotted neckerchief is not Daft Jamie; it is William Burke's nephew, his brother Constantine's boy, Richard, and he is in the tight grip of a furious shopkeeper.

'Tell me where you got that waistcoat, laddie, or I'll

give you something to think about.' The man has a handful of the green fabric in his fist.

The squirming boy has a look of defiance on his face.

Helen hangs back; a gut feeling tells her this is not the time to be seen. She wants to step forward to intervene, to rescue the lad, out of family loyalty, but she fears where this might lead. Others, though, bored with the grind of life, relish a street commotion, and she is jostled by a growing crowd, pushed out of the way, obscuring her face from the boy.

'Oi! Leave the poor laddie alone,' shouts a woman, sleeves rolled up to her elbows. 'It's just a waistcoat.' There are shouts of agreement.

The man swings round to face his audience. 'It's not just a waistcoat,' he says, his voice rising in fury. 'It's Jamie Wilson's waistcoat. And I demand to know where he got it from.'

Helen bites her lip as the crowd begins to mutter.

'Daft Jamie's?' says the woman. 'How do you know that?'

'I'll tell you how I know,' snaps the man, his eyes ablaze. 'I know because I gave it to him. It was mine. I gave it to Jamie because I took pity on the lad. That grease spot,' he jabs a finger at the lad's chest, 'that's gravy from a meat pie I ate only a few weeks ago. And those snuff stains? Everyone knows Jamie is partial to snuff.'

The crowd murmurs in apprehension. The boy is now beginning to look fearful.

'I ask you again, laddie,' says the man, his voice quiet and menacing, 'where did you get it? Did you steal it from poor Jamie? He was fair delighted with it and wouldn't be parted from it willingly.'

'No, no! I swear I didn't,' says the lad, his eyes wide. 'My uncle gave me it.'

Helen feels sick.

'A likely tale!' someone shouts.

'But that's Jamie's kerchief too!' shouts another.

The crowd gasps at this. All eyes now focus on the spotted piece of cloth knotted around the boy's neck.

'Just who is your uncle, laddie?' says the man, moving closer to the boy.

'Aye! Who is your uncle?' demands a voice from the crowd. 'And where did *he* get it from?'

No one is looking at her, so Helen steps back. Everyone is focused on the boy and the clothes that William gave to his brother.

'And, more to the point, where's Jamie?' a woman shouts. Everyone begins speculating on Jamie's whereabouts.

'No one's seen Daft Jamie for days...'

'I saw his mother and his sister out looking for him. They're worried sick...'

A sudden silence falls, as if everyone is catching up

with their thoughts. They look at one another, shocked and anxious. Helen continues to slip further back, stepping away from the crowd. She needs to get home; she needs to warn William.

'Jamie's missing and here you are walking around in his clothes bold as brass,' the shopkeeper says.

Helen sets off down the street.

'Take the boy to the police!' somebody yells to much agreement.

'He's not the only one missing,' shouts a woman. Helen freezes and swings back round. She immediately recognises the girl who was with Mary Paterson that day. 'My pal Mary's not been seen for weeks. No one's seen head nor tail of her since she was out drinking in Canongate. I went to the police ages ago.'

This creates more indignation, more intakes of breath, more chatter.

For a moment, Helen wonders if this is it. If everything will unfold right now and the folks of Edinburgh will piece together the whole series of grisly events, become an angry mob and turn on her. But suddenly Richard Burke sees his chance and makes a run for it, his escape a flash of green pushing through the crowd and sprinting up the street to cries of outrage. And while all eyes are on the bolting boy, Helen sees her chance and runs down towards the Grassmarket and home.

Chapter 26

Helen hears a clamour from the close as she races home, a wild hullaballoo that increases in volume as she descends the common stairs. She opens the door to a scene of drunken revelry; the dingy room is in a shambles, shrouded in smoke; it is as though she has stumbled into Hell itself. And there, as proud as Old Nick himself, sits William, belting out a song with his eyes closed, stamping his foot rhythmically while an old woman in a red-and-white striped dress whom Helen has never seen before twirls and twirls, shrieking with laughter and wailing off key. Her face is purple and sweaty, and her skeletal white arms wave above her head. Helen quickly grasps that this inebriated old crone is to be the next victim.

Hare is dancing with Lucky, his feet, clumsy and heavy, pounding the floor. Their new lodger, Mrs Gray, sits by the fire, smoking a pipe and watching the proceedings, a tiny child cowering in her lap. Lucky's baby lies cocooned in a bundle of rags in the corner, fast asleep, dead to the world.

'Well, well, look who it is,' says Lucky, grinning dangerously.

'Helen, my dear!' says Mrs Gray when she sees her come through the door. 'Come join the Hallowe'en carousing. No evil spirits would dare haunt us tonight!'

Helen looks to William, but he doesn't cease his singing, and she wonders how she will make them stop, make them listen to her as she imagines whisperings about Daft Jamie spreading like wildfire through the town. Lucky stares at her, as if smelling her fear, and goes quickly to her side, wrapping an arm tightly around her waist.

'We need to get Mrs Gray out of here. She can lodge with me tonight,' she says, her hot breath tickling Helen's ear.

'I need to talk to William first,' says Helen, firmly shrugging off Lucky's grip.

The song finishes, and the old woman claps and cheers, and William beams and takes a bow, stumbling so much he almost topples over his stool.

'Come now, Mrs Gray,' announces Lucky, reaching down to scoop up her baby from the floor. 'Let's get you and the little one settled with us for the night. We can leave Mrs Docherty here with the Burkes. You'll get some peace with us!'

'No, no, no! I keep telling you, he's not a Burke!' slurs the old woman, shaking her head at Lucky. She points a wavering finger in Lucky's direction, her eyes rolling wildly. 'Why do you keep calling him Burke? He's a Docherty too, just like me! His mother was a Docherty.' She then turns to Burke. 'That makes us related! Doesn't it? Distant cousins or something.'

'That's right!' says William, clapping his hands together and grinning broadly. 'Come sit on my lap, Auntie Madgy!'

The old woman roars with laughter and whirls over to William like a spinning top. She falls onto his knee, her spindly arms wrapping around his neck, and buries her face in his chest.

Repulsed by this sordid sight, Helen swoops over and wrenches the old woman off William's lap. The force of Helen's jealous anger and the frailty of the woman cause her to be thrown to the floor with violent velocity, where she lies groaning in agony.

Immediately, Lucky begins to hustle a startled Mrs Gray out of the house. 'Let's get the babies away from all this commotion,' she says as they leave, the door slamming behind them.

'You gave Jamie's clothes to your brother?' shouts Helen in William's face.

'Aye, what of it?' he retorts.

'People have noticed, William. The boy was walking around in Jamie's green waistcoat.'

'So what?' says William, rubbing his chin.

Hare's ears prick up. 'To Constantine? You gave the clothes to Constantine?'

'For his sons. His boys have nothing.'

'Are you bloody daft?' says Hare, now looming over William.

William springs up, throwing the glass in his hand to the floor where it smashes, and grabs Hare tightly by his throat. He in turn grabs William by the lapels of his jacket. But William Burke is stronger. He pushes Hare backwards, but they do not see the old woman still on the floor, writhing like an insect, and they stumble over her, falling heavily on her legs. There is a ferocious struggle; the old woman desperately tries to pull herself out from underneath the sprawling bodies, but as William retracts an arm to throw a punch, his elbow catches her in the eye, and she is thrown backwards once more, striking her head on the corner of the bed. Blood instantly pours from a gash, trickling dark and rich down her pale face. She touches a hand to her temples and seeing her hands smeared in her own blood begins to screech.

'*Murder!*' she hollers with such force that Helen is convinced the whole street will hear. '*Murder!*'

'Shut up!' she yells. She crouches down and clamps

a hand over the woman's mouth. But the woman's breathing is becoming faster, desperately sucking on Helen's fingers.

'Here, take some of this,' says Helen, releasing her momentarily to grab a bottle of whisky from the floor. She pulls out the cork and, holding the woman's head, pours the liquid down her throat. The woman chokes and splutters, but Helen persists.

'Drink it!' she urges. She forces the bottle further into the woman's mouth, glass smashing against teeth. From somewhere deep within, a malevolent fire is ignited inside Helen. It begins with a tiny flame but then, as it burns, it grows into something uncontrollable, something destructive: something truly hellish. She realises that her heart is beating furiously not with fear but with exhilaration. Nothing will make her stop. The old woman's eyes bulge, her hands flail in desperation, but Helen forces the bottle still deeper down her throat. Further and further, until whisky bubbles from the woman's nose.

Suddenly, William is pushing Helen out of the way. Hare appears and grasps the old woman's nose tight with one hand and places the other across her mouth. William lies on top of her, but she fights and kicks, and in Hare's drunken stupor he loses grip, so that she has a brief opportunity to cry out. Hare throttles her and then slaps his hand to her mouth so violently that her head smacks off the floor. Without thinking, Helen reaches in to grip her nostrils, and soon the job is done; the old woman stops fighting and, finally, is still. For a few minutes they hold their position to make sure she is dead before letting go. The two men fall away, exhausted, but Helen cannot move. She stares at the woman, whose eyes are wide open as if forever frozen in the throes of horror, her faced bloodied and bruised.

The only sounds are the crackle and burn of the fire and the distant comings and goings on the street, voices bellowing in the close outside, and the rasp of their heavy breathing. Helen touches her forehead and neck; sweat is pouring off her.

'The bitch bit my hand,' says Hare, sucking on his palm.

'Aye, she had some fight in her,' agrees William, adjusting his hat. 'Not as much as Daft Jamie, mind. He gave it his all, that one.'

Helen thinks of Jamie, his broad smile, his familiar face in a crowd. Poor Jamie. And she imagines how frightened he must have been in that moment, fighting off two men hellbent on murder. Then she looks at the old woman and realises she is no better than them. She too is a murderer. She grabs the bottle of whisky and takes a long drink, comforted by the fire in her throat. She wipes the sweat from her brow with the back of her hand.

William stands and begins to haul the body over to

the corner beside the bed. Helen goes to help. Hare remains on the floor examining his hand. 'She drew blood,' he says. 'Like being bitten by a rat.'

'Shouldn't we close her eyes?' asks Helen, as if this small act of respectfulness exonerates her brutal murder. 'We should. We should close her eyes.'

William doesn't reply, so Helen leans over and presses down on her papery eyelids. But they won't stay closed; they keep springing back, staring blankly in protest.

'Never mind that. Take her clothes off,' says William.

Wordlessly, Helen obeys. She pulls off the woman's worn old boots and fumbles for buttons and ties on her skirt. Under her ragged clothes, she is just a withered corpse, more bones than flesh. Life has drained quickly from her veins, and she appears waxy, like a shrivelled doll.

'Hide her under the straw,' says William, grabbing handfuls to bury her. 'We can take her to Knox in the morning.'

'What if someone sees her?' says Helen.

William sighs. 'I need to sleep,' he mumbles, then he slumps heavily on the bed, places his hat over his eyes and within moments is snoring loudly. Helen looks to Hare, but he has already passed out by the fire, clutching his injured hand to his chest. She takes the whisky and crouches down on the floor beside the hidden body. As she raises the bottle to her lips, in the still of the moment, she sees her hand is shaking.

Chapter 27

While Burke and Hare sleep, Helen keeps watch. Her mouth is sour with the taste of whisky, which she consumes with more fervour than ever before. It is as though she can't get enough to calm her down. She forces herself to keep her eyes open and wonders what she fears the most. Someone coming in and discovering Mrs Docherty? Or William, now in the clutches of despair, being persuaded by Lucky and Hare to finish her off. She has no strength left in her tonight, and if they come for her, the fight will be over quickly.

In a drunken, delirious stupor, sliding in and out of consciousness, she sees her dead and naked body being pressed into a box. What is real and what is nightmare is becoming entangled. She feels herself turning upside down; beside her swing Joseph, Mary Paterson, Daft

Jamie, Mrs Docherty and many others, all naked and hanging by their feet from meat hooks like the cattle at the abattoir. Their skinned bodies gleam a marbled red and white, and Mary Paterson's long red hair skims the sticky, bloody floor. Doctors in spattered aprons enter the room and begin hacking at their flesh with knives, jovial and indifferent, busy in their work. As they come closer, Helen opens her mouth to scream and jolts awake. She takes a swig of whisky and then another until the bottle is drained.

She is aware of the men close to her. They are awake once more and have resumed their revelry; staggering and crashing around, sometimes they argue, sometimes they laugh. They mutter words she cannot make out. Other people, neighbours perhaps, seem to be in the room, and the cacophony continues. Glasses are smashed. Furniture topples over. But Helen doesn't move. Her eyes close again, and when quietness descends once more, she falls into a fretful sleep. She dreams she is hammering on a door, crying out for help, but no one comes. Then, suddenly, she realises that the hammering is not her but the sound of someone pounding on their front door.

She staggers to her feet, dizzy and disorientated, to find a smiling Mrs Gray with her bairn in her arms.

'Hello, dear,' she says brightly. 'Did I waken you?' Mrs Gray is squinting at Helen and attempting to see into the room beyond. 'Is everyone still sleeping?'

Helen turns to look behind her, but there is no sign of Burke or Hare. 'I don't know,' she stammers, bewildered.

'Don't mind me, dear,' says Mrs Gray, pushing past her.

Helen quickly follows and, as the dreadful events of the night before start to emerge in her memory, positions herself by the bed. 'I didn't expect you back so early, Mrs Gray,' she says nervously. 'Let me clean up before you come in; it's not safe for the baby.'

Mrs Gray looks around the room. It is in a terrible state with broken glass and upended furniture all over the floor. 'Quite the night, it appears,' she sniffs. 'What on earth happened here? Was there a fight? And where is everyone?'

Helen immediately realises that the men must have gone to make arrangements for the removal of the body, perhaps to find a tea chest. 'I ... I really don't know. I was just about to tidy up,' she lies. She fetches a broom and makes a dismal attempt at sweeping the floor.

'Why don't I give you a hand?' says Mrs Gray.

'No!' Helen snaps.

Mrs Gray looks at her strangely.

Helen softens her voice. 'You shouldn't have to clear up our mess.'

'I just need to find wee Johnny's stocking. We left in such a hurry last night I must have dropped it somewhere.' She surveys the room as Helen shifts awkwardly. 'Where's the old woman?'

For a moment, Helen is caught out by this mention of a living, breathing Mrs Docherty.

'She left,' mumbles Helen, rubbing her hot face. 'Last night.'

'Is that so?' says Mrs Gray, a quizzical look on her face. 'Most peculiar. She told me she was going to stay for two or three nights to look for her son.' She fusses around the room once more. 'He came here from Ireland some weeks ago, you know. She thinks he's here in Edinburgh somewhere.'

'Oh, I didn't know that,' shrugs Helen. She carries on sweeping and watches Mrs Gray from the corner of her eye as she makes her way over to the corner of the room, the bed beside the straw pile.

Helen rushes over and blocks the way. 'There's nothing over there,' she blurts.

Mrs Gray stops. Her eyes narrow and she pushes Helen firmly out of the way. 'What are you hiding, Helen?' she says as she puts the baby down and gets on her hands and knees to look under the bed.

'Aha! There it is!' she says, standing up. Helen closes her eyes. 'Johnny's stocking,' she says, waving it in the air. 'I told you it was around somewhere . . . Well, if the old woman has gone, I can move back over with you and William. I prefer it here. I don't care for Mrs Hare, and I certainly don't take to her husband. He's a sinful man.'

The baby starts gurgling. He has crawled over to the pile of straw and is tugging at something.

'What have you got there, Johnny?' says Mrs Gray. And then she gasps in horror, for the little boy is playing with the fingers of Mrs Docherty.

'Holy Mother of God,' says Mrs Gray, snatching up the child.

Before Helen can say or do anything to stop her, Mrs Gray has reached a hand down and pulled back a large clump of straw to reveal the body of the old woman, curled up in a ball, her face bloodied and bruised.

'It was an accident!' cries Helen.

Mrs Gray steps backwards, crushing glass underfoot, and looks, horrified, from the body to Helen. 'What hell is this?' she gasps. 'An accident, you say? I think not.'

'I . . . I don't know how it happened,' pleads Helen. 'She had too much whisky. She fell.'

But Mrs Gray is having none of it. She clutches the baby to her bosom and marches out of the room into the passageway, up the common stair and out into the close, with Helen running after her, pawing at her shawl.

Lucky appears in the gloom.

'We can pay!' shouts Helen. 'Ten pounds a week. You can help us.'

Mrs Gray spins round.

'They sell them,' Helen whispers, 'to the doctors.'

'*God forbid!*' says Mrs Gray.

'What's all this commotion?' says Lucky, now standing close to Mrs Gray and glaring at Helen.

'The old woman,' blurts Mrs Gray, pointing back towards the apartment. '*Murdered*. See for yourself. Her bloodied body lies in there.'

'Tell her, Lucky, tell her what we do,' begs Helen.

Mrs Gray looks aghast at the two women. 'You too, Mrs Hare? I should have known. And you have the nerve to ask me to join you?' She edges away, her face contorted in alarm. 'You want me to take money for dead people? *Is that what you people are?* Barbarians, the lot of you. And to think I was staying with you, with my child. It is foul murder, I tell you!'

'I cannot help it!' Helen shrieks.

'You surely *can* help it,' says Mrs Gray emphatically, 'or you would not stay in this accursed house.'

'Come, come, Ann,' Lucky says smoothly, 'come back to the lodging house and take some breakfast with us. We can talk things through in a cordial manner.'

'Oh, no,' says Mrs Gray, shaking her head. She presses her baby tighter to her chest. 'I'll not sit anywhere with the likes of you. I'm a good Christian woman, and I'm going to the police. I'll not see murder done and remain silent.'

And with this she turns away and hurries up towards the West Port.

'What do we do?' moans Helen. 'Should we go after her?'

'They need to get the body out of there,' says Lucky, looking back to the lodging house, 'or you and William are done for.'

'*William and me?* It's all of us!' shouts Helen, running after Lucky and grabbing her shoulder. 'You said we should be sisters in all of this!'

Lucky swings round, her face white with fury. She grabs a fistful of Helen's hair and twists her head downwards. 'You shouldn't have told her, you imbecile.' She spits outs the words, her lips inches from Helen's. 'It happened under *your* roof, Helen, and William Burke is *your* man.'

She releases Helen and marches away, wiping her hands on her skirt and cursing loudly.

Chapter 28

It is late when the knock on the door comes. Helen rocks backwards and forwards on a stool. William, cool, disinterested, continues to sip from a bottle. The knocking persists.

'Just follow my lead, Nelly,' he says. 'Say what I say.' Slowly, he goes to open the door.

Helen's hands are shaking so violently that she sits on them. She feels her heart thumping.

'Mr Burke?' says a man's voice. 'May I come in? I'm Police Sergeant John Fisher.'

William steps back and with a dramatic flourish of his hand allows them to enter, because the man is not alone. With the sergeant is Mrs Gray, lips pursed, arms folded, and another policeman, smartly dressed in a long dark overcoat with brass buttons, his boots polished to a lustrous shine, holding a lantern.

'And, pray, what can I do for you, Police Sergeant Fisher?' says William, his tone cocky.

'I'm here to enquire after the whereabouts of one of your lodgers,' says Fisher easily.

'Is that right?' says William. 'And which one would that be? This woman here perhaps?' He points a finger at Mrs Gray. 'I turned her out last night, as I'm sure she's told you. But I wager she hasn't told you the whole story.'

'And what's that, then?' asks Fisher.

'Disorderly conduct,' sniffs William.

Mrs Gray shakes her head. 'Lies,' she says. 'They got rid of me so they could murder.'

Fisher lifts a hand to silence her. 'Mrs Gray tells us that there was an old woman here – a Mrs Docherty? Come over from Ireland to look for her son, I believe?'

'Oh, she's long gone,' says William casually.

'I see,' says Fisher. 'And when did she leave, Mr Burke?'

'This morning. Early it was, about seven,' says Burke.

'Indeed?' Fisher glances around the room. 'Seven this morning.'

'Aye. And plenty folk saw her leave. You can ask anyone round here.'

'You won't mind if I take a look around?'

'Be my guest.' William sits down, leans back in the chair and places his feet on a stool, ankles crossed.

'The straw pile beside the bed,' says Mrs Gray, staying by the door and pointing. 'Look there. That's where the body was. Where my poor boy touched her hand.'

The two policemen wander over, and Fisher begins to poke around. Helen can barely contain herself. She yanks her hands out from under her and twists her fingers compulsively. The candle on the mantelpiece casts shadows on Burke's face. Helen looks at him, but he won't meet her eyes, and, in the darkness, she cannot read his expression.

'There's nothing there,' says William with a smile, his teeth gleaming. 'You're wasting your time, gentlemen.'

'Ask him about the box, then,' shouts Mrs Gray from the door.

'What box is that now, Mrs Gray?' William glowers at her.

'Your neighbours saw you hauling a box out,' says Mrs Gray. 'Mrs Docherty perhaps? Taking her to the doctors, were you?'

William sighs. 'You don't give up, do you, Mrs Gray? There's no law against moving things in boxes, is there? You need to learn to mind your own business.'

'Thank you, Mrs Gray,' says Fisher. 'I can manage.'

'I can see there is no body here, Mr Burke,' continues Fisher, 'but how do you explain the blood?'

Helen looks up at William. But he doesn't flinch.

'I don't know about any blood,' he says quietly, picking a fingernail. 'Nelly, do you know about any blood?'

She swallows.

'I told you!' says Mrs Gray defiantly.

'Mrs Burke?' repeats Fisher.

'Me? Blood?'

'Yes, you, Mrs Burke. Come and take a look, if you would, please.' Fisher beckons her over. As Helen shuffles over, William gives her a nod and Fisher shares a look with the policeman, who gives him the lantern and then goes over to talk to William.

The two men converse in low voices. Helen wants to listen to what they are saying, but Fisher is speaking. 'Do you see the blood? Here – and here?' He indicates the dark red patches on the floor and amidst the straw.

'I don't know anything about that,' says Helen. 'It must've been the other woman. Yes, I'm sure it was. I should have cleaned it up. She was here about a fortnight ago. I haven't washed anything since.'

'Not Mrs Docherty's, then?'

'Oh no. I saw Mrs Docherty again, this afternoon,' lies Helen.

Fisher gives a little smile. 'Oh, you did? And where did she go to . . . after she left here?'

'The . . . The Pleasance.' Helen doesn't know what to do with her hands. She tries putting them behind her back, and then when this feels uncomfortable, she folds her arms in front of her chest. 'Yes. That's where she's staying. I saw her in the Vennel,' she rambles. 'She was very sorry, you see, for having been so drunk.' She tries to smile at this, the way Burke is smiling.

'And she left at seven?'

'Yes, yes, that's right. Seven, last night.'

'Oh?' says Fisher. He is surprised. 'You say seven *last night*?'

Suddenly, the room feels very cold and very quiet. Helen looks over to Burke who is not smiling any more. She feels a ferocious heat in her face. Everyone is staring at her.

'Ah, now, Nelly,' says Burke with a rueful shake of his head. 'You're getting jumbled up.'

'Am I?' says Helen, almost in a whisper. Tears well in her eyes. 'Seven – that's what you said. Seven, last night.'

There is such a long pause that Helen wonders if the unfolding scene is in fact only in her head. She feels dizzy. She cannot remember what is true and what is a lie any more. She sees Mrs Docherty dancing, spinning and laughing, the red and white stripes of her skirts spiralling round like a barber's pole, and then she is naked, deathly white, yet still dancing, with blood spilling from the gash in her head down her face and into her open mouth, coating her teeth.

'What did I say?' she says, blinking. 'Did I get it wrong?'

'I think, Mr and Mrs Burke, that I'd like you to come with me to the police office. Best just to get things straightened out.' Fisher's voice is calm, but he seems different now, almost nervous.

William doesn't argue, doesn't put up a fight. He stands up and allows himself to be ushered out of the room by the policeman. Helen follows. As they head up the stairs and out into the wynd, she is aware of eyes watching them from windows and doorways. She catches sight of a woman in the dark close beyond: a woman smoking a pipe.

'Wait,' she says.

'Yes, Mrs Burke,' says Fisher.

'The Hares . . . William and Margaret Hare. They live down there, at the lodging house.' She points towards Tanner's Close. 'They were here last night too. They saw her leave. Ask them.'

Chapter 29

Unable to sleep and tormented by his thoughts, Thomas has become a night walker. He finds solace in the dark, in slipping unseen through the streets of Auld Reekie. Sometimes he ventures into the New Town, whose inhabitants slumber and dream in cosy feather beds through the long night. In the Old Town cruisie lamps and penny candles burn steadily at all hours. Work never ends there, and the poor must snatch sleep on bare floorboards, shivering under straw or a rough blanket.

For Thomas, it is the simplicity of placing one foot in front of another that comforts him; brooding thoughts can be redirected by a distracting silhouette at a window or a shadowy close never before seen. Sometimes he wonders if he is really searching for a glimpse of Mary Paterson or a lame boy calling out for a bit of snuff. Over the last few weeks, he has felt restless yet listless, struggling with his studies and growing distant from his boisterous companions and their mischief and merrymaking. The excitement surrounding the acquisition of fresh subjects for dissection has been replaced with dread at whom might be in the box and the realisation of how they met their end. Since Daft Jamie weeks ago, there had been no further deliveries – until yesterday. The same two men had appeared in the afternoon, a heavy tea chest on a porter's back. Thomas noticed that their manner had shifted from when he first met them all those months ago. Gone was the polite hesitance and awkwardness; instead they were bold, insolent and drunk. They presented the dead as if they deserved to be congratulated, like a cat bringing its master dead birds, and there is a malevolence in their eyes that frightens him. He hadn't dared to open the box. He simply paid them the rate of £10 and told the porter to put the crate into the cellar, as far away from him as possible. He would not open it alone, he decided. This burden was too great to carry by himself. Dr Knox had made it clear that the provenance of the bodies was of no importance to his work, that the people, their lives, their deaths, mattered not. What the dead could do for his reputation was all that mattered.

Now, as Thomas wanders past a shop window, he

catches a glimpse of his reflection illuminated by the full moon. He is more cadaver than man: spectral white and alarmingly dishevelled. He takes no care of himself and sees no reason to. When he finds himself standing on the North Bridge, staring up at the castle keeping watch over the city, he wonders if it might make sense to throw himself off instead of persevering in this misery. He remembers his friend, who did this quite successfully the previous year, smashing into the ground below at speed. His bones were so shattered he would have been no use as a specimen. Better than cutting his throat, Thomas muses, which would leave him rather too intact. He imagines Dr Knox smiling and rubbing his hands, scalpel at the ready to dissect him with his usual fervour. To Knox, he muses, we are all just meat.

'Thomas!' a voice shouts from the other side of the bridge.

He swings round to see Victor sprinting towards him, looking quite out of breath.

'I've been looking for you everywhere,' he pants. 'There's a policeman looking for you.'

'For me?' His blood runs cold.

'He needs the keys to get into Knox's rooms. Says there's a body in a box he needs to look at.'

'A policeman?' Thomas doesn't know whether to be terrified or relieved.

'Yes. They sent a messenger to your accommodation.' Victor looks at Thomas carefully. 'I know you like a night-time stroll, but Thomas, old chap, you weren't going to jump, were you?'

'No, no,' says Thomas, patting his friend on the back. 'I wasn't going to jump, Victor. Now let us go.'

After retrieving the keys from his room, Thomas arrives at Surgeons' Square. It is still dark, although there is a gentle shift in the clouds that suggests the sun is beginning to rise. Two men stand outside the door, one holding a lantern, the other hugging his arms around himself. Their breath clouds white in the frigid air.

'Good morning,' says the man with the lantern. 'Thomas Fergusson?'

'Yes,' says Thomas.

'I'm Sergeant Fisher,' says the man. 'And this is Dr Black, police surgeon.'

Thomas acknowledges each man with a nod as he unlocks the door. 'And what can I do for you, gentlemen?'

'We believe bodies are delivered to these rooms for the anatomist Dr Robert Knox. Is that correct?' asks Fisher.

'Yes, although several anatomists receive bodies – not just Dr Knox.' Thomas leads them into a small reception room where he sets about lighting lamps.

'Quite,' says Fisher. 'However, we have been informed that Dr Knox is especially generous with his payment for bodies, hence our coming to you first.'

Thomas nods.

'And have you taken delivery of a body recently, sir? Yesterday perhaps?'

'Why, yes.'

'May we see it?'

'It's in the cellar. I haven't looked at it yet.'

Fisher frowns. 'But you bought it for Dr Knox?'

'Yes, I paid the two men who brought it in.'

'Paid for it without looking at it? Is that usual? Surely you would desire to check the quality of the goods, so to speak, before paying the gentlemen? Ensure that the box did in fact contain a body?'

'It wasn't my usual practice,' admits Thomas. 'I was short on time yesterday. But the men have delivered subjects for dissection many times before, so–'

'You supposed they were trustworthy?' Fisher completes his sentence.

'Yes, something along those lines.' Holding a candle aloft, Thomas leads them out of the room and down some steps towards the back of the building, to the cellar below. It is a dank, musty room with miscellaneous tools, a table on its side and some empty crates. There, in the middle of the floor, sits a large tea chest.

'Sir?' a voice calls from upstairs.

'Down here, Findlay,' shouts Fisher. 'My assistant,' he explains to Thomas.

They hear footsteps, and then a tall policeman holding a lantern ducks and enters the room accompanied by a rather shabby-looking woman.

'Ah, Mrs Gray,' says Fisher. 'Now let us open the box.'

'The lady might find this distressing,' says Thomas.

'Fear not, young man,' says Mrs Gray, raising a palm. 'As God is my witness, I have seen wickedness at work, and I am here to help put an end to it.'

Thomas cuts the cords around the box with a knife, and then Findlay begins to prise off the lid with a crowbar. As the lid is raised, the stench that hits them is one of liquor and decay.

'Good God,' says Findlay, raising a hand to his nose. 'It is foul.'

The men shuffle forward to peer inside.

Dr Black lifts the head upright, then takes the lantern from Findlay and holds it close to the face, regarding it with some concentration.

'A newly deceased body, Dr Black? Not one that has been interred?' asks Fisher.

'I would say so,' agrees Dr Black.

'What depravity leads a living soul to end another's life and discard them in a box?' remarks Findlay.

'Destitution at first,' offers Thomas quietly, 'then greed, and then, maybe, something else.'

'The Devil,' says Mrs Gray, standing in the shadows.

'Indeed,' says Fisher, shaking his head. 'Mrs Gray, please come forward if you feel you have the stomach for this task. I wonder if you could look at this body and tell me if you recognise it.'

Mrs Gray swallows and then steps into the light cast by the police surgeon's lantern.

'Aye,' she says. 'That is Mrs Docherty and no mistake. The very same who I saw carousing with William Burke and Helen, and who lay dead in the straw the following morning in their house. As God is my witness, I swear this to be true.'

'There is blood around the nose and mouth,' says Dr Black, tracing the features of Mrs Docherty's face with a finger in the air. 'And there appears to be lividity here on the neck. I shall of course do a thorough examination, but it would appear to me that this woman met with a violent end.'

'It is always two men,' says Thomas. 'The same two who bring in the bodies. We were led to believe they were merely the middlemen, that they had been given the bodies to dispose of.' He is astonished at how easily these words slip out of his mouth. This glib, uncomplicated lie sounds so plausible, he knows he will have no case to answer. And nor will Knox. There is nothing to prove otherwise. But he must live with it.

'William Burke,' says Mrs Gray. 'And the other one is

Hare. A William, also. He was there with his wife, Lucky.'

'Findlay, I think it's time we brought Mr and Mrs Hare into the police office,' says Fisher. 'They seem to have some involvement in all this.'

'There have been so many others,' admits Thomas. 'None with blood or marks on them, but their bodies are all gone – dissected, I mean.'

Fisher looks at Thomas. 'When you say *many*?'

'At least sixteen,' says Thomas. 'Perhaps more. I've lost count.' This, at least, is the truth.

'All gone?' says Dr Black.

'All gone.'

Chapter 30

Lucky paces the day room she shares with other women prisoners and their infants at Calton Jail. Jack, asleep in her arms, is oblivious to the bleak surroundings. Close to his mother's heart, soothed by its rhythm, he is unaware that it beats fast because she is nursing an intense rage. Being surrounded by other women who have led hard lives laced with crime intensifies her own aggression; she sleeps little, eats sparingly the cold porridge and thin broth they are served and instead feeds ravenously on her own wrath, most of which is directed at Burke and Helen, with a little reserved for Dr Knox, who she fancies is sitting by a roaring fire in a fancy house, laughing uproariously at them all. With no whisky to distract her, no bodies to source, she remains tightly wound, often lashing out at other prisoners for such misdemeanours as a sour glance, a misplaced remark, an accidental nudge or perceived slight. They don't shy away from retaliating, and so she is the frequent instigator of vicious fights. The prison wardens have already warned her she will be put in irons or forced to walk on the treadwheel if she keeps losing control. Many within the confines of these high walls fear her, including the wardens. There are whisperings of her crimes with Burke and Hare, and she knows she is an object of abhorrence, but it only fuels her anger.

There is little contact with Helen, who is kept away from her in a separate storey so that Lucky only catches glimpses of her when they are taking their exercise or moving from refectory to sleeping cells. Mute, shoulders stooped, face bruised from beatings, Helen has become a spectre. Burke and Hare are in another wing; with no chance to communicate, Lucky is ignorant of what they have said, what they have confessed to, and whether she has been implicated.

She and Hare had not had long to establish the story they would tell before the police came to take them. But she had made sure Hare knew that the less they spoke, the better the outcome.

***

'They've got nothing on us,' she reminded him after seeing Helen and Burke being led away. They were sitting in the kitchen, Hare with his head in his hands,

Lucky smoking her pipe. 'And it was in Burke's house; the old woman was *his* guest.'

'It'll be me going to the gallows for all the killings,' he wailed, wringing his hands and then reaching for a bottle to swig from. 'Not you. You'll escape it,' he said, wiping his wet lips on his sleeve. He was in the depths of self-abnegation and wouldn't listen to a word Lucky was saying. 'For you're a woman.'

'Listen to me,' she said. 'Say nothing unless there's a bargain to be made.'

Hare was curious. 'A bargain?'

'They'll have found the old woman's body by now at the doctor's rooms. One corpse' – she raised a single finger in the air – 'because everyone else is long gone, hacked to pieces. There's nothing left to show they ever existed. No bodies: no evidence.'

'What if the doctors say it was us? They must know.'

Lucky laughed wryly at this. 'What do they know, exactly? Knox won't say a word. He wouldn't lower himself. And his little helpers won't say anything either. They won't betray him or ruin themselves for this. They'll say they didn't know a thing. And the lawyers and judges will keep them out of it. The dirty little secrets of their comrades will be locked away so they can nod at one another at their balls and fine luncheons.'

'And then what?'

'If no one's talking, they'll need to bargain for it,'

Lucky mused. 'Your freedom for evidence against Burke. Bide your time. Be patient. Keep your mouth shut.'

Hare nodded, eyes darting, fear written all over his face. 'What if Burke talks first?'

Lucky took a long, slow draw on her pipe as she considered this. 'He's no Judas,' she murmured, ribbons of smoke wafting from her nostrils. 'But that's his problem. Not ours. Once a deal is struck, we make it clear that the pair of them are behind all of this. They are the masters, we the pitiful, terrified onlookers.'

When the police arrived the next morning, hammering on the door, Lucky was ready, but Hare was fast asleep and awoke in a panic.

'Don't act like a guilty man,' she hissed before opening the door. 'You can't remember anything. You have a poor memory. *Say nothing.*'

They were marched to the police office, then to the Canongate Tolbooth, where they were placed in separate cells before being transferred to Calton Jail. There, she had no chance of encountering him again. Her statement was a sparse patchwork of vague half-memories. She said little and feigned fear of Burke. She denied a long friendship with him and rejected the suggestion that she and Helen were anything more than acquaintances. Now, she had to wait. She knew, if Hare wavered, she would be joining him on the gallows.

***

Many weeks have passed, and November has drifted into December, with its pervading damp, freezing air and gloomy days that struggle to yield any light. There is no news apart from hearsay and whispers, and this gives Lucky too much empty time, for her mind is a predator's, fixated on hunting and killing.

One day, her pacing of the room is interrupted. A visitor wishes to talk with her. She is ushered into a different room, one with a table and two chairs, where she is told to sit and wait.

A dour-looking man, dressed in black, enters.

'Margaret Hare? Of Tanner's Close, West Port, married to William Hare?' he says in a sombre tone.

'I am, sir.'

He pulls out the chair on the other side of the table, looks down to check its cleanliness and then sits, crossing his legs.

'I have news, Mrs Hare. Your husband has elected to turn King's Evidence.'

She says nothing. She watches as he plucks a hair from his coat sleeve.

'Do you know what that means, Mrs Hare?'

Lucky raises an eyebrow. 'No,' she lies. She has a fair idea.

A flash of a smile. 'Your husband has agreed that

you and he will testify against Burke and Helen McDougal. And in exchange for your disclosure of events, you will receive immunity from prosecution.'

She sits forward. 'Immunity? You mean protection?'

The man nods.

'For me too?'

The man nods again.

'And the others?'

'The others? Who might you be referring to?' says the man. 'Mr Burke and Helen McDougal, or the many others you killed?'

'Burke and his woman,' snaps Lucky.

'William Burke will stand trial for the murders of Mrs Docherty, Jamie Wilson and Mary Paterson, and Helen McDougal for the murder of Mrs Docherty.'

Lucky absorbs this triumph. 'And then what?' she pushes. 'After the trial?'

'And then you will be free to go,' he says, standing up once more. He doesn't push the chair back in. He steps away from it as though it is contaminated and then pauses at the door. 'I must warn you, though. We can *attempt* to keep you and Hare as clean-handed as possible during the trial, but convincing the good people of Edinburgh of that is another matter. Out there,' he waves a hand to the world beyond the prison, 'there are, shall we say, feelings of discontent towards your actions. These sentiments are growing stronger every day as information makes its way out onto the streets. Your release might not bring the freedom you imagine, Mrs Hare.'

Chapter 31

The folk packed into the courtroom in the High Court of Edinburgh have listened to proceedings all day and all through the long night. It is Christmas Day now, and they are waiting for the jury to return their verdict. Helen is exhausted; she feels sick and tremulous with nerves. The skin on her hands is raw and bleeding, but she feels a compulsion to scratch it. She has barely followed any of the trial; it has been utterly perplexing. So many people have come and gone; some folk she knows and recognises, others she has never seen before. They all had something to say. Many said terrible things about her and about William. Lies have been spoken too, bold, awful lies, despite all having sworn to tell the truth. Lucky Hare, who came to the stand, babe in arms, evaded questions every time the infant coughed or cried, and barely said a word.

Hare never caught her eye but wheedled and wormed his way around the questions, not even answering all of them; he denied that he'd killed that old woman, claiming that he only witnessed it. How could he say that? Helen cannot understand why Lucky and Hare are not sitting beside them, here in the dock. Why were they allowed to speak against them and then ushered away as if they have no part in this?

Burke has said little, and she does not want to trouble him with her concerns. But now one of the men on the bench is speaking, and he has placed a black cap on his head. He glowers at Helen, and she feels the quick rise and fall of her chest as she hears the words 'cold-blooded murder' and 'not proven'.

Not proven. What does it mean? Her eyes dart around the room as the man keeps talking; there is an eruption of applause and cheering which seems to spread out into the street. She turns with a questioning look to Burke who sits beside her.

'Nelly, you are out of the scrape,' he explains. His eyes, bloodshot and puffy, gaze at her with concern. She stares at him blankly. 'You are free,' he whispers.

That is not why everyone is cheering. She realises they are clapping because William has been found guilty. But she cares not for herself. What will happen to William?

'Make no mistake,' the man continues. 'The jury

have found the libel against you *not proven*; they have not pronounced you *not guilty* of the crime of murder.'

The crowd murmur at this.

I am guilty, thinks Helen. Am I guilty? Her mind wanders. I am guilty but they won't kill me.

But then the man asks for quiet, and the courtroom falls silent. Burke is concentrating on what is being said; he stands, solemn, resolute.

'William Burke, you now stand convicted, by the verdict of a most respectable Jury of your country, of the atrocious crime charged against you . . . You will be carried from the bar, back to the Tolbooth of Edinburgh, therein to be detained, and to be fed upon bread and water only . . . until Wednesday the twenty-eighth day of January, and upon that day to be taken forth to the common place of execution, in the Lawnmarket of Edinburgh, and then and there, between the hours of eight and ten o'clock before noon, of the said day, to be hanged by the neck, by the hands of the common executioner, upon a gibbet, until he be dead, and his body thereafter to be delivered to Dr Alexander Monro, Professor of Anatomy in the University of Edinburgh, to be by him publicly dissected and anatomized . . . And may Almighty God have mercy upon your soul.'

Helen hears someone sobbing, unable to catch their breath, then realises it is she who is crying and her face is wet with tears.

'No,' she whispers. 'William, it cannot be.' She reaches out to touch his arm, hoping he might take her hand, but he doesn't, so she clutches his moth-eaten coat instead.

'The burden has fallen from my shoulders, Nelly,' he says quietly as he sits down. His head is erect, his chin high, and he gazes intently ahead, as if looking at something distant, something that only he can see. 'Don't weep for me. At last, like Christian, I can continue with my journey.'

Helen's mind is a tangled knot, and she cannot think what William is talking about. She has a vague memory of Christian, of *The Pilgrim's Progress*, but it is from another time, another life. She has forgotten who they once were. There is no time to say anything more as he is bundled out of the courtroom. He doesn't look back. Helen is surrounded by strangers, with expressions of hatred and disgust. She can hear the mob outside as she stands up. Bitter, furious words are thrown at her as she leaves the court building, and then, as she stumbles towards a carriage, a woman throws something hard at her. It hits the side of her head, and she begins to bleed profusely. She is caught by a policeman who pushes her inside the carriage and slams the door shut as the crowd roars.

'Burke her!' shrieks a woman. 'Burke her like they did poor Jamie.' There is a cheer of approval.

Helen cannot see anything from within the dark enclosure of the carriage, but she can hear fists and objects being hurled against the sides as she cowers on the floor, too terrified to move.

When they return to the prison, she is led to a cell alone, away from everyone else.

'Let me stay,' she pleads. 'Let me stay here in the prison. Don't make me go out there.'

The warden shakes his head. 'Oh no, dearie. You'll be released tonight when it's dark and the mob have dispersed, and then you'll be a free woman. Isn't that what you wanted?'

'Can I see William?' she begs. 'My husband.'

'Burke! You can see him alright. You can see him swing on the twenty-eighth of January with everyone else. You can push your way to the front and take your chance then.'

He shuts the door and locks it, and she can hear him laughing as he proceeds down the corridor.

Chapter 32

It is a bitterly cold evening; frost already sparkles on the ground, and the woman crossing the North Bridge is swathed in a blanket that covers her head and shoulders. Beneath the folds is her baby. The freezing temperatures keep everyone huddled together indoors, which is fortunate for this woman. Lucky Hare has left Calton Jail a free woman. It was all so remarkably easy. She kept Hare's side of the bargain by giving meagre evidence in the High Court and then was told she must wait several days before being spat back out onto Edinburgh's streets. Hare is still imprisoned; there are more legal procedures to be concluded, and there have been threats from Jamie Wilson's family, who are furious that he has turned King's Evidence and will likely walk free. But Lucky cares not, for she has no intention of waiting for him. She will not bide with her husband again. She cannot, for risk of being hounded by the mob, and so she is truly free. She thinks neither of Burke in the condemned cell waiting for his death, nor of Helen who was released some days ago. There have been whisperings that they will be cornered and lynched in the street; even Knox has been threatened. It is not safe to stay in Edinburgh any longer, but first she must return home to retrieve her hidden belongings.

When she arrives at Tanner's Close, it is deathly quiet, and nobody notices her slip down the wynd towards the house. She hasn't been here since the morning she and Hare were awoken by the police, but it is clear others have. The door hangs, broken on its hinges, and the glass in every window is smashed; the mob have been here, and they have ransacked and torn the house to pieces. She steps inside and quickly realises there is nothing left. Every last stick of furniture has been taken, and anything fixed – the floorboards, the walls the fireplace – has been smashed or ripped out. Lucky doesn't fear the mob, but for the first time she truly understands her fate, and that of her son, if she remains in the city. They will tear her limb from limb, as they have desecrated her house.

She leaves swiftly and goes round to the yard. Hare's pigs have been taken, but thankfully the mob haven't thought to plunder the outer buildings. Clutching Jack to her chest, she opens the cellar door and slips inside, pulling the door behind her, in case anyone should come. In the murk, she awkwardly feels her way along the damp wall to a pile of straw, where, hidden deep within, in the very darkest corner of the room, she retrieves a sack. She is pushing her hand inside to check the contents when she feels a touch on her arm and then a small freezing hand gripping her wrist. She jumps back in horror, but she cannot see who is there.

'Lucky?' a small voice croaks.

'Helen?' says Lucky quietly. 'What in God's name are you doing in here?'

There is a sound of shallow, panicked breathing.

'I've nowhere to go,' says Helen at last, the words laboured. 'I was looking for you, I thought you were out of the jail, when the mob came. I hid in here under the straw and I heard them shrieking and screaming, tearing up your house. I thought I was going to die, but they didn't come in here.' She grips Lucky's arm tightly. 'No one will help me, Lucky. I went to Constantine, but he turned me away. And the police, they just laugh. I don't know what to do. All I can do is hide.'

'I'm not helping you,' says Lucky. 'If we're seen together, the mob will string us up. Let go.'

'Don't leave me,' Helen whispers, her grip tightening. 'Please, I beg you. Just help me get away from here.'

'Why would I risk my life to help *you*?' says Lucky, wrenching her arm from Helen's fist.

Placing the baby on the straw, she pulls something out of the sack. Helen cannot see as Lucky arranges Mary Paterson's hair on her head and pulls it tight over her scalp. But, just at that moment, the wind catches the cellar door, and it swings open, spilling moonlight over Lucky and her long red tresses.

Helen gasps. 'What is *that*? A wig?' she says. 'Is it red? Wait, you look like . . .' She falls silent for a moment until she begins to laugh. At first it is quiet, but then it becomes maniacal. 'Mary Paterson? You made a wig with her hair? You really are the Devil, are you not, Lucky? A fiend. William knew it too.'

'What does that make you, Helen? An angel?' sneers Lucky, once again lifting Jack to her breast and wrapping the blanket around them both. 'And where is your precious William now? Cowering in jail until they hang him. Oh, there's a sight I would've liked to see.'

'What will become of me?' sobs Helen.

'I do not care if you perish at the hand of the mob, Helen. That's the difference between you and me,' says Lucky. 'Some of us are victims, some of us, survivors. We should have killed you when we had the chance. Put you out of your misery and made some use of that pathetic carcass of yours. At least then we'd have gained something from your existence. If I could kill you now and sell you to Dr Knox, I would.'

Then she turns and strides out of the cellar, leaving

Helen in the straw, lost in despair, and sets off back up the close towards West Port, feeling emboldened by her disguise. Hurrying up Victoria Street, head down, she knocks into a man holding a bundle of parcels and a lantern. The parcels fall to the ground, and as he bends down to retrieve them, Lucky is unaware that the blanket has slipped from her head.

'Please excuse me, madam,' he says, glancing upwards. He stares first at her long red hair and then her face. She is about to continue onwards when he puts out a hand and touches her arm.

'Mrs Hare?' says the man, now upright.

Lucky curses herself for not wearing a bonnet. She frantically rearranges the blanket.

'Oh, you can't hide from me. I'd recognise that luscious hair anywhere,' says Mr Dickie from the wig shop. 'You *have* been busy since we last met. Going somewhere, my dear?'

Lucky doesn't linger a second longer. She pushes past him and bolts up Victoria Street, towards the High Street, a rising panic in her chest. The baby, unsettled at being jostled, begins to howl, drawing attention to them. Her mind is racing. She has the money that she hid in the sack, enough, she hopes, to escape Edinburgh, although to where she does not know. Hare had spoken of returning to Ireland, but there will be people watching those routes, waiting to pounce. Her feet pounding, she heads down the High Street, past the closes where Daft Jamie roamed and Mary Paterson skipped, past the ale houses and drinking dens alive with the gossip of their crimes, until just beyond the Canongate she sees a waiting mail coach. Boxes and packages are being loaded on; people are climbing aboard.

She approaches a man who is attending to the horses. 'Where are you travelling to?' she asks, masking her Irish accent with a Scottish one.

'Leith,' says the man. 'For the steamship to London. If you want to travel, you'd better get aboard, as we're ready to leave.'

'Does it depart tonight? The ship?' she asks.

The man nods and walks round to help her climb aboard. 'No baggage, madam?' he asks, curious. He doesn't recognise her, but he gives her a smile. Perhaps it is the hair again, those copper strands that hang loose and tousled around her face. Men are always drawn to it. 'Just you and the bairn?'

'Just us,' she says, settling into her seat. She glances around, but the other passengers are preoccupied; she keeps her eyes down and fusses over Jack, who is staring at her, wide-eyed but no longer bawling.

As the carriage sets off, she peers out of the window to catch a fleeting glimpse of Calton Jail silhouetted against the sky, where she imagines Hare sits, wallowing in self-pity and recrimination, lost without her instruction. And Burke, in chains, doubtless reconciling with God and asking for mercy, counting the days he has left on this earth. But she, Lucky, feels no remorse. She needs neither man nor God for guidance or absolution: she is London-bound. Free.

Part II
Edinburgh, 1850

Chapter 33

Duncan Fletcher stares at the skeleton before him in the busy foyer of Edinburgh's Medical School. Behind him, students and professors criss-cross the tiled floor, chatting and laughing or deep in thought. He reads the display card, and his eyes widen.

It is smaller perhaps than he imagined. He touches the glass case, imagining he can reach through and touch the ribs, the spine and pelvic frame. Suddenly, like a child, he fancies he might awaken what is left of the man and he jerks his hand back. The skull has a disturbing horizontal cut circumnavigating the cranium; the eye sockets seem to stare back at him. The teeth are fixed in an eternal grin. Duncan's gaze shifts downwards to the hands, and he pictures himself lifting one, as if to shake it in a polite greeting. He imagines examining each finger, rubbing his thumb over the smooth knuckles and ridges. The rhyme of his boyhood resurrects itself with a thrilling shiver.

Up the close and doon the stair,
But and ben wi' Burke and Hare
Burke's the butcher, Hare's the thief,
Knox the boy who buys the beef.

'Strange to come face to face with a murderer,' says a cheerful voice behind him. 'Are you a new student of anatomy?'

Duncan spins round to see an older gentleman beside him. 'No, no, I'm not,' he blusters. 'I'm waiting for a friend who is. But this specimen caught my eye. I grew up hearing the grisly tales of this man – he is something of an Edinburgh bogeyman, isn't he?'

The man nods. He seems pensive, as though he is holding something tightly within. 'Yes, William Burke. He was quite the fiend. His skeleton is here as our current anatomical museum is somewhat overflowing with specimens. But it seems fitting, does it not, that he should be here to greet all who grace these hallowed halls.' He says this with a sharp irony rather than reverence.

'I wonder, do you remember his hanging?' Duncan asks, hoping not to offend the gentleman with this assumption of his age.

The man seems to take no offence. 'Oh, yes. I was

there along with twenty thousand or so others, all baying for his blood. I watched it happen. I can remember it as though it were yesterday.'

'Heavens! That must have been quite an experience. I daresay his fate was justified . . . grave robbing and so on.'

'Oh, he didn't rob graves. Not one grave. That's a common misconception that I fear will endure for all its ghoulish associations. No, no, no. He *murdered* – pure and simple. You will hear it was sixteen people. And of course their first victim who was sold after dying of natural causes. But it was more. Many more.'

'Street folk, wasn't it? Vagrants who wouldn't be missed?'

'Is that what you think?' The gentleman swivels his head to look at Duncan, eyebrows raised. 'Is that how people justify this sorry tale?'

'Oh, I don't know,' mumbles Duncan; it appears he has said something indelicate.

'These "street folk" didn't matter?' continues the gentleman. 'Their lives were inconsequential and so death was all they deserved?'

Duncan flushes. 'No, no, I fear I have misspoken. I meant that they were alone and so no one went out to look for them.'

The gentleman's expression is stern. 'But they weren't alone. And they *were* missed. No one is so alone that they die without *someone* caring. And people did look for them. Make no mistake, young man, those victims had lives. They were alive and living and breathing with families and friends and they had that ripped away. Some were young and beautiful, full of life and vitality ...' His face is animated now, his voice cracking.

'Of course,' says Duncan, chastened. 'But it was for a greater purpose. Arguably. In that their deaths contributed to all this.' He waves a hand to demonstrate the grandness of the university school of anatomy. 'And ultimately helped us all. Their deaths were not in vain.'

'That's what we tell ourselves, isn't it?' The gentleman turns back to the glass case. 'That those murdered people aided the advancement of medical science. That students must practise on corpses to be sourced by whatever means available before we release them upon the living. And here he hangs in a glass case – William Burke, notorious murderer – never to be forgotten. Unlike his victims who are now reduced to faceless, unloved paupers. But not Burke. He will be a trophy for the anatomy school for centuries to come while his comrades, his partners in crime, escaped unscathed. I am forced to see him every day of my life. To remember. And so I should – remember, that is.'

Duncan stares at the man a little longer than is perhaps courteous, but there is something intriguing about him. He seems profoundly sad, agitated by something. Something unfinished. 'Hare, you mean? His partner in crime?'

'Ah, well, there were others, of course. Two women who are lost in history forever. They walked away, unscathed, and never had to face justice like Burke here. Their guilt remains buried deep in this sorry tale. Forgotten.'

'Duncan!' Another voice cuts into the conversation. 'There you are.'

'Ah, Charlie,' says Duncan.

'I see you've met our resident murderer,' says Charlie with a flourish of his hand as if bowing to the skeleton.

'Well, yes,' says Duncan. He turns to introduce his friend to the gentleman he had been talking to but sees he has turned and left and is now walking down the corridor. 'I was just talking about him to that gentleman there.'

'You mean Dr Fergusson?'

'You know him?'

'Of course! That's Dr Thomas Fergusson, the eminent anatomist and surgeon,' says Charlie as they set off towards the door. 'An eccentric, brilliant sort. But aren't we all?'

'We were discussing Mr Burke.'

'The story goes that when Dr Fergusson was a young man, he assisted Dr Robert Knox himself,' says Charlie, pulling on his gloves and hat. 'Rumour has it that he was the one who actually bought the bodies from Burke and Hare. I gather the poor fellow hasn't been the same since. He was quite disturbed by the whole affair. Shame, really. He was only doing what needed to be done in the name of progress. Anyway, onwards to luncheon, my friend!'

Chapter 34

The nightmares begin the evening after the encounter with Burke's bones. Always the same, Duncan wakes frantic and in abject terror. It begins with some soirée, where Duncan is enjoying himself taking tea in a fine parlour or wandering through a grand house, until across the crowded room he sees William Burke, his fixed smile like the skull, the same missing teeth. He glides with ease through the assembled people, politely doffing his hat to the ladies who titter behind gloved hands and exuding a magnetism that draws everyone to him, to shake hands, to gawp, to simply to be near him. But, from across the room, Burke has his sights set on Duncan and is moving ever closer. Duncan tries to back away, panic surging through his body, but stumbles and falls to the floor. When he looks up, Burke is bearing down on him, his hands moving towards his face; but his hands have no flesh and are bony and terrifying. Behind him, two faceless women spur him on. At that petrifying moment, every time, he awakens, sweat dripping from his clammy skin.

'You look so tired, Duncan,' says his aunt Jessie. 'You're working too hard.'

Bright spring sunshine streams across the breakfast table of Duncan's aunt and uncle's apartment in Great King Street.

'Are you not sleeping?' she pushes. 'What ails you, dearest?'

'I must admit, I am sorely distracted by something,' says Duncan, grateful to unburden himself.

'Tell me,' she says after taking a sip of tea. 'Your uncle and I won't have you suffering alone, will we, Frederick?'

'Do you remember the William Burke hanging?' asks Duncan.

His uncle puts down the periodical he has been reading and clears his throat. 'Of course,' he says. 'A shocking business. I was a young reporter then, much like yourself. The *Caledonian Mercury* printed much on the case – even Burke's full confession. Why do you ask?'

'I met the anatomist Dr Thomas Fergusson last week at the medical school when I was waiting for

Charlie. We engaged in conversation while looking at the skeleton of William Burke. It, or rather "he", hangs there in a display case.'

'A fitting end,' says Jessie, 'for his body to be given to the surgeons to dissect, was it not?'

'He said at least sixteen people died, maybe more,' says Duncan. 'Burke was hanged for his crimes, but what of the others – the accomplices of Burke who, according to Dr Fergusson, were not punished. What happened to them? Does anyone know?'

'You mean Hare,' says Frederick. 'He turned King's Evidence. Got away with it. He left Edinburgh and was last seen somewhere in Dumfries or Carlisle. No doubt returned to Ireland. It was quite the scandal at the time.'

'And the others?' says Duncan.

'Dr Knox, the anatomist at the centre of it all, his reputation was damaged beyond repair,' says Jessie.

'If my memory serves me, an angry mob gathered at his house, threw stones at his windows and burned an effigy of his body,' says Frederick. 'He was driven into hiding for some time, I believe. He kept quiet for the most part and hoped to weather the scandal, but he was tainted by it. His ethical stance took quite the beating. Many thought he must have known, must have seen evidence, bruising or markings and so forth on the bodies but chose to ignore it. Those who had known him distanced themselves. He became a pariah here in Edinburgh.'

'Where is he now?' asks Duncan.

'That I don't know,' admits Frederick. 'Glasgow? London perhaps.'

'But there were women, were there not?' asks Duncan.

'You mean the wives,' says Jessie, reaching out to pour herself another cup of tea. 'Mrs Burke and Mrs Hare, who walked free.'

'I'm not sure how involved they actually were,' says Frederick.

Jessie lets out a small sound of disbelief. She stands up, carrying her cup and saucer over to the window. 'It sounds as though Thomas Fergusson has some insight into it,' she says looking out over the New Town and to the Firth of Forth in the distance. 'Was he at the school of anatomy when it happened?'

'Yes, he was,' says Duncan. 'Charlie said that he was an assistant to Dr Knox and that he had been there, had even met the pair. But he said something that has imprinted itself in my mind. He said of the women that their "guilt was buried deep in that story". I wonder, did those women escape rightful justice? Were they more involved than we might have previously thought?'

Jessie turns and peers at Duncan over her teacup. 'I think they were up to their necks in it,' she says decisively, replacing her cup in the saucer. 'I have always been of that opinion. How could they not have been? They offered a level of safety that only women can.'

'Come, come, Jess, what on earth do you mean? *A level of safety?*' Her husband shakes his head.

'I'll tell you exactly what I mean. People trusted them *because* they were women,' she says. 'There were moments I am sure when they were instrumental in luring victims. But how do you prove that?' She shrugs. 'And so, yes, while they certainly escaped the death penalty, whether they escaped other forms of justice is beyond our ken. The mob rose up swiftly in a most determined pursuit of them. Perhaps they didn't survive. Emotions were running high at the time.'

Duncan tries to picture an angry crowd, intent on administering violent justice. What would that have looked like? Did they attack them? Tear them limb from limb? Surely that could not have happened.

'But what if they did survive?' says Duncan. 'What if they got away, started new lives and have been able to live as though none of it happened? And that's assuming they decided to follow paths of redemption. What if they're still committing evil acts?'

Frederick takes off his glasses and rubs the bridge of his nose, Jessie perches on the edge of her seat, and both stare at Duncan.

'It's not beyond the realms of possibility,' says Jessie.

'They would have had to go far away, though, to escape recognition. Their crimes featured in the press across the entire country, not just here in Edinburgh. Everyone knew about it.'

Duncan considers this. 'What would you say if I tried to pursue it? A story for the paper?' He looks earnestly at his uncle. 'Enough time has passed, don't you think? And I would pursue only the women. Hare might be too dangerous. But I could try to trace the paths they took, find out where they went and if they're still alive. It could be a report for the *Mercury* or an essay for you, Aunt Jessie, for the *Edinburgh Magazine*.'

'It's got promise,' says Frederick. 'At the time, the story certainly sold papers, and I can't see the appetite for such a macabre tale having diminished in any way. But, Duncan, it is more than likely that they are both dead. It has been twenty-one years since Burke was hanged.'

Jessie smiles. 'On the trail of Mrs Burke and Mrs Hare,' she says. 'Don't be too hasty there, Frederick, to claim ownership for the *Mercury*. I could see our readers being equally interested. After all, we have a large female readership, and this would certainly appeal to them. Women's involvement in crime is sensational.'

Frederick grins broadly at his wife and taps his fingers on the table. 'Are we in competition, my dear?'

'But a word, dear,' says Jessie, turning to face Duncan,

her expression serious. 'Take the greatest of care. You say that pursuing Hare would be too dangerous, as if finding the women is somehow safe. Don't be naive. From my memory, those women were anything but mild-mannered. They were ruthless sorts who would do whatever they had to, to better their lives, including murder. And if they are still alive, a transformation of spirit seems unlikely. They might not take kindly to someone digging them up for a modern dissection of their lives. You might want to consider where this could all lead, so I urge you to proceed with caution.'

Duncan smiles a little at her analogy and shakes off the image of Burke's skeletal hands reaching for him. 'I'll be fine,' he says, kissing her lightly on the cheek. 'I shall relish the adventure.'

Chapter 35

Duncan is the furthest he has ever been from home. He travelled for several days across miles of countryside until he reached the village of Doune with its ancient castle, and now he is walking alongside the river Teith, following a path that leads to the mill at Deanstone. It is a mild spring day and he turns his face to the sun, enjoying its thin warmth; the river ripples and babbles beside him, and he feels excited and full of energy. He has been wrestling with self-doubt about this entire escapade since he received his aunt and uncle's blessing, but he tries to push it firmly aside, for, as he reminds himself, he has craved this opportunity to prove himself away from the mundane clerical duties of working for his uncle at the *Mercury*. He is, he muses, an observer of people, and will one day, like Dickens himself, become a voice for the marginalised, the unseen and unheard. Perhaps he could propel social change through writing about the plight of the poor and the human cost of progress, like those who were the sacrificial lambs to anatomy. It is the pursuit of truth that matters to him most of all, and his words must count. Besides all of that, the nightmares about Burke and Hare's escapades persist, the two faceless women always a foreboding, shadowy presence in the scene, and he knows he must get to the bottom of their stories to quell their nighttime visits.

He began his investigation some days ago by reading *The West Port Murders*, a detailed account written soon after the whole affair, and then, out of respect to the victims, carefully listed their names as far as is known. Several of those souls have no name but are referred to as 'The Old Woman' or 'The English Peddlar.' In some cases, several possible names are listed – 'Mary Paterson or Mitchell', 'Margaret or Madgy Docherty, also known as Campbell'. Duncan keeps this list at the front of his notebook so that every time he opens it, he is reminded of their brutal deaths and of his purpose. As he walks along the riverside he recalls the circumstances of his recent encounters in the West Port.

***

The descent into the Grassmarket was like entering Hell itself. Having rarely ventured into this part of the

Old Town, it was as though he was passing through a hidden door to another world – one suffering from the most shocking level of deprivation. The filth and overcrowding, the sheer number of people and animals milling around the wynds and warrens was overwhelming. The boarding house once owned by William Hare and his wife, at the far end of Tanner's Close, was now nothing more than a ruin; nature had reclaimed it brick by brick. Dilapidated walls, piles of rubble and glass, scattered roof tiles and unruly vegetation were all that remained. So pungent was the smell belching from the nearby tannery that his eyes had begun to water. The yard was now strewn with rubbish and the putrid remnants from the tannery and the abattoir. He stood for some time, a kerchief over his nose and mouth, staring at the sorry sight, then walked back up what was left of the close. Tiny barefoot urchins jumped and splashed, unsmiling, in an open gutter; their faces were gaunt, their rags and matted hair infested with vermin, grimy bodies covered in sores.

'You mustn't play here,' he heard himself say to the children. 'It's not clean.' But they merely stared at him as though he was an apparition in their world. He expected them to beg for money, but it seemed they had no words, no concept of a better life. He realised that, for these people, cleanliness was simply unknown and unobtainable. And so he wandered on, looking up at the sky from time to time as a blessed relief from the abject misery around him. Drunken creatures lay slumped in doorways, legs outstretched across the wynds, oblivious to passersby. Water here was a precious commodity, and the queues at the pumps snaked down the road as women stood waiting their turn, clutching empty buckets. The grim reality of their lives shocked him to his very core.

Duncan pressed on, his copy of *The West Port Murders* clutched in his hand; he was determined to find a Mrs Ann Gray who was not only listed as a key witness at the trial but had also been suggested to him by his colleagues at the *Mercury*. He had been told that it was known she lived in the Cowgate, or 'Little Ireland', as it was also known. Back and forth he wandered, trying to locate a drinking den where it was believed she lived upstairs.

Finally, it was a cobbler, working in a tiny room, who came to his aid. 'Are you looking for someone?' the young man said, his accent a singsong blend of Scots and Irish. He was wearing an apron and eyeing Duncan's shoes hopefully. But Duncan's shoes were not in need of repair.

'Yes, thank you,' he said. 'I'm trying to locate a Mrs Ann Gray.' He reached into his pocket and pulled out his card. The cobbler looked at it, mystified. 'I heard she lives around here somewhere,' Duncan added, and then realising the card was ridiculous, slid it back in his pocket.

'First floor.' The cobbler pointed upwards to a broken window. 'The door on the right.'

Looking up, Duncan could not believe the building was habitable such was the state of disrepair. Like a perilous tower of children's blocks, one loose brick and all might tumble down at any moment.

'Mrs Gray – she's blind,' the cobbler said. 'Doesn't go out. There's other people live there with her, though. Her lodgers.'

With a nod of thanks, Duncan bravely ventured into the building and up to the first landing.

'Mrs Gray?' he called, knocking firmly then pushing the door open. The room had a low ceiling and was lit only by two tiny lamps. It took a few moments for Duncan's eyes to become accustomed to the dark. The smell was foul; the lamps were burning fish oil. There was no visible source of heat, and the room was viciously cold. Several people were sitting in the shadows, but then a voice came from the furthest corner, where a small, birdlike woman was sitting on a bed wrapped in a shawl, wispy white hair trailing down her shoulders.

'Who is that? Is that you, Joseph?' she said. 'Have you brought my water?'

Duncan approached the bed and could see the woman's eyes were a glazed milky white, rendered useless from countless infections. Although she couldn't have been much older than his own aunt, Mrs Gray looked worn out by a hard life.

'No, Mrs Gray,' Duncan had loudly and clearly. 'My name is Duncan Fletcher. I'm a writer – a reporter at the *Caledonian Mercury*. The newspaper.'

He wondered if she was slow of mind, whether she could understand him and follow what he was saying.

'The *Caledonian Mercury*,' she said, confused perhaps. 'Is that a newspaper?' And then something dawned and her demeanour changed. 'Ah, Burke and Hare . . .'

'How did you know?'

'It was, and remains, the only thing any newspaper would want to talk to me about,' she said. 'Come and sit here, boy, I will tell you everything I know.'

He remained standing as there was nowhere to sit other than on the unclean floor, but he moved a little closer.

'And I won't take a penny,' she said raising a finger. Duncan had not even considered paying her for information. 'How could I take payment to speak the truth about those fiendish deeds? I wouldn't take payment then for my silence and I won't now for telling the truth. I was young back then, but the shock of it all turned my hair white.' At this, she tugged at a few strands. 'I can no longer see, but that man's face is etched in my mind for eternity. And his evil wife. It was thanks to me they were caught! I reported them, and what did I get for my efforts?' She swept a hand around her wretched room and smiled broadly, revealing stained and rotten teeth. Not as good as Burke's teeth, Duncan mused.

'You knew his wife, Helen McDougal? Mrs Burke?'

'Mrs Burke indeed,' Mrs Gray growled. 'He was already married, had a wife back in Ireland. And she, that woman, had been married to my father. No, she was Burke's bidie-in. That is all. No wife. Not in the eyes of God.'

'I wonder, might you have any idea what happened to her?' Duncan asked. 'The newspapers reported many stories about her, but I'm trying to establish if she's still alive, after all these years.'

Mrs Gray considered the question for some time, sucking in her lips so that her cheeks hollowed and distorted her face.

'Dead,' she said quietly. 'Torn limb from limb, murdered at the hands of a mob. No one would protect her. Not her people, no one. The papers made up stories about what happened to her, but I know the truth: she was killed by the women from the mill at Deanstone, near Doune. She tried to hide who she really was, but the truth followed her wherever she went. And they put an end to her. I heard it from my own sister's mouth. She lives out that way with her husband, and they saw it happen.' Mrs Gray leant forward, her dead eyes glistening in the lamplight. 'They *saw them kill her*. They saw them throw her dead body away like rubbish. For that's all she was. Rubbish!'

***

Duncan considers those words now as he continues his journey along the river Teith, towards the cotton mill at Deanstone. Was the old woman just havering, repeating the rumours that were embellished over many glasses of whisky and repeated by the Edinburgh newspapers? Those kinds of salacious tales were certainly popular. Were they concocted to satisfy the anger of the mob? He had resolved to get to the truth and so he would pursue the trail of Helen McDougal until it was quite exhausted. The pursuit of truth, he thinks to himself, is surely what readers really want: not fast-spun fiction to sell papers. The people can see through that.

Soon, tucked back from the road, he sees a farm cottage, just as Ann Gray had described: a 'but 'n' ben'. A gate blocks his path, and it takes him some time to establish how to open it. It appears to be tied fast with rope.

'Can I help you?' says a voice. A woman wearing a bulky plaid shawl is walking towards him. Duncan sees immediately that she has a look of Ann Gray but is much younger and healthier, with a fresh complexion and bright, seeing eyes. She eyes Duncan carefully and then simply lifts the knotted loop of rope over the post and pushes the gate open.

Duncan blushes. 'I'm from the city . . .'

'I can see that,' says the woman with a smile.

'Are you Mrs Margaret Nicoll?'

'Aye,' she says, looking taken aback. 'Maggie, please. And who might you be?'

'Your sister told me I could find you here. I'm Duncan Fletcher. I've come from Edinburgh in the hope I could talk to you. I wondered if I could ask you about Helen McDougal?'

Maggie's smile drops and she looks shocked. She smooths her hands down her skirt. 'You'd better come away indoors, then, Duncan Fletcher.'

Chapter 36

'You've come a long way,' says Maggie's husband, John. He is sitting at the kitchen table, a plate of oatcakes and cheese in front of him. 'Just to ask about Helen McDougal? That murderer, eh?'

'The train makes travel much faster these days,' Duncan says with a smile, 'and, well, I'm writing an article for the *Caledonian Mercury* – a newspaper in Edinburgh, Mr Nicoll. Not just about her, but the other woman too. Mrs Hare. About where they went, what happened to them after the trial.'

'An awful business,' says John with a shake of his head.

Maggie stares at Duncan and bites her lip. Then she turns and busies herself around their kitchen, placing a heavy iron kettle on the range and arranging chipped cups and saucers. It is a small, sparse room with a low ceiling, but it is spotless. The brick floor has been swept, the table scrubbed, and the sunlight streams through a polished window. It smells clean too, with fresh laundry folded neatly over the clothes airer hanging near the range.

'You'll take some tea?' she asks.

'That would be very kind,' says Duncan. 'I hope this is not an inconvenience.'

'I have a little time to spare,' says Maggie briskly. 'How fares my sister? I've not seen her in so many years. Ten, perhaps more.'

Duncan wonders how to reply. He thinks back to her sitting, blind and uncared for in that pitch-black room. The stench. The cold. The lack of clean water. The miserable souls she shares her abode with. This humble cottage is paradise in comparison.

'Oh, she is full of spirit,' he says.

Maggie seems satisfied with this minimal reply. Perhaps, thinks Duncan, they were never close.

'She told me that you saw Helen McDougal set upon by a mob of women from the mill,' says Duncan, now fishing out a pencil and pocketbook from his jacket. 'That they killed her most viciously and dumped her body.'

John pushes his plate away and puts his elbows on the table. He glances over to his wife who is bringing a teapot and milk jug to the table.

Duncan looks at John and then to Maggie; he notices their shared looks of concern. 'Was your sister mistaken? Forgive me, perhaps this account is wrong.' He considers the brutality of the subject matter and feels suddenly quite ashamed at his directness. He is about to apologise when Maggie clears her throat.

'No,' she says. 'My sister is right. We saw it. But it was a long time ago. We did tell Ann a little of what happened that day when we saw her last. We went down to visit her in Edinburgh, not long after it all happened. But she always was one to tell tall tales. Add to them, maybe.'

Duncan frowns. 'I see.'

'We'd not long been here, on this farm, when it happened, and we didn't want to say too much,' adds John.

'I wonder, would you mind, I mean, can you tell me more about what actually happened that day?' Duncan stumbles over his words, his pencil poised. 'It would be helpful for me to build a clear picture so that I can describe it for my readers.' And he likes the sound of that. *His* readers.

John looks strained. 'It's not something we want to remember . . .' he begins. 'And we certainly don't want our names mentioned.'

'It was just down there on the road,' begins Maggie, her eyes focused on pouring the tea through a strainer into a teacup. 'The women at the mill, some of them are a rough lot. It was my fault, I suppose. All of it. You see, I knew Helen. She'd been married very briefly to my father after my mother died. Then when he died, not long after, she took off with that man, William Burke. She came here some months after the trial, perhaps hoping to build a new life after being a fugitive, but I recognised her immediately. I didn't speak to her, so she didn't know I'd seen her. She was hoping no one would recognise her and she made up a new name, Agnes Nimmo. Even found herself a new man.' Maggie shakes her head. 'But it was her alright.'

'It was a foolish decision on her part to come here,' says John. 'Or any part of Scotland. They say she'd tried living elsewhere but was found out and had to leave.'

'Well, I mentioned it to a few people, as you do,' says Maggie, 'and like wildfire it spread. She'd only been in the mill for one day, and the women tricked her into telling them the truth. Called her by her true name, caught her off guard, and her face gave her away. Then they said they wouldn't hurt her if she told them the truth, said they'd protect her and put everyone right, which she did, believing they'd be merciful. But that was never going to happen.'

'It was quick, and it was brutal,' says John, looking at Duncan over his teacup. 'I was out in the fields over the way and heard this terrible commotion.'

'All Hallow's Eve,' says Maggie. 'It was dusk when I came out of the house, and I could see them, a whole crowd carrying lanterns. Some had come down from the village just to watch. They were shrieking like a pack of wild animals. They threw stones at her and hit her with sticks, pulling at her hair. And stripped her of her clothes too.'

'They all but killed her,' said John. 'It was like nothing I'd seen before.'

Duncan stares at John, aghast. 'So they didn't actually kill her? They just left her for dead?'

A long pause sits between them all. Duncan glances between husband and wife, and senses there is something pressing on them.

'Perhaps it's time to tell the truth, John,' says Maggie quietly. 'Heaven knows the guilt of it all has caused me anguish over the years.'

'No, Maggie. That *is* the truth.' says John, throwing his wife a fierce look. 'She was dead, and we watched them throw her body in the river. That's all there is to it. No one asked any questions. The authorities didn't ask what happened to her; they didn't want to know. It was justice for what she did. It put an end to it, and that's all there is to it. Isn't that right, Maggie? Why must it be stirred up again?' He stands, puts his hat on his head and opens the door. 'I must return to work. Good day, Mr Fletcher,' he says, without shaking his hand.

'I should go,' says Duncan.

'We just don't want any trouble,' says Maggie. 'Not round here. People talk, you see, and this is our home.'

'I understand.' Duncan stands up.

Maggie sips her tea, not meeting his eyes.

'Mrs Nicoll,' he says quietly. 'What else happened? I sense there's more.'

Maggie shifts in her chair. 'What I'm about to tell you must stay between us. John must never know that I told you. We can never be named. Because, folk round here, if they knew what we did, they'd turn us out. I want to rid myself of this terrible secret. It's dogged me for twenty years.'

Duncan sits back down. 'I won't write what you tell me, I give you my word.' He closes his pocketbook and tucks it into his jacket.

'It was a time of great anger at what they'd done,' she says. 'And that anger would rise up again.'

He instinctively knows not to say anything now. Instead, he must wait. Listen. He must give her space to speak.

'They set fire to the woman,' she whispers. Duncan's eyes widen, and Maggie immediately puts her hand to her mouth as she though she regrets what she has said, that this is the first time she has ever put the events of that day into words.

'They shouted that they were burning her like a

witch,' she says. 'After they'd beaten her and thrown rocks at her head, they doused her in oil from the mill and set her on fire. Then they ran off. Left her flaming in the dusk like a torch.' Maggie's eyes fill with tears, and she takes a sip of tea. 'I don't know why they ran off. Maybe they were horrified at what they'd done. Thought they might get caught. But we couldn't leave her. We couldn't listen to those wails and cries. No matter who she was or what she'd done. She sounded like a tortured animal. But you must understand, Mr Fletcher, we couldn't let anyone know that we'd helped a murderer. She had been married to my own father, you see? My own flesh and blood. And it was me who had revealed to everyone who she really was.'

'Of course,' he says kindly. 'So what did you do?'

'We managed to put out the flames with blankets. But she was in a terrible state. Her skin and hair had melted. She was completely disfigured. Inhuman. If it had been an animal from the farm, we'd have put it out of its misery. But we couldn't do it to her. Not to a living person.'

Tears begin to stream down her cheeks at the memory. 'We tried to help her. But, oh, what a sight. She was in agonising pain, and we knew we had to get her to a doctor. So when it was quite dark, we shrouded her in blankets and took her on the cart.'

'Where?'

'We didn't know where to go, but we knew there was a workhouse with a hospital, or an asylum, a new one, in Stirling. St Ninian's. So we took her there, kept her hidden as we travelled, and that's where we left her.'

Duncan looks at Maggie. He pieces together what she has said, and suddenly there is a moment of horror and excitement. 'What happened to her? Did she survive?'

Maggie shrugs. 'I don't know. We rang the bell, said we'd found her lying on the road, that we thought her name was Agnes. And we left before they could ask any more and never went back. We just put it behind us. Got on with our life here at the farm. No one asked what had happened to her after the mob burned her. They assumed she was dead and that the body had been discarded or someone had thrown her into the river, and that's what I told my sister. The folk round here, you have to understand, we're good Christian folk. The whole business, what they did, Burke and Hare and their wives, they were savage murderers. And she'd walked free. But if it got out that we'd saved her, saved a murderer, even after all this time, we'd be turned out of this cottage. We'd be hounded out of the village. Our lives would be over because of her.'

Chapter 37

Emotions attached to a moment in time are like ghosts: they haunt you. Duncan felt Maggie's lingering distress at what had happened to Helen McDougal that Hallowe'en night. But as he stares at the page of his notebook, he has written only two words: Agnes Nimmo.

He sits in the carriage, watching the Perthshire countryside pass, and observes that he has been thrust into an ethical dilemma that he didn't consider before he set out in his 'pursuit of truth'. If he writes about any of this, people's lives, like those of Maggie and John, even now after all this time, could be grievously affected. He gave Maggie his solemn word that he would not write about the attack and transportation of Helen McDougal, that he would put their welfare above that of a newspaper story, but he is deeply disappointed.

If he were cruel and heartless, he would disregard their request and write it anyway. But Duncan knows he could not live with himself if they came to harm due to his words.

He has all but decided to give up on the whole enterprise by the time the coach arrives in Stirling. As it's a fine day, and he has time to spare before catching his train back to Edinburgh, curiosity takes him for a walk. He asks a smart-looking gentleman the way to St Ninian's Poorhouse and Asylum, and, despite the wary look he receives, is duly directed to the edge of the town away from the noise and the hustle and bustle. There, standing in extensive grounds, is an impressive building with the date '1829' carved into the stone above the door, alongside the words 'St Ninian's Combination Poorhouse'. To Duncan, it certainly does not look like a house for the poor from the outside, rather a palace or a duke's grand residence. As he walks through the gates, he notices several people moving calmly and purposefully around the landscaped gardens; they are taking in the air or working in some capacity, some tending to a vegetable patch while others play bowls and tennis, or simply enjoying the fresh air and the views. This was not as Duncan had imagined it would be.

But as he approaches the door, he feels a stab of doubt as to why he is even here. It is, he tells himself, simply to corroborate Maggie's story of Agnes Nimmo, but to do this he will have to assume another identity. He takes a deep breath. Lying does not come easily to him.

He rings the bell, wondering what story he can spin to glean as much information as possible. The door is opened by a sullen-looking girl dressed in a pinafore.

'Good afternoon,' he says. 'I'm trying to locate a distant relative. I believe she came here some twenty-one years ago, when this establishment was newly opened. I'm hoping to find out what happened to her.'

The girl narrows her eyes. 'What's her name, sir?'

'Agnes,' says Duncan, remembering Maggie saying this was all they revealed about her when they left her.

The reaction is immediate and undeniable. 'One minute, sir,' she says and closes the door again. 'Mrs Gow!' he hears her shriek as she hurries away.

When the door opens again, it is not the same girl. Immaculately dressed in stiff black clothing, this woman wears a bunch of keys around her narrow waist. Her eyes look tired, as though she has been deprived of sleep, and they regard him suspiciously through small round spectacles.

'I must apologise for keeping you waiting, Mr–?'

'Gray,' says Duncan quickly. 'Mr Frederick Gray.' He wonders if the lie is written all over his face. But, to his great relief, she steps back and ushers him into a vast, sterile reception area.

'I am Mrs Gow,' she says, 'wife of our Superintendent,

Dr William Gow. I believe you are enquiring about a woman called Agnes, yes?'

From some distant room behind one of the many locked doors, Duncan hears faint moans. It is an unsettling sound, but Mrs Gow seems undeterred and stares at him expectantly. Duncan refocuses his mind on the lie. 'Yes. I have been conducting research on my family tree,' he says, his confidence beginning to grow. 'I have uncovered a distant cousin on my deceased mother's side called Agnes. It is believed she fell from polite society, shall we say. Ran away after a disastrous marriage and was reputed to have brought great shame upon the family. No one traced her, but I have been making enquiries of my own and believe she came to this area about twenty years ago. Sadly, I was informed that it was likely she ended up in the poorhouse, and this being the largest establishment in the area, I thought I'd start with you.'

'I am not sure I can help you, Mr Gray,' says Mrs Gow. 'Agnes is a very common name.'

Duncan hesitates, but he steels himself. He cannot come this far and walk away with nothing. 'Perhaps you could check your records for me?' he says, arranging his face into his most beguiling smile.

Something in her face hardens. 'I have been here since the inauguration of St Ninian's, Mr Gray, and I can assure you that I remember the names and faces of every individual who has come to us. And there have been many women called Agnes. I would need more information to identify her for you. I am sorry I cannot help you further.' She turns to usher Duncan out.

'I have reason to believe she was seriously injured in a fire,' says Duncan.

Mrs Gow looks taken aback. 'How could you know that?' she says, and then realising what she has said takes a deep breath.

'So you do know of her?'

'Yes.'

'Why did you lie, Mrs Gow?'

'I didn't lie. We have had many patients called Agnes but only one who was injured in a fire. How did you come to know of her condition?'

Duncan doesn't want to give Maggie and John Gray away, nor does he think it prudent to raise the question of Agnes's true identity. He must assume that the staff here would never have known who she truly was.

'I have been making a lot of enquiries,' he says. 'Someone in the town suggested that there was a Agnes who was brought here after a fire, that she was disfigured in a most horrible way. The date seemed to fit with when she left Edinburgh. It was around Hallowe'en, October 1829. That's all I know, but, of course, stories like that do become the subject of much gossip and elaboration in small towns and villages.'

Mrs Gow nods. 'That is very true, sir. But what happened to her was indescribably cruel.'

'Can you tell me more of what happened? She was my cousin, my flesh and blood, and I won't rest until I know the truth.' Duncan is surprised at the strength of feeling in his voice.

'We don't know anything about her or how or why she was burned. Only her first name. She was brought to us in that terrible state, but no one knew anything. Perhaps it was due to an unfortunate accident, but we suspected foul play. She was unable to tell us anything at the time, and now, well, she barely speaks. So we'll never know.'

'Now? You talk of her in the present tense.'

'Well, yes, of course.'

'You mean she's still alive?' says Duncan, eyes wide with incredulity.

'Mr Fletcher, Agnes been under our protection and supervision ever since the night she arrived. The longest of all our patients.'

A creeping sensation turns his blood cold. 'Alive?' he mutters, more to himself. And he realises he had not considered this. He had assumed that she could not have survived her injuries for any length of time, let alone nearly twenty-one years. Helen McDougal, the wife of William Burke, is alive and well, in this very building.

'Here?' he gasps. He swings around, almost expecting

to see her wander down the corridor. Perhaps she was one of the figures in the garden tending the vegetables. 'Might I see her?'

Mrs Gow tuts, and Duncan judges by her reaction that there is more to this particular case than those other patients outside. 'I think that would be a mistake. She is an extremely vulnerable woman,' she says. 'I would not like to cause her any distress.'

'I have no wish to cause her any upset,' says Duncan. 'We don't even need to say who I am. I would like only to see her and know that she is safe and well cared for. Please understand, Mrs Gow, it would bring me great comfort. And if it helps, I am sure my family would be happy for me to make a considerable charitable donation in light of the care you are giving.'

Mrs Gow seems to brighten at this. 'A donation would be most gratefully received. But I must warn you, Mr Gray, that Agnes is one of our most damaged patients. What we suspect happened to her all those years ago was inhuman; she will never recover. She suffered a serious head injury and makes little sense in her chattering. Her will can be strong, her brain hot and troubled, but we continue to work on that. However, unlike many of our patients who recover and leave the institution, she can never be released.'

'I understand,' says Duncan respectfully. 'You have my word I will be discreet and follow your instruction.'

He wonders why he is so keen to lay his eyes on this woman, this murdering accomplice, if all the reports are to be believed. This woman who was married to a brutish murderer, who escaped justice and walked away from their terrible crimes despite her complicity. Is he determined to establish facts for the sake of his pursuit of the truth, or is there something deeper, more sinister, at play: some twisted curiosity at the plight of others?

Mrs Gow selects a key from the chain around her waist and leads Duncan along the long dark corridor towards the ladies' wing.

Chapter 38

'St Ninian's is a progressive institution, Mr Gray,' says Mrs Gow. 'My husband and I believe in good moral treatment, one that encourages self-control not just for those in the lunatic ward but in the poorhouse too. We believe in fresh air and nourishment – nourishment for the soul as well as for the body.' She gives Duncan a nod at this statement, as though it underlines all that she believes. 'Routine, orderly behaviour, exercise and rest are paramount to aid spiritual and physical recovery. Here, we apply order to the disordered mind. My husband is also a leading figure in the practice of phrenology and the administration of a variety of modern treatments.'

Duncan struggles to keep up as she goes up stairs, unlocking and then locking several doors, taking them further into the complex maze of the building. They pass expressionless attendants, who don't meet his eyes, and off each corridor he catches tantalising glimpses of rooms through glass windows. He sees bright dormitories and large rooms where women sit in rows engaged in some domestic occupation. He passes a laundry room and a ballroom and another where people are playing cards. Duncan is not sure if he is seeing into poorhouse or asylum rooms or whether they are combined: where does poverty end and madness begin? The tranquil atmosphere is certainly surprising. He begins to wonder if Mrs Gow is carefully choosing what she wants Duncan to see.

'Because of her injuries, Agnes has more exacting needs, but I can reassure you that she is one of my husband's special patients. He takes a close interest in her welfare, often spending hours with her in observation and examination for his personal research. They have a particular bond, and he allows her to call him by his Christian name. It is a privilege he ascribes only to her.'

Duncan considers his misunderstanding of asylums. He had visions of chains and straw on the floor. Of abandonment, restraints, mistreatment and cruelty, of madness locked away from polite, civilised society, as something unspeakable. But this is quite the opposite.

The final room, at the very end of a long corridor, is a spacious, bright dayroom with chairs and tables and a delightful view over the grounds. Alone in the corner, with her back to them, stands a small woman talking to a canary in a birdcage.

'Here she is,' says Mrs Gow. 'She, like many of our patients, takes pleasure in petting animals.'

As Duncan walks towards her, she turns to look at them, and he realises she is not the monster he had imagined. Rather, Helen McDougal is tiny, almost like a child. She wears a simple grey dress and a plain white bonnet. As he moves closer, he sees the skin on her face is waxen and shiny. One side droops, is misshapen like a melted candle, and where once there were features such as a nose and eyes, there are merely holes. One eye is lost to the disfigurement; the other is barely able to open. No wisps of hair appear under the bonnet pulled tight around her face, making her look more like an infant than an adult.

'Agnes,' says Mrs Gow quietly, 'this man has come to see you.'

Helen rests her better eye upon Duncan.

There is no movement of expression; such subtleties of emotions are lost forever. But Duncan can see the good eye move slightly. There is something mesmerising about it, as though it is the doorway to her past life.

'Hello,' he says. 'I've come from Edinburgh to see you.'

The pupil moves. Then she moves her mouth as if

attempting to speak. It clearly takes great effort.

'William,' she says with a hint of longing in her voice. It is not a question; it is a statement.

'No, Agnes,' interrupts Mrs Gow loudly. 'She means my husband; she's quite devoted to him.' she explains for Duncan. 'No, this isn't William, Agnes. The Superintendent will see you later. This man is called Mr Frederick Gray.'

But Agnes isn't listening. She has lost interest in the visitor and, like a grotesque mechanical doll, returns her attention to the canary. Duncan wonders with a shudder if Agnes had actually meant William Burke, her long dead husband. But he says nothing.

'Get thyself rid of thy burden,' she whispers to the caged bird.

Duncan moves closer, listening intently. He watches her through the bars of the cage; her chin is lifted so that her good eye can focus on the movement of the little bird. Her pupil darts and tracks its tiny staccato movements. In her stumpy fingers she grips little seeds which she feeds awkwardly through the bars.

'What's that you say?' he murmurs. 'Is this your canary? What's it called?'

'William,' she says. Her face cannot smile, but he senses she is smiling inwardly. 'William.'

'A canary is a lucky bird,' he says, staring directly into that eye, that eye that has seen terrible things, that eye that once rested upon William Burke and William Hare.

'Lucky?' she says suddenly. The glassy surface of her eye becomes watery, and her shoulders begin to convulse as she breathes in panicked gulps. 'No!'

'I'm sorry,' says Duncan, 'I didn't mean to upset you.'

'It's all right, Agnes,' says Mrs Gow. 'No need to excite yourself.' And with these words she calms down and focuses once more on feeding the canary.

'I think we should go now, Mr Gray,' says Mrs Gow quietly.

Duncan nods and moves away. They are walking out of the room when a male attendant walks past them and enters Agnes's room. As they head down the corridor, Duncan hears his loud voice.

'It's time for the doctor to see you, little Nelly,' he says. 'Now, now, don't be difficult. A cold-shock shower will cool that hot little brain of yours.'

Duncan stops dead in his tracks. Nelly? He called her Nelly. Short for Helen. He turns to Mrs Gow. 'What did he just call her?'

And he hears a chilling moan of distress.

Mrs Gow quickens her pace. 'Call her?' she says. 'I don't know what you mean. Come, come, Mr Gray, it is time to leave. Agnes needs here treatment.' She leads him swiftly back through the corridors towards the front entrance, her shoes clipping on the polished floor.

'He called her Nelly. Why did he call her that?' he says, catching her up.

'You are mistaken, Mr Gray. Perhaps the attendant was speaking to someone else.'

'There was no one else in that room,' he says. 'And why is she frightened? What did he mean by a cold shower? What is he going to do to her?'

'As I warned you, Agnes can be wilful,' says Mrs Gow, marching on.

Now, as they move back through the corridors, Duncan's senses are heightened: every shriek and wail is intensified, and his nostrils are overwhelmed with the reek of carbolic soap.

'Some of the treatments my husband advocates can be momentarily uncomfortable for the patients, but I assure you it is for their own benefit. It encourages their obedience.'

They arrive back in the reception area. Duncan feels frantic. 'Mrs Gow, I must insist you answer my question. Who is that woman?'

'Are you quite well, Mr Gray?' she says, her head cocked to one side.

'Yes, I am,' snaps Duncan. But he isn't. His sense of what is real and what is not has become blurred.

'I can assure you that the woman you saw is called

Agnes Nimmo,' says Mrs Gow evenly. 'She is the woman you said was your cousin, did you not, Mr Gray? Perhaps the attendant has a special name for her. An affectionate nickname. Many do. That is all there is to it. But you do look pale. Perhaps you would like to stay a while and recover?'

'I didn't tell you her surname was Nimmo,' he says.

'I'm quite sure you did, Mr Gray,' says Mrs Gow, opening the door. 'Good day to you.'

Duncan does not feel well. But to stay any longer in this place would be too awful; and so he allows himself to be ushered out of the building, and no sooner has he walked out than Mrs Gow wordlessly and firmly closes the asylum door behind him.

Chapter 39

What is justice? ponders Duncan, slumped in his seat on the train back to Edinburgh. He has never had cause to think of such things before in his privileged life. But now he realises that justice might exist as a shapeshifting, abstract moral construct that dances around ideas of *what we deserve* and of *what is fair*, of allocating punishments as a measured system for wrongdoing. But what some deem justice, others claim is too lenient. And are we ever satisfied that it has been truly served? After the rope drops and the neck snaps, do we walk home from the gallows satisfied? For that matter, can we ever know if killing someone is enough? The finality of death perhaps provides justice for the living, the ones left behind, but we can never know if what exists after death is not better than the world we inhabit now. Death might indeed be preferable to life. Duncan shakes this absurd notion away. He is allowing his imagination to get the better of him. But, he concedes, he does not truly believe in the binary concept of Heaven and Hell, despite the admonitions from the pulpit every Sunday.

Surely knowledge of a criminal suffering in life for what he or she has done is preferable to relying on what comes afterwards.

Duncan rests his pounding head against the cool glass of the carriage window, and as the train passes through a landscape of muddy brown fields, he tries to make sense of the plight of Helen McDougal. Is Agnes really Helen? Could Maggie have been wrong all those years ago? Was it a case of mistaken identity gone horribly awry? But then there were so many coincidences, weren't there?

He feels such a conflict within: he acknowledges his feelings of compassion for the pathetic creature he saw whispering to the canary, dragged away for icy showers to break what is left of her will, but he reminds himself that from what he has read and heard she *was* complicit in those murders. She did not falter in her commitment to Burke despite his crimes. The idea of Helen McDougal living as a free woman is abhorrent to the people of Scotland. If she is indeed Helen, then is her incarceration in the asylum a fitting end to her story? He remembers Mrs Gow's reference to the hours her husband spends locked away with her. What happens, he wonders, with unease, behind the closed door?

He relives walking through those endless, echoing corridors. What had initially felt spacious and clean became overwhelming and frightening. Much like Burke, Helen's body is now the property of a doctor who seeks to use it for medical research. She is a living cadaver to be used in the advancement of knowledge. It seems to Duncan that Helen's fate is arguably worse than Burke's.

He realises that he cannot write about this. For now, her story must end here. For Helen's existence and whereabouts to be revealed, published in a newspaper, would inevitably lead to something vengeful and catastrophic; and, for Duncan, it is unthinkable that he should be the cause. As the train arrives back into the familiar hubbub of Edinburgh, he finds himself relieved to return to the safety of his home city and to leave behind the horrors of Helen's life. Perhaps, he thinks, as he walks along Princes Street, beneath the reassuring bulk of the castle, he will return to his simple clerical duties at the *Mercury* and satisfy himself with the pursuit of stories of little consequence. Perhaps that is all he is good for.

Chapter 40

A melancholy descends on Duncan over the following days. He is unsure whether it is related to his feelings of personal failure and his decision not to write about Helen's fate, or if it is knowing that she is still alive, albeit enduring an existence like the caged canary. Beyond the asylum walls, he alone knows the truth. The knowledge which he so craved now presses on him, and it is a crushing weight.

He says little to his aunt and uncle about his visit to Stirling and Doune and remains vague about his progress with his account of Mrs Burke and Mrs Hare. Instead, he buries himself in more prosaic duties: opening correspondence, filing documents, writing out advertisements and public notices, and preparing the announcements of births, marriages and deaths in the city. It is repetitive work, but for the moment it is all he can face. Walking is of great comfort to him. He pounds the streets of Edinburgh whenever he can, exploring the hidden nooks of the New Town and further afield. He regards the spires and rooftops of the Old Town from a distance, venturing only as far as the High Street for work. It is on one of these walks that his eye is drawn to a handwritten sign in the window of Robert Frazer's jeweller, not in a hidden side street, but in plain sight on South St Andrew's Street beside the grand square. The sign reads: *Extensive Sale By Auction of Valuable Jewellery And Private Museum of Natural History Antiquities.*

He knows this establishment well and remembers many trips as a boy to visit the strange curiosities, antiques and automata housed at the back of the shop, in the jeweller's museum. A showman of sorts and a kind and generous man, Mr Frazer opens the museum to anyone who cares to see inside and will talk enthusiastically about all the wonderful objects he has collected over the years in his emporium. Buoyed by the idea of a nostalgic moment or two, Duncan pushes the door and steps inside.

It is not Mr Frazer who greets Duncan as the bell behind the door heralds his arrival, but a lady, wearing pince-nez and a striking scarlet dress. He takes off his hat and takes in his surroundings. It has been many years since he was last here and he realises that it has fallen into a poor state of repair; it feels surprisingly small and cramped.

'Good afternoon, sir,' she says, looking up from an examination of figures scrawled in a large ledger. 'How can I help you?'

'Good afternoon,' replies Duncan. 'I see from your sign that you are holding a sale.'

'Indeed, we are, sir. We are closing, I'm afraid. After thirty years, Mr Frazer, my father, is to retire.'

'I am very sorry to hear that,' says Duncan. 'Perhaps I might be of assistance? I work for the *Caledonian Mercury* and could arrange for the placing of an advertisement. I could personally write it for you.' He smiles.

She looks at him blankly for a moment. 'That is very kind of you, sir. I will inform my father of your suggestion. I have been so busy arranging the stock for sale and for the preparation of a catalogue, I had not considered doing such a thing.'

'An advertisement would be most advantageous for a successful sale,' says Duncan with an air of confidence. 'While there is a small fee, of course, it would ensure more people attend the sale, and I imagine there will be many in the city who have fond memories not just of the shop and your fine jewellery, but of the museum too. I am one of them.'

He takes a step towards the backroom. 'May I?'

'Please do,' she says, standing up to show him through to the museum.

He walks through the arched doorway and enjoys inhaling the familiar musty smell. Glass cabinets from floor to ceiling cover every inch of the walls and are packed with curiosities. Duncan grins. To see these objects again is like being reunited with old friends. There are stuffed birds, fragments of Roman pottery, fossils and shells, masks and tiny bottles, each with a story to tell. Now he is able to look directly at the objects his childhood self could only strain his neck to see. He recalls his father hoisting him up for a closer look. Sometimes Mr Frazer would produce a little key from his waistcoat pocket and open the doors of a cabinet. Then he would reach in, lift something precious from the glass shelf and let Duncan touch it. The thrill of being allowed to hold a shark's tooth in his small hand, tracing its fearsome pointed end!

His eye is drawn to the furthest corner, to a display of miniature coffins, and he gasps with delight, remembering how much they had entranced him as a boy. They are smaller than he remembers, perfectly crafted, with little corpses in each one, dressed in exquisite clothes.

'You're not the only one to be transfixed by those ghoulish little objects,' says Miss Frazer.

'I imagine so,' says Duncan, gazing at them. 'They

take me back to my boyhood. They captured my imagination all those years ago, so I'm sure I'm not the only one in Edinburgh to feel the same way.'

'We have one very regular visitor. A man, I guess of a similar age to you, but very shabbily dressed,' she adds disapprovingly. 'He comes here most weeks to see them. I wouldn't usually allow his sort to come in, but my father won't hear of turning him away. He says they're for everyone to enjoy. If it is possible to enjoy seeing such peculiar things. This particular visitor is most upset that we are to sell them. He has pleaded with us not to let them go such is his fondness for them.'

'Yes, it will be interesting to see who buys them,' remarks Duncan. He scans along the row and counts them. There are eleven. 'Remind me, where did they come from?'

She folds her arms and sighs. 'My father would know the answer to that.'

'Found on Arthur's Seat,' says a voice behind them. They turn to see the thin figure of Mr Frazer. His pallor is grey and his suit hangs from his diminished frame, but his smile is broad.

'Ah, Father! I was just going to come to find you. This gentleman works for the *Caledonian Mercury* and is inviting us to place an advertisement for the sale.'

'Duncan Fletcher.' Duncan hands Mr Frazer his card. 'I am also a devoted boyhood visitor to this very museum. It brought me great pleasure, and it is especially delightful to see these little coffins again.'

Robert Frazer shuffles forward and raises a shaky hand towards the display. 'They were found by some schoolboys out looking for rabbits' burrows. They were buried in shallow graves, as it were. We don't think they had been there for very long, maybe just a few years when they were discovered. I bought them from the father of one of the boys.'

'They are remarkable, are they not?' says Duncan.

'There were many more,' adds Mr Frazer, 'but they were damaged beyond repair. The boys in their excitement didn't treat them carefully when they brought them off the hillside, stuffing them in their pockets and so forth.'

Duncan frowns. 'How many were there originally?'

'Seventeen,' says Mr Frazer.

The number resonates with Duncan. 'Seventeen?' he repeats.

Mr Frazer turns his gaze to Duncan. 'Burke and Hare,' he says, his eyebrows raised.

There is a pause. Duncan feels a sudden prickle at his neck. It seems he cannot escape those names.

'I don't recall the connection to Burke and Hare,' says Duncan, 'but of course I was only a boy.'

'Oh, yes,' enthuses Mr Frazer.

'But they were said to have murdered sixteen people,

yes? Perhaps more, but sixteen is the number they mention in all the literature.'

'Ah,' says Mr Frazer, 'but there was an additional one who they didn't actually murder; he too was sold to Butcher Knox. Seventeen souls who missed out on a Christian burial. But these little coffins were buried in their place. Perhaps . . . We shall never know, I suppose.' He sighs as though to clear the air. 'Come through to my office, Mr Fletcher, and let me give you the particulars for an advertisement. I have a lot to sell, you see.'

Duncan nods but continues to stare at the miniature corpses, lying peacefully, their arms clamped to their sides. But then he realises that they all have their eyes open. Staring at him. Pleading with him. For despite their delicate caskets, these souls cannot rest in peace.

Chapter 41

The first blow to his head is a mighty whack that sends Duncan staggering in shock, and when the second one comes, he crashes to the ground. He instinctively cradles his skull with his arms as more punches come raining down upon him. And then, as though in a place far away, he hears their voices.

'What's he got on him?'

'Here, check that pocket.'

'Grab the watch and chain.'

'There's money in the wallet. Get it.'

'Hurry before anyone comes.'

The world is a spinning, chaotic blur. He can feel his face begin to swell and the metallic taste of blood in his mouth. He knows from the voices that they are women: definitely not ladies. He smells them as they lean in close to his face, reeking of sweet, stale sweat. He dares to open one painful eye as their fingers poke and jab, rummage through every inch of his clothing. These creatures wear no bonnets, and their raggle-taggle clothing is soiled. He sees their breasts, more womanly flesh than he has ever been close to since he was a child. They are unlike any females he has ever encountered, more animal than human. And then they are gone.

Duncan breathes deeply and raises his throbbing head.

'Hey, you there, are you all right?' says a male voice.

Duncan feels muscular arms lifting him upwards to a sitting position. 'I'm fine ... I think,' he mumbles. 'Thank you.' But he isn't sure if he is fine. Right now, dazed and bewildered, he barely knows his own name.

'Someone is chasing them,' says the man. 'They'll catch them this time. Here, lean back against the wall. You've been badly beaten.'

Duncan rests his head on the damp brickwork, then instinctively presses his hand to his chest.

'They got your watch and chain, didn't they? And your wallet?'

'It matters not,' says Duncan quietly.

'Oh, yes, it does,' says the man. 'I know them. This isn't the first time.'

'They are women.'

'What of it? Did their punches feel any less painful because they are women?'

Duncan tries to smile, but it hurts his jaw.

A policeman appears, hurtling down the close towards them. 'Are you hurt, sir?' he says.

'Yes,' says Duncan, 'but I shall survive.'

The policeman bends down and offers him a handful of jumbled objects. 'Are these yours, sir?'

Duncan peers at the silver chain and watch and the worn leather of his wallet. 'Yes,' he says with some surprise. He looks inside the wallet; no money has been removed. 'Thank you.'

'All part of the job, sir. We have the culprits and will be charging them with street theft and assault.'

'No,' says Duncan sharply. 'Don't do that. They might have children to feed. It won't help them.'

'Won't help them?' scoffs the policeman. 'We enforce justice, not social benefit. We shall do what is right by the law. You might reconsider taking a walk in these dark closes in the future, sir.' He turns and heads towards daylight and the High Street beyond.

Duncan gets to his feet, wincing in pain.

'Easy there,' says the man. 'Where are you headed?'

'To work – to my office at the *Mercury*.'

'I thought I recognised you. I spoke to you just the other day, helped you find a woman. Mrs Gray.'

Duncan looks at the man more closely. 'You're the cobbler? From the Cowgate.'

'That's right. My name's Joseph,' he says, putting

out his hand. 'Joseph Campbell. I was just hawking on the High Street when those two harpies came bolting out the close. I knew they'd left some poor soul behind. They've done it many a time before.'

'Well, you've come to my aid twice now, Joseph Campbell,' says Duncan, shaking his hand as firmly as his aching body can. 'Let me buy you a drink. I could certainly do with some fortification. I'm Duncan Fletcher.' Joseph grins. The dirt on his skin has settled into the fine lines around his eyes. He is very slim, but he is handsome, and there is a warmth, a kindness about him.

'A drink is always welcome, Mr Fletcher,' he says before helping Duncan limp up Fleshmarket Close and onto the High Street, where they head down the hill to the pleasing sight of The Ship Tavern.

Chapter 42

They make an odd couple, the well-heeled gentleman and the scruffy cobbler, sitting in a corner of the tavern. A good fire burns in the hearth, and it is a convivial atmosphere, in sharp contrast to the dark close of their encounter.

'Why would you care what happens to those women?' asks Joseph, looking at Duncan inquisitively.

Duncan takes a sip of his ale. 'I'm no stranger to the plight of the poor in this part of town.'

'So it's acceptable to you to attack and rob an innocent man?'

'I didn't say that. It's merely understandable. I can imagine poverty leading to desperation, particularly if you're a mother with children to feed and no other way to earn money. As Christians we must be tolerant and have insight into what drives their actions.'

'How desperate do you think they truly are?'

'Well, that I don't know,' admits Duncan. 'How could I possibly know that?' He thinks back to the children playing in the open sewer of Tanner's Close, their emaciated, grubby faces. 'But hunger, I can imagine, must be a driving force.'

'You're assuming they have mouths to feed?'

'Well, yes ... I must say, you seem wholly unsympathetic to the plight of these women. Surely they need our compassion not our condemnation.'

'Let me tell you something about Jane McEwan and Ann Leydon,' says Joseph. 'They have no bairns to feed. They live in a boarding house in the Cowgate like many other souls, but instead of finding honest work like hawking, they prowl the streets looking for folk to rob. They make no attempt to live a decent life. Instead, they attack the old and infirm, the drunk, and they care not if they leave them for dead, stealing their last penny or even their shoes. Yes, they may be hungry, but they are thirstier still. They spend what they have on drink, and it makes them a malevolent presence round here. They lurk around the streets, watching for victims, threatening anyone who crosses their path, and show no mercy, not one shred of it. They have operated a reign of terror here for too long.

'You just happen to be the first man of wealth they've attacked in broad daylight. Your loss – your watch and money – at least you know there's more where they came from. But the folk round here, they're left with less than nothing.' He shakes his head in disgust. 'No, it's time their spree was stopped. Because they're getting too bold. What next? Murder?' He looks at Duncan as though challenging him to argue back, but Duncan shifts uncomfortably in his seat and fiddles with the glass on the table in front of him.

'And you come here with your high and mighty Christian values defending them. Yes, there is poverty here, but defending women like that, feeling pity for them because they have chosen a life of crime, does not help the plight of the poor.'

Duncan takes a sip of his ale. 'You're quite right, of course. I didn't realise,' he concedes, rubbing his cheek. He can feel the swelling where he was hit. He presses the cold glass to his face.

'Why would you?' says Joseph. 'But that's the problem. The rich dip a toe into our lives and think they know how to fix it, but they never think to ask those who live and breathe it. After all, what would we know? Us hard-working, decent folk who have been born with no advantages, nothing. Just our wit and determination to live – to live a modest life.'

'I apologise.' Duncan feels mortified at this lecture. 'You are correct. I am on the outside looking in. As though your world was a curiosity, a museum piece behind a glass case. I observe, but I haven't lived it. I know that I've been very fortunate.'

Joseph acknowledges the admission, and the pair sit quietly for a moment.

'Why did you want to see Mrs Gray?' says Joseph. 'The other day.'

'For a story – an account I wanted to write about Burke and Hare's women,' says Duncan cautiously. 'You know, the murderers who sold the bodies to the medical men.'

'I know who they are,' says Joseph. 'Or were.'

Duncan watches Joseph's reaction. He is curious to know what he thinks. He is quite sure there will be a strong opinion.

Joseph takes a gulp of beer, swilling it in his mouth before swallowing. 'And why would you want to write about them? Out of sympathy?'

Duncan hesitates. In the space of just a few minutes, Joseph has made him view everything differently. 'No. I suppose I just thought it might make an interesting story for the paper,' he says sheepishly. He feels his face getting hotter and hopes Joseph doesn't notice.

'And what have you discovered so far?' says Joseph.

Duncan feels a rare empathy with this man; he feels compelled to open up to him, to tell him the truth about what he has learned of Helen McDougal.

'Well, so far, I've been to a lunatic asylum outside

Stirling, and they have a woman there, a patient who it seems *might* be Helen McDougal, the wife of William Burke. She is in a very bad way.'

Joseph's eyes flicker.

'But I don't know about the other one yet,' says Duncan. He is about to go on to explain that he has been unsure about continuing, that the whole idea has come to a dead end, but that seeing the coffins today had been too strange a coincidence to shrug off; that he wonders if he is being guided by an unseen force. But he stops himself. It sounds foolish, just superstitious nonsense. He doesn't want Joseph to think badly of him. He's already scolded his ignorance.

'Lucky Hare,' says Joseph, interrupting Duncan's thoughts. 'I think I might be able to help you there.'

Duncan looks up. 'You can?'

Joseph drains his glass and stands up. 'Follow me.'

Chapter 43

St Mary's Wynd is little more than a slum. Most of its buildings seem to have been abandoned: roofs are caved in, slates slipping downwards like dominoes to expose rotten beams and crumbling brickwork. Chimney pots lie smashed on the cobbles, and the old signs that once heralded the presence of thriving businesses are now just remnants of a forgotten time. Yet, unbelievably to Duncan, there are people living here, slipping in and out of hidden places like ghosts.

He hesitates, peering into the darkness beyond; he can hear the distant sound of a wailing baby.

Joseph senses Duncan's reticence. 'It's safe here,' he says. 'No one is going to attack you this time, I promise. Not with me around.'

Duncan breathes a sigh of relief and continues. They

come to a door which Joseph opens without any indecision, beckoning him to follow. Inside is a musty room lit by tallow candles and lamps that burn the most foul-smelling oil. Duncan immediately puts his hand to his nose, but it is his eyes that feel most irritated by the fetid air. In the pervading gloom, he glimpses groups of men and women huddled around tables. He has heard of such drinking dens but would never have dared enter one alone. Joseph nods and smiles at the patrons as though he knows them of old. Perhaps, considers Duncan, he has mended their shoes.

At the very back of the room, in the darkest of corners, a man sits alone, nursing a drink.

'Mr Dickie?' says Joseph. 'I've brought someone to see you, someone who'd like to hear about Lucky Hare.'

Mr Dickie looks up. He is wearing a wig that resembles something in a painting of old, powdered and grotesque. His face is smeared in a greasy white paint, and he has dabs of rouge smeared on his wrinkled cheeks. His lips are a bright, artificial cherry red, and there is a beauty spot on his chin, a smudged circle as though applied with a tremulous hand. His glazed eyes swing from Joseph to Duncan, and his mouth breaks into a wide smile revealing a jumble of bad teeth.

'Now that is a name I don't hear often,' he says. 'Buy me a drink and I'll tell you all I know.'

'Sit,' says Joseph to Duncan, and he turns towards the hatch.

Mr Dickie regards Duncan with curiosity. 'And why, pray, do *you* want to know about Lucky Hare? It's been many years since she frequented these streets. You can't even have been born then.'

'I'm a writer,' says Duncan shyly, sliding into a chair. 'I want to know what happened to her, where she went after the trial, where she is now. If she's still alive.'

Joseph returns with a glass of whisky and pulls a stool in close. Duncan is relieved that he is sitting beside him.

'I cannot be sure if she is still alive,' says Mr Dickie. 'But she had evil pulsating through her veins, that one. I am fortunate I am still here to tell the tale. She might have had me killed. *Burked me!*'

'Tell him about her and the wig,' says Joseph.

'I tell him what I choose to tell him,' slurs Mr Dickie. He takes a swig of whisky and shudders as he swallows. Some of the liquid leaks from his mouth, but he doesn't notice. 'I had a most successful business in my younger days,' he says. 'I supplied all the great actors who came to this city with their wigs and hair pieces and face paints. Do you know I made the wigs for the great Miss Stephens and Mr Horn, performing *The Marriage of Figaro* at the Theatre Royal when I was just an apprentice perruquier.' He raises his chin and hands dramatically, as though on stage, facing an auditorium. Then he lowers his head, as though bowing to a cheering audience.

Duncan looks to Joseph, who raises his eyebrows in a signal to be patient.

Mr Dickie lifts a single, gnarled finger and continues. 'But the most infamous customer I ever had was the wife of the murderer William Hare. When Mrs Hare came to me I knew the minute she walked through my door that she was wicked. It was as though Satan's wife herself had appeared.'

'What did she want?' asks Duncan.

'She wanted me to make her a wig, of course. With the dead girl's hair. I didn't know at the time, I hasten to add. I learned that afterwards, when it all came out.'

'She brought you hair to make a wig, but you didn't know where the hair had come from?' says Duncan.

'Of course I didn't know it was Mary Paterson's hair,' spits Mr Dickie. 'Lucky Hare told me the hair had been bequeathed to her. From a dead relative.'

Duncan is horrified at this; he looks from Joseph to the old man. 'Does that happen? I mean is that normal?'

Mr Dickie cocks his head to one side. 'What exactly is normal, young man? In my line of work, the most peculiar things occur. I have made wigs from horse hair, even goat hair. If you are blessed with a marvellous head of hair, why wouldn't you leave it to your nearest and dearest when you die? It wasn't anything out of the ordinary to me. And this hair, Mary Paterson's hair, was quite exceptional. It was long and thick and the richest radiant red . . .' He drifts off into a memory.

'Why did she want it?' asks Duncan. 'A wig? Why would Lucky Hare want such a thing?'

Mr Dickie snaps back into the present and leans forward; Duncan can smell a noxious decay on his breath. 'Oh, I saw the gleam in her eye when she came to collect it. She understood the power of that hair to bewitch men: like Mary Paterson herself. What started out as a game became a way to make money. Lots of it. Rumours began to spread like wildfire after the whole business was well and truly over. Rumours that Lucky herself walked the streets of Edinburgh at night wearing the wig. And had encounters with men for money, like a common whore. That she took pleasure from it – from masquerading as Mary Paterson.' Triumphant with this dramatic statement, he slumps back in his seat. 'But she stopped when she had her child. I didn't see her again after she came to collect the wig. Not until the very night she left Edinburgh.'

'Go on,' urges Joseph.

'Perhaps it was fate,' he muses. 'We collided in the street, her and I. I knew the hair before I even saw her face. I would know that wig anywhere. After all, I had created it. She was clutching her mewling offspring and ran off up towards the High Street. But I followed her. Oh, yes, I followed. She didn't see me, but I saw her board a carriage that was heading to Leith to catch the London steamer.'

'London,' says Duncan quietly. 'An obvious place to disappear, I suppose.'

'Perhaps,' concedes Mr Dickie. 'But just a year or so later, an actor friend of mine came to Edinburgh from London. And one night after his performance we shared a drink or two. I told him my tale of Lucky Hare and the red wig, and he went quite pale. Said he'd stayed in a boarding house in London off Drury Lane, which was run by an Irishwoman with long red hair – who went by the name of Mrs Mary Paterson.'

Duncan gasps. He feels his heart racing.

'Of course, we can never be certain it was the same woman,' continues Mr Dickie, 'but what an extraordinary coincidence, wouldn't you say?' He smiles wickedly, enjoying the moment. 'Now then, gents, how about another glass of that excellent fire water for this old trooper?'

Chapter 44

It is early morning, and Duncan is sitting beside Joseph on a train bound for London. It is bitterly cold in the third-class carriage, and he pulls his coat tighter and tries to get comfortable, which is impossible given they are sitting on hard wooden benches like church pews. This express train, he thinks to himself, will arrive at 10 o'clock tonight, which is nothing short of miraculous, considering travel by any other means would take several days. However, the accommodation is most disagreeable. He had wanted to buy them second- or even first-class tickets, but Joseph had refused. 'Come now,' he had said firmly. 'If you truly want to comment on our lives, you must experience it: walk in our shoes.'

Duncan observes their fellow travellers. Around twenty men are crammed into the carriage, their faces expressionless, bodies rocking rhythmically to the steady movement of the train. The two women are wrapped in thick woollen blankets, and Duncan considers they are more sensibly prepared than he is as he pulls his arms tighter around himself. Joseph is slumped with his hat tipped over his eyes, his chin down, his arms folded.

Duncan gives him a nudge. 'Joseph . . . are we making a mistake, do you think?'

Joseph pushes up his hat, revealing sleepy eyes. 'Didn't we go through all this last night?' he says.

'Yes, I suppose so. But what if Mr Dickie was lying or exaggerating? For whisky? And what if we do find her? What then? What on earth do we do? I'm not sure if I haven't taken leave of my senses setting forth on this escapade.' He rubs his bruised cheek.

Joseph sits up and stretches his arms. Duncan flinches at the sound of cracking bones. 'You said yourself you're trying to get to the truth. So, this way, you'll know. We just want to see if she's there, don't we? If she exists. At the moment she's just a myth, a story from the past. It's more than likely she's dead, and you've got nothing for the other one, nothing that can be reported anyway, so you may as well give Lucky Hare a go.'

Duncan is unconvinced. Last night, Joseph had persuaded him that he was the key to discovering more.

He could wander into any drinking den, he said, and nobody would look sideways. Duncan, on the other hand, was too conspicuous in every possible way. Joseph would be his spy, his agent to the truth. All he needed was his train fare and a bite to eat here and there. Last night, all of this had sounded exciting and intrepid. But, right now, Duncan feels he would rather be sitting at his desk writing out the advertisement for the sale at the jewellery shop. He feels in his pocket for his notebook and fishes it out. In all the drama of the night before, he had quite forgotten about it. He reassures himself that a day or two's delay will make little difference.

'As I see it,' Joseph continues, 'we're just going to lay eyes on her. Yes?'

Duncan nods as he flips through the pages.

Joseph glances over his shoulder at the writing. 'What's all that for? Messrs Frazer and Co., Jewellers? Is that the place near the Scott Monument? The one with the museum in the back?'

'You can read?' says Duncan. Joseph nods. 'I'm sorry, that was quite rude of me to assume otherwise.' Duncan flushes.

Joseph shrugs. 'Why should you think otherwise? I hardly look like a scholar, do I? I didn't go to school. My father couldn't read, but the priest could. He taught me and a few other boys to read the Bible and other texts. I can write a little but not very well. Why are you writing about the jeweller's shop? It's the one that's closing, isn't it?'

'Yes. I'm writing an advertisement for the sale.'

'What will they do with everything? All the items in the museum?'

'Sell them to the highest bidder. Mr Frazer should do very well, I should think. He has many unique pieces.'

At that moment, they become aware that the train is pulling into a station. Their fellow passengers are standing and jostling, organising their belongings. Joseph looks as though he is about to say something further when they have to stand to let a young lad past who has been squatting in the corner. Duncan finds great relief in standing up and continues to do so long after the lad has passed by, stretching his limbs and allowing the blood to move freely to the parts of his body that are numb with cold. The train comes to a full stop, and there is a flurry of movement as the passengers disembark to relieve themselves or grab a hot pie and a cup of tea. With the carriage now quiet, they have the bench to themselves. Duncan bends to look out of the window and then turns to Joseph, who appears deep in thought.

'Have you a wife and family at home?' he asks, sitting back down. 'I didn't think to ask last night before making this plan.'

'No. I am quite alone in the world.' Joseph says this without a trace of emotion. 'I have only myself to worry about. You?'

'No wife, no. My parents are dead; they died when I was very young. My aunt and uncle raised me, so I board with them.'

'My parents are dead, too,' says Joseph. 'My mother died hours after I arrived into this world and my father died when I was but thirteen. Only eight years ago but it feels like yesterday.'

'My sincere condolences. A difficult age to lose a parent,' concedes Duncan. 'Was he a cobbler like you?'

'He was. A highly skilled and god-fearing, hard-working man, came to Edinburgh from Ireland in search of work. He was the very best of men. I remember him in everything I do. Because he taught me, cared for me, raised me.'

'What was it that caused his death – if you don't mind my asking?'

'The truth?' says Joseph, picking at a fingernail. 'Despair.'

Duncan says nothing. The carriage begins to fill up with passengers, but for now they have the corner to themselves. A whistle sounds. Doors slam shut and the train begins to pull away from the station.

'Your father, he suffered from melancholy?' he asks.

'He simply could no longer remain alive, such was

his anguish,' says Joseph, taking off his hat and running his fingers through his dusty hair. 'I have often wondered what he hoped it would achieve. Was he seeking improvement by dying? Assuming there was something more pleasant to come? Not purgatory, surely. Or was it simply to terminate the misery? Either way, he chose to end his existence in this world.'

'Suicide?' Duncan says gently under his breath. He does not wish anyone to hear, and fortunately the group of men nearby are engaged in lively discussion, drowning out all other conversation.

'Self-murder, that's what they call it, isn't it? The sin of silent, fatal despair: a crime against God?' He turns over his hat in his hands. 'I don't see it as that. He held no quarrel with God. It was mankind that let him down. And once that happened, sadness followed him like a deathly shadow.'

'I'm so sorry,' says Duncan, shocked at the honesty of this disclosure. The train picks up speed and settles into its soothing rhythmical motion. They sit in silence for some minutes listening to the gentle clack of wheels on track and the merriment in the seats behind them.

'It was me who found him,' continues Joseph, so quietly it is hard to hear him over the noise. 'Me, his only son. Just a boy, too. It's not the memory of his lifeless body that haunts me. How he did it isn't even important; it's the fact that he chose to destroy himself.

That he felt he had reached the end. I couldn't help him. I wasn't enough. Just existing, for him, just breathing was too hard.' He pauses, considering his next words. 'I wonder if somehow I made his life worse. I certainly didn't make it better. I brought him no succour. That I must live on, knowing that, is painful.'

Duncan can see tears glistening on his long eyelashes.

'When they took him for burial, it was at night, the sin too great for anyone to see. The shame of it. The secrecy. No one wanted to call it suicide,' he says the word with deliberation, 'because we are too afraid of that, aren't we? No, temporary insanity seems to sit better. Then we didn't have to give the Crown all his worldly goods.' A bitter laugh escapes at this. 'Not that he had any.'

Duncan cannot take his eyes from Joseph's face, stricken with the grief of the memory.

'His torment is over,' offers Duncan. 'He is at peace; you can take some comfort from that at least.'

'Do you know where they buried him?' Joseph says, staring at Duncan. 'In the furthest corner of the churchyard. Where the other *self-destroyers*, the *sinners* are dumped. That's how they punish the dead. They told me he was lucky to be in the churchyard at all. No words were spoken, no prayers for the dead.'

Joseph's jaw is taut, and two tears meander down his

face. Duncan swallows hard. He has never witnessed emotion this raw and honest, but there is no discomfort. He feels only compassion.

'For a long time, I couldn't sleep, thinking of him lying there in that muddy corner in the rain and the snow,' says Joseph. 'Buried like a dog he was, my father. But at least he was buried, unlike some unlucky souls.' He wipes his face with the back of his hand and turns to look at Duncan, his handsome face blotchy with blooms of pink on his cheeks. Then he sighs as though with relief. 'Do you know, that's two firsts since I've met you, Duncan Fletcher. I've never told anyone that before. Not a living soul has ever listened or wanted to listen. And here I've sat pouring out my father's story. I'm not sure why.'

'I have never known anyone brave enough to say the unsaid,' says Duncan. 'To speak honestly about something so private. I admire your bravery. And the second first?'

'I've never been on a train before,' says Joseph with a grin.

The two men smile at each other in a fleeting moment of solidarity and then turn their heads in opposite directions, to gaze, in silence, at the passing countryside.

Chapter 45

Vinegar Yard is a decrepit alleyway tucked behind Drury Lane's Theatre Royal. And it is there, in a public house called the Whistling Oyster, that Duncan and Joseph will seek fortification after their exhausting journey from Edinburgh. London is every bit as overwhelming as Duncan imagined it would be. The impact on the senses the minute they step off the train is like a brisk slap in the face. The smells, the noise, the sensation of soot and miasma at every turn is exhilarating and terrifying at the same time. The cab driver is wary on hearing their request to travel from King's Cross to Drury Lane.

'Full of unsavoury types there. Are you quite sure, sir?' he says, eyeing Duncan in particular. 'At this time of night?'

Duncan wonders why he seems so hesitant; surely it

can't be any worse than the slums of Auld Reekie.

The driver doesn't linger a moment longer than he needs to after he drops them off, whipping the horse with gusto to escape this inhospitable nook of the city. And now, looking around the malodourous maze of streets in the shadows of the theatre, Duncan understands the driver's concern. If he thought that the slums of Edinburgh's Old Town were miserable, this is surely ten times worse.

'Here,' Joseph says, leading them towards the Whistling Oyster. 'This will give us a chance to gather our strength ... And stop staring! You're drawing attention to yourself. You look like a lamb surrounded by hungry wolves.'

Inside, the tavern is predictably dark and smoky, but, Duncan concedes, it is lively and warm. The patrons are not as he had expected. This is no squalid drinking den, with guilt written across bleary faces; rather, it resembles a microcosm of society from well-dressed gentlemen in top hats to bohemian types – actors and artists in garish garments – to working men with coal-smeared faces, grubby waistcoats and trousers. The women, however – and there are several even at this late hour – are painted night creatures with ribbons tied through their twisted, tousled hair. Draped over chairs and men's laps, their flesh is on show, with lacy skirts hitched up higher than is proper to reveal stockinged legs. Their lewd manner makes Duncan recoil, bringing back the sensation of the women in Fleshmarket Close with their warm, pungent bodies pressed to his.

'You're doing it again,' murmurs Joseph. 'The staring.' Duncan lowers his eyes. 'Give me some coins and I'll get us a drink.'

Duncan fumbles in his jacket pocket for his coin purse and pulls it out. His fingers are freezing, and opening the damned thing is awkward.

Joseph rolls his eyes. 'Let's just tell all the pickpockets, thieves and cut-throats that you've got money, shall we?'

Duncan pulls out a few coins.

'Sit there,' instructs Joseph, pointing to a secluded corner.

'I believe I am too tired to function properly,' groans Duncan before throwing himself down in a seat and removing his hat. Slowly, he begins to acclimatise and take in his surroundings, even to take pleasure in it. There is a sense of merriment, joy, in the room. It is full of colour and spirit, so different to anything he has experienced in dour Edinburgh. It is as though he has stepped into one of Dickens' novels. The faces are dynamic and expressive. Their stories would be fascinating, he thinks. He suddenly feels very shy and ordinary.

Joseph returns with two glasses of ale and a plate balanced precariously on top. 'I thought we could do with some sustenance.'

Duncan helps retrieve the plate and looks at it in disappointment. 'Oysters. I can't stand oysters.'

'I assume you noticed the name of this place?' Joseph scoffs. He wastes no time in grabbing a shell and tipping the contents down his throat. 'You can pick at the bread.'

'Where should we even begin?' says Duncan, cradling his glass. 'Whom should we ask?'

'I've already done it,' says Joseph. He takes a hefty swig of his ale, wipes his mouth with the back of his hand and then leans back. Duncan tries not to show his surprise. Joseph seems strangely focused on the task in hand. There's a readiness, a capability, and Duncan doesn't know whether to be grateful for this confidence or intimidated by it.

'Done what, exactly?'

'I asked the publican when I was fetching the drinks,' says Joseph, now tearing at a piece of bread.

'Asked him what?'

'If he knew of a boarding house round here, one that was run by a woman called Mary Paterson. Said I was a distant relative and wanted to see her.'

'And?'

'He said he'd never heard of a Mary Paterson.'

'Oh,' says Duncan with an exhale of disappointment, or perhaps relief. 'She may have changed her name again.'

'Well, according to him, there's a Mary-Ann O'Donnelly and a Mary Murphy and a Mary Millar living round here and more. So many Marys.'

'Like a needle in a haystack,' mutters Duncan.

'Looking for some company, gents?' says a female voice. A woman, a fair bit older than Duncan and Joseph, appears by their table. Dressed in faded rags, her tight corset accentuates her tiny waist and pushes her tiny breasts upwards into two fleshy moons.

What Duncan had regarded from afar as a lascivious creature, on closer inspection he sees as a desperate poor soul. Under the thick greasepaint, her skin is pock-marked and scarred, and she has some nasty sores on her neck.

'Well, now, do you happen to know someone called Mary?' asks Joseph with a cheeky smile.

The woman throws back her head and shrieks with laughter. 'Mary, you say? There's a million Marys in London! And who are you, anyway? Joseph?'

Joseph grins. 'You might not believe me, but my name is indeed Joseph.'

The woman cackles again. 'That must make you the bleeding donkey,' she says, pointing a bony finger at Duncan and laughing uproariously at her own joke.

Then she tilts her head to one side in a coquettish manner and purrs, 'I can be called Mary, if you like.' She sits down so close to Duncan she's almost on his knee. He tries to shift along the seat; he does not like her touch.

'I'm no virgin, though, I can tell you that,' she warns, giving Duncan a nudge with her elbow. 'May I?' She points at the oysters.

'Be my guest,' says Duncan with a sigh.

'Watch your pockets there,' says Joseph to Duncan.

'Oi,' snaps the woman, reaching for a shell. 'I ain't no pickpocket. I do other things for money.' She winks and pulls at the oyster with her teeth.

'You might remember a Mary Paterson, an older woman,' says Joseph, trying to catch her attention. 'Maybe with a Scottish accent or Irish. Has a son. She ran a boarding house round here for actors.'

The woman looks at him blankly. 'Oh, I dunno. Never mind her. Why don't you think about me instead?' She begins to stroke Duncan's face with her long, filthy nails, now wet with oyster juice. Duncan cringes and tries to pull away.

Joseph shakes his head. 'Too many Marys.'

Desperate to say something, anything to distract the girl, Duncan remembers Mr Dickie's story of the wig.

'She had very long, very distinctive red hair,' he offers, removing the woman's clammy hand from his face.

Something flares in her eyes. Fear perhaps? She snatches her hand away and her body stiffens. 'Oh, I remember her, alright, her with the red wig,' she says hoarsely, her mouth distorted. 'Pretending it's her own hair. We all knew it was a wig on that raddled old head of hers. That bitch and her boy. Savages, the pair of 'em.' She places a hand to her throat. 'She's had a few places near here. Filthy! Keeps changing men, she does, the wicked old hag. But she's not here no more. Good riddance, I say.'

Duncan is intrigued. By this woman's visceral reaction, he senses that this could well be Lucky Hare they are discussing.

'Dead?' suggests Joseph. He, too, is staring at the woman intently.

'I wish she was. Nah, she moved up in the world, that one, got married again and shifted herself and her beast of a son out to Whitechapel to the workhouse there.'

'Oh, come now,' says Duncan. 'How has she moved up in the world if she's ended up in the workhouse?'

The woman shakes her head and laughs. 'She's not in there to bleedin' work, mister. Oh no! That bitch is running the place.'

Chapter 46

Joseph and Duncan find rooms for the night in a cheap hotel overlooking Covent Garden, and although Duncan sleeps like the dead, he is awoken at some ungodly hour by the rumble of carts and the shouts of the sellers setting up their stalls. Like an excited child on Christmas morning, he remembers with a thrill that he is not in Edinburgh, but London. He dresses with speed so he can pull back the moth-eaten curtains and watch the city awaken from its slumber. He opens the window and breathes in the air, which although noxious still reminds him he is in a place so different and invigorating he could be in a foreign country. A watery sunlight is leaking through the early morning fog, and the streets before him are alive with a fascinating chaos of horse-drawn wagons and makeshift stalls weighed down with an abundance of fruit and vegetables. Barrow boys wind their way through the crowds, narrowly avoiding the women with vast baskets crammed full of spring flowers. Such bustle and commotion make for quite the joyous scene, and Duncan could happily pull up a chair and sit here all day, but he is interrupted by a knock at the door.

'Come and see this,' says Duncan, waving Joseph over to the window. 'It is quite something out there.'

Joseph glances absent-mindedly at the busy marketplace. 'We must go,' he urges. 'Come, where's your coat and your hat?' He picks them up from the bed.

Duncan is surprised at his urgency. 'Why the rush?' he says.

'I have spoken to the proprietor of the hotel, Mrs Warren, and she has drawn me a map of roughly the direction we need to go.' He thrusts a piece of paper in front of Duncan. 'We can breakfast on the way.'

Duncan looks at the scribbled map which makes little sense to him, but what is most curious is Joseph's agitation.

'I propose we take a cab,' says Joseph, heading towards the door.

'Actually, I would like to walk,' says Duncan, thinking of Mr Dickens' jaunts around the city. 'I would like to see something of London while we are here, after which I can reflect upon my observations and record them in writing. We can ask people on the way for directions.'

Joseph turns to look at Duncan. 'You are quite giddy this morning,' he says. 'Here, I thought you wanted to find Lucky Hare.'

'Of course, I do. But our mission is simply to establish where she is – to lay eyes on her, as you said. If that's possible. Isn't it? And then we'll head home.'

Joseph looks down. 'Aye,' he concedes, 'and a walk might do us good after sitting for so long yesterday.'

'There's just one small problem,' says Duncan, indicating his shoes which sit side by side at the foot of the bed. 'One of my shoes is in a bad way.'

Joseph reaches down, picks them both up and inspects them carefully. The sole on one shoe is gaping; he pulls it open like a yawning mouth. Wordlessly, he reaches into his pocket and pulls out a stitching awl with its formidable sharp point, a needle and thick thread.

'You carry your tools with you?'

'What sort of cobbler would I be if I wasn't prepared to at least mend my own shoes, let alone mend others' for money?' He perches on the bed and sets about sewing the upper back to the sole, working so deftly that Duncan is transfixed. 'You need a new heel,' he says, checking the bottom of the shoe, 'but that will have to wait until we get home.' He hands the shoes back to Duncan, who scrutinises the immaculate stitching.

'Astonishing,' he says. 'Thank you, what do I owe you?'

'A steak pie should do it,' says Joseph with a smile.

They set off at a sprightly pace, dodging the plentiful horse dung and cesspools. But today Duncan does not notice the unsanitary conditions; instead, he is captivated by the wonders that surround him, from the colour of the bricks to the unfurling blossom on the trees – so much further ahead in the season than back in Edinburgh. He looks up with fascination at the architecture of the historic old buildings, noting the renovations and improvements that are being made. After a brief breakfast in a coffee house, they continue on through the famous archway at Temple Bar before ambling into the beating heart of the city of words: Fleet Street. When Duncan catches sight of the dome of St Paul's Cathedral he grabs Joseph's arm to show him.

'Would you look at that!' he cries. 'The mighty St Paul's! The work of Sir Christopher Wren himself. Isn't it marvellous?' He turns to look at Joseph, beaming, but his companion seems deep in his own thoughts.

From there, they walk onwards, every so often glimpsing the murky waters of the Thames and the distant ancient spires of the White Tower.

'London is a remarkably eccentric city, don't you

agree?' says Duncan, slowing down yet again to take in the array of shops and businesses. 'It is so much more cosmopolitan than I could have imagined. So much more vibrant and vital. Somehow I feel freer here, away from the shackles of grey, presbyterian Edinburgh. Perhaps because the climate is so much milder, too. No biting east coast wind cutting us in half.'

Joseph nods distractedly. 'We shouldn't linger. Let us press on.'

'I have wanted to visit London since I was a boy,' Duncan prattles on, 'and I must say, despite the deprivation, everywhere we look, advancements are being made. Look here – they are demolishing the slums to make way for beautiful wide streets.'

'They certainly are,' remarks Joseph, grim-faced. 'However, it would appear we are seeing the same city but through very different eyes.'

'How so?' says Duncan, glad that Joseph is finally engaging with him on a discussion of the city.

'You see the gilt that is slapped over the dirt,' he says. 'A society that favours the rich and wants the poor to disappear. They are tearing down the slums, but where are the people who live there supposed to go? Like beetles they must scurry out as their homes are destroyed. But it does not solve the problem; it merely sends them elsewhere to continue their rotten existence. What the wealthy desire is a London that has all the power and riches without any of the hardship on show; to be swathed in a plush velvet curtain, behind which they sweep the dirt.'

'I had not thought of it like that.'

'I am educating the educated, it seems,' says Joseph.

Duncan feels a surge of irritation. 'Yes, but might we be allowed to enjoy our jaunt, too? Without the constant commentary on the plight of the poor?'

'Is that not why I am here?' says Joseph, slinging a protective arm around Duncan's shoulder. 'As your pauper guide and protector?'

'So it would seem,' says Duncan with a wry smile.

They head north, further away from the river towards the area of Whitechapel. Duncan is quieter now as they are confronted by vast warehouses, houses crammed tightly together and factories belching acrid black fumes that catch the back of their throats; the colour and energy of the city has been smothered by industry and brutal poverty.

'This is suffocating,' says Duncan, looking around in horror.

They stop to ask a woman directions to the workhouse. Wrapped in a threadbare shawl, huddled in a doorway, she raises her sunken eyes to them and points wordlessly towards the adjacent street. Following her outstretched finger, they head onto Charles Street and immediately see the workhouse building casting its long shadow over all who linger nearby. Beneath the archway, on which the words *Avoid Idleness and Intemperance* are inscribed, loiter two elderly vagrants and a family with three children wearing little more than rags.

'What now?' says Duncan. 'We can hardly ring the bell, can we?'

'Swap coats with me,' says Joseph.

'Why?'

'I have an idea. I am going to trade places with one of those tramps.'

'What? And go in there?'

'It's the only way. Give me your coat and hat to trade – yours is warmer than mine so can be sold.'

Duncan knows it's a benevolent act as well as purposeful, but he is reluctant to part with his smart coat. 'And what shall I wear?' He is embarrassed at how petulant he sounds.

'Take mine,' says Joseph.

The two men fumble with buttons and wallets and belongings as they set about swapping coats and hats. Duncan is about to pass Joseph his own when he remembers his notebook. 'Wait, I almost forgot,' he says, quickly retrieving it from the breast pocket.

He watches as Joseph crosses the road and speaks to one of the men at the gate. They disappear off down a nearby lane, and when they reappear, the tramp is now wearing Duncan's immaculate hat and coat and a beaming smile under the layers of dirt on his face. Joseph is now clad in the tramp's dowdy coat and hat. The tramp gives Joseph a wave and trots off down the street in the other direction.

Joseph returns to Duncan, and as soon as he is close, the stink of the garment reaches Duncan's nostrils.

'My coat,' moans Duncan, watching the tramp disappear. 'And now, dear God, Joseph, you smell like the Thames.'

'Your precious coat will earn that man enough money to avoid the workhouse for a spell,' says Joseph. 'I just need to make sure my face and hands are as grubby as my clothes. Let us find a dustbin.'

They don't need to wander far, for two streets away there is a mound of domestic detritus that is being sorted and picked through by women and children. Some of the smaller children are scrabbling up an ash heap and then jumping off into a cesspool below with shouts of delight. Duncan finds he is no longer shocked at this; it reminds him of the street urchins in West Port.

Joseph scoops a handful of cinders and smears it over his face in a thick layer. 'Does it cover my lack of beard?' he says.

'Yes,' says Duncan, the crook of his arm over his face. 'But I don't like this. We shall both die of some disease if we breathe in any more of this noxious air. Let's abandon the whole idea.'

'It's just for one night,' says Joseph, turning to head back to the workhouse. 'The tramp who is now wearing your coat told me that's all they hope for. One night of basic shelter and food in the casual ward. But of course they must work for it. I'll be back out tomorrow, and I can tell you everything I've seen and heard.'

'It doesn't feel right, Joseph. You don't have to do this – certainly not for my sake. I should be going in there. Not you. And what shall I do while you're in there?'

'You going in there would not work, Duncan. They'd see through your New Town ways in a heartbeat,' says Joseph with a smile. His teeth gleam white against his dirt-smudged face. 'Go and find a boarding house in a more comfortable district. Or stay here. Observe everything for your report. The most humbling thing any man can do is view the world through someone else's eyes. But promise me you'll not run away back to Edinburgh. Not until I get out! At least you don't have to worry about fitting in now – you look like quite the part in my tatty coat.'

'Wait,' says Duncan, a hand on Joseph's arm. 'What am I to you that you would take this extraordinary risk for me? You barely know me. We don't have to do any of this. We can stop this game and leave.'

Joseph gives him a half-smile. 'Believe me when I say this is not for you, my friend. It's for the greater good. For those who lost someone at the hands of those murderers. Perhaps it's all been leading to this. I owe it, I mean *we* owe it to them. To see for ourselves if that woman is still here.' And then he crosses the road, determination in every stride.

Duncan watches him walk away. He is unnerved by this turn of events; at Joseph's resolve to get inside the workhouse.

'Well, for pity's sake, be careful!' he calls after him. 'I don't want you to die in there.'

'Och, if I do die, I'll come back to haunt you, Duncan Fletcher,' says Joseph over his shoulder, with a wink.

The street is busy with comings and goings, and no one so much as gives Duncan a second look as he waits, leaning against a warehouse wall as Joseph joins the queue of hopeful vagrants. Duncan feels unsure of what to do with himself. Quite suddenly, everything feels sinister. He does not like being alone in this strange city.

Joseph doesn't have to wait long. A bell above the entrance rings out a gloomy toll that heralds the opening of the front door, then a tall young man with dark hair opens the gate. He talks to each person in the queue, his face quite flat in expression. Duncan watches carefully. The ragged family are ushered in and then taken off in one direction, but when the first tramp and then Joseph follow on, they are ushered in a different direction. It is hard to get an unobstructed view, and before he can see any more, the gates swing shut and Joseph disappears. But just as Duncan is about to turn away, he notices an older woman at the door. She is dressed in a formal uniform with her hair scraped into a bun under a bonnet, but the hair is quite unmistakably red. For the first time, Duncan feels a raw, terrible fear for Joseph, and, worse still, like a child who has lost a parent, he feels utterly alone.

Chapter 47

Duncan turns up his coat collar. The rain is coming down in sheets now, and the bright thrill of the London morning has shifted into something more ominous. He is grateful for Joseph's coat, not just for its warmth but for the invisibility it affords him to mingle amongst the working men of Whitechapel. He is pretending to be something other than himself, and he finds a sort of liberation in this disguise, this secret identity. He decides against changing his accent; he doubts he could carry it off convincingly, but he may just tone down his turn of phrase. There is something else that this garment stirs: knowing it is Joseph's. Duncan feels comfort wearing something of his – as though his confidence, his warmth, affability and intelligence are wrapped around him, like a blanket. He thrusts his hands into his pockets, and the thumb of his right-hand touches the cold, sharp metal of the needle Joseph used to mend his shoe. He feels for the neat bundle of thread and unearths a piece of paper. Duncan sees it is the map, scribbled hastily to show them the way to the workhouse. He thrusts it back into the pocket, and then as he continues to walk, his head down against the elements, something crosses his mind. The awl. The dagger-like tool used by Joseph to widen the holes for stitching his shoes is not there with the needle and thread. He stops abruptly and pats down the coat pockets inside and out, but there is no sign of it. Where could it possibly be? Why would he take it with him into the workhouse?

In need of a moment to think, he heads inside a nearby inn. The Bell and Anchor is nothing like the Whistling Oyster; it is devoid of any bohemian charm or conviviality whatsoever and has an atmosphere akin to a railway station's waiting room. Drinks are served from a hatch, and its patrons are hard-living, heavy drinkers who pay no heed to him. With a glass of ale in his hand, Duncan takes a seat close to the door. He takes off his hat and rubs his face, and when he looks at his hands, they are disgusting – the soot and grime of the city has settled like a polluted scum on his skin. Without Joseph at his side, cajoling and teasing him about his middle-class ignorance and naivety, he feels overwhelmed. He sips his drink, hoping it will soothe his tumult.

One thing is clear to him: if Joseph has taken the awl with him into the workhouse, without the needle and thread, he is not planning on mending shoes. With its sharp point, it could easily be used as a weapon. Perhaps he wants it close to him for self-defence; that would make sense. But Duncan cannot get it out of his head that there is something more dangerous at play.

Conversations from the past twenty-four hours tumble in his mind. He cannot quite fathom Joseph's determination to come with him on the quest to find Lucky Hare, let alone to take it upon himself to adopt a disguise with the intention of getting into the workhouse. His mood this morning was different, too; he was quiet, focused; and his eyes betrayed a hunger. Like a hunter getting close to a kill. And for what? For Duncan to write a report that might allude to the whereabouts of Lucky Hare? If they even have located her.

Duncan has known Joseph for such a short spell, it is hard to make a measured assessment of him. But it was he who had pushed for this foray to London, he who had been so keen to get to the workhouse this morning. Duncan dwells on what he said before he left him, something about owing it to those who lost someone, that perhaps it had all been leading to this. Where has this sense of destiny come from?

And there is something else nagging at him, like a

midge buzzing in his ear, something Joseph had said when he was talking about the tragic suicide of his father. Those words: 'at least he was buried, unlike some unlucky souls'. What, he wonders, did he mean? Which unlucky souls? Everyone, even those who had taken their own lives, would be buried in some way. And then it dawns on him.

Cadavers.

Those who had been dissected and picked over by the anatomists, exhumed by the resurrectionists or murdered by Burke and Hare: they had not received a burial. For the first time, he allows his mind to contemplate their fate. He had heard gruesome tales from his friend, Charlie, who had spoken casually, brazenly, of the work he was doing. To him, the corpses he worked on were anonymous objects, something useful to help him achieve his ambition of being a surgeon. Duncan had never heard him speak of them with respect or acknowledge that they were people who had lived real lives. They were just criminals, vagrants or unclaimed paupers. Once, Charlie had told him that he had held the hearts of two men in his hands, weighing them, and that he had felt like God. Duncan shudders at the memory.

Over the following weeks, after immersion in spirits, the bodies were carved, sliced, dismembered, their tissue poked and scraped, their innards slithering onto the floor. Decimation. Their organs were ripped out of their bodies by bloody hands like pieces of meat. And then, any 'unusual specimens' would be stored in jars and housed in a museum to be peered at as ghoulish curiosities. As far as he knew, procedures had changed since the dark days of Burke and Hare, and now cadavers were buried in a cemetery. But back then it was a different story: unregulated, callous. Any fragments of bones or tissue were scooped up, jumbled together with other remains and dumped – with no burial in consecrated ground or memorial service, and utterly no respect for the human beings they once were. Duncan imagines this happening to one of his family members and feels sick.

He pulls his mind back to Joseph. Was it possible that Joseph Campbell had some association with all this? With one of Burke and Hare's victims?

He pulls out his notebook and opens it at the first page and traces a finger down the scribbled names of the victims, but it is the very last one that makes him catch his breath: *Margaret or Madgy Docherty, also known as Campbell.*

Was Joseph a relative of Margaret Docherty, the final victim of Burke and Hare? Duncan recalls the story of the Irishwoman whom William Burke had lured to her death, who had come to Edinburgh to search for her son.

Joseph had mentioned that his father had come over from Ireland and that he had killed himself after suffering profound despair. Could it perhaps have been because of the murder and dissection of his mother? Unresolved grief and no grave to visit would have fuelled his anguish.

With a sense of dread, Duncan drains his glass. He is now convinced that Joseph is not here for an adventure, or a passing interest in some inconsequential newspaper report, or for the 'greater good' as he had put it. This has been the plan all along, and Joseph Campbell is here for one reason alone: retribution.

Chapter 48

A fleck of blood glistens crimson upon the pale cheek of Mary Feist, matron of the Whitechapel and Spitalfields Union Workhouse. She glances at her reflection in the mirror she keeps in her spartan room. And as she removes her bonnet to adjust the position of her faded red wig, she thinks back over the morning's events, trying to remember whose blood it is. There had been an altercation with an old man who had soiled his bed, not for the first time. Despite his pleading, her anger had raged so fast and so ferociously that she had dragged him by one puny arm down to the yard, made him strip off his mucky bedshirt and then beaten him mercilessly with her cane. He had done the same thing the week before, for which she had reduced his bread provision, but clearly that hadn't been enough. His shrieks with each strike suggested he had finally learned his lesson, and no blood had been spilled.

She casts her mind back again. Yes, it was Alice Maides. The hiding she had received had split her head open, from the strap buckle this time – a most effective tool for instilling discipline, particularly with insolent youths. The girl had stolen a piece of bread belonging to another child, and such acts of subordination needed swift action. The blood on her cheek was from that girl. Mary feels gratified with herself as she replaces her bonnet.

The vermin here live much too well and do much too little, Mary thinks, as she reaches for the bottle of gin in the cupboard. She pours herself a generous measure, gulps it in one, and before the burn has eased in her throat, pours herself another. Paupers are useless creatures, lazy wicked animals that need to be herded and controlled. Some individuals are so contemptible she cannot bear to look upon their matted hair, dirty faces and broken souls.

She does not pity them; she despises them. According to Mary, now a widow, running the workhouse with her son, Jack, discipline is the only way to exert control in this institution. And, in turn, control means they can operate their own enterprises without detection. Jack patrols the wards and the corridors carrying the switch that belonged to his dead stepfather, swiping the ears of anyone who needs reminding of their place. A hefty bunch of door keys is also an excellent tool for this purpose. The late Alfred, Mary's husband and master of the workhouse, had excelled in instilling discipline but had taken too many liberties with the younger females, and Mary did not take kindly to her husband's indiscretions. He had also become too free with his fists, like so many of the others before him, particularly when intoxicated. And so she had done what she always did when someone in her life became troublesome: she had helped him on his way. She had waited until he was senseless with drink and then, aided by Jack – who had nothing but hatred for Alfred, having suffered many beatings at his hands as a boy – they had stopped his breath. Burked him. She smiles at the memories.

Alfred's death was a great relief to all. Not a single soul had mourned, such was the antipathy towards him. There had been no surprise at his passing. Nor any interest in how he had passed. And as her opinion had always been that a good body should never be wasted, Mary and Jack had struck a deal with the undertaker. They switched his body with the dissected remains of a pauper returned from the anatomists, sealed the coffin and sold Alfred's fresh corpse to the anatomy school for a handsome payment. All she had to do was dab her dry eyes as the coffin with the unknown remains was lowered into the ground. It was a scheme her husband had conceived two years ago, and it had supplemented their incomes nicely. Many people died in the workhouse, mostly from natural causes, and if they lay unclaimed in the deadhouse for two days, they could then sell them. And if some snivelling relative materialised, they were ready to make the switch.

Mary's thoughts are interrupted by a knock at the door. It opens, and, in the reflection, she fleetingly sees the face of William Hare.

'Did you see him? The man in the casual ward,' says Jack. 'Just arrived.'

Her son's resemblance to his father is uncanny, and she has caught her breath many times thinking William has finally found her. Jack is a foot taller than her now, with the same dark hair and insufferable swagger as his father, but it is his eyes that remind her most of William. She last saw William Hare in a courtroom – and where he is now, she neither knows nor cares. She suspects his self-pity will have been his undoing.

'What of it? I've not had time to cast an eye over the newcomers yet.'

'You should see this one. Young, fit and healthy, with good teeth we can sell. He's just what those doctors were asking for. They want their cadavers in one piece.'

'I dare say they do. And keep your voice down.'

They often had requests, but the days of Robert Knox were long gone. Now there were rules and regulations about shifting the dead, and there were inspectors sniffing around. They couldn't simply murder to order. But where there is money there are ways and means.

Although they are surrounded by the sick and feeble-bodied wasting good air, ending life isn't always easy in the workhouse. There are over five hundred paupers, never mind the staff – far too many eyes and ears everywhere. Burking, while clean, isn't without its risks. Spirits induce the sleep required, but they can't be administered to workhouse inmates. However, opiates can be used, and once stupefied, their victims can be transported away under cover of darkness to have their life terminated somewhere they won't be disturbed.

If intact bodies are being monitored by the inspectors, they resort to dismemberment, so that a single body can be distributed amongst several anatomy schools. This business works well, and Jack has become adept at butchering. Siphoning off vagrants, casual visitors to the workhouse, is another effective scheme, for they are already ghosts; they are unseen, they leave no trail and their disappearance goes unnoticed.

'A healthy young body is good news,' says Mary, still looking in the mirror. She decides to leave the splash of blood on her face and turns to face Jack. 'No names, no medical record, nothing written down. And keep him away from the other casuals,' she adds.

'Already done. I put him in the itch room. Alone,' confirms Jack. 'No one else in here has seen him.'

'Give him some bread, so he trusts the food. And a pile of oakham to pick until we're ready. We can lace the broth later. Don't let him leave – there's no need for him to bathe. Keep the room locked and the key about you. Tell no one he is in there.'

Jack nods.

She reaches into a cupboard and takes out a bottle of laudanum, which she conceals in the pocket of her skirt. 'We'll deal with him tonight. Get word to Moth to meet us in the usual place.'

Chapter 49

Duncan is beside himself. He cannot sit still for worry about Joseph. He cannot go to the police, for where on earth would he begin? It is all hypotheses at this point. If he were to reveal his suspicions that Joseph is either in danger or about to threaten the workhouse matron with a cobbling tool, it will only incriminate his companion. And he doesn't really know if Joseph is planning some act of revenge. Perhaps his imagination has got the better of him. After all, he is tired and in a strange place, and such things can play tricks upon the mind.

He resigns himself to waiting. And watching. He positions himself opposite the workhouse gates, crouched in the doorway of a dilapidated shell of a building, like a tramp, staring at the building facing him as though the walls might peel back like skin to reveal the rooms and the workings. Occasionally, he sees a fleeting shadow or movement at the windows, but apart from occasional bells ringing – he assumes to signal beginnings or endings of mealtimes or rest – there is nothing to indicate what is happening beyond the brick façade.

The street is busy with people and traffic, but no one pays attention to another pauper on the streets of Whitechapel. There is a steely greyness to the afternoon with a relentless mist of fine rain, and when the chill enters his bones, making him stiff, he stands and paces up and down, his hands thrust deep in his pockets, never taking his eye off the workhouse for too long in case he should miss something, some sign that Joseph needs him. He considers banging on the door and fabricating some bizarre story to ensure the immediate removal of Joseph, but he knows this would raise too much curiosity, and he has no idea of where that might lead. Is waiting cowardly? he asks himself, burying his chin into his collar. What would Joseph want him to do? That is easy. Joseph would want to be left well alone. The man needs no fussing or mothering. Duncan wonders how it all came to this – how his own vanity and ambition has put another life at risk in this whole sordid tale of death – and he swallows down his own guilt that he has been the creator of this wretched situation.

As evening falls, there is a shift of mood and tempo on Charles Street, Whitechapel. The industrial briskness, the shouts of hawkers, the horses and carts all give way to something darker. Perhaps it is due to the fog which has descended like a heavy blanket over everything, altering the light and distorting faces. Or perhaps it is the influence of gin and ale that transforms walking to staggering, talking to shouting and the mild-mannered to the feverish. Voices become exaggerated, emotions are heightened, and it seems that with too much gin, everything, no matter how petty, results in a drunken brawl. Wary of passersby, Duncan is curled up in the doorway, trying to remain focused on the workhouse and block out his fears. He wraps Joseph's coat tightly across his chest and rests his head on the wall. Sleep is the last thing he wants, but his body has other plans, and so he drifts in and out of consciousness, haunted by faces from the past twenty-four hours: the people on the train, the cab driver, the woman in the Whistling Oyster. But they all merge into a terrifying woman with red hair.

'Oi! You there.'

Duncan feels a sharp kick on his foot. He wakes with a jolt, and it takes him several moments to remember where he is. His neck is aching, his mouth parchment dry. He looks up. A man glares down at him.

In white trousers, a long dark tailcoat and top hat, the policeman looks plump and well fed, in stark contrast to the impoverished souls drifting around the streets nearby. 'Are you mad – shouting and wailing like that?' he barks.

Duncan realises he must have been dreaming.

'Get yourself to a dosshouse, lad,' says the man dismissively.

Duncan comes to his senses, and then panic floods through him as he does not know how long he has been asleep. But it is not yet dark, so it must still be early evening. 'What time is it?' he mumbles.

'It doesn't matter what time it is. You can't sleep here, even if you are waiting for the workhouse in the morning,' says the policeman. 'Flower and Dean Street is your best bet.' And he raises a gloved finger as though a path might open up through the slums like the parting of the Red Sea.

'I'm waiting for someone,' says Duncan, standing up.

'Oh, are you indeed?' he says. 'And what's her name, then?'

'No, no,' Duncan protests. 'I think you've misunderstood me. My friend, he's meeting me here, and I need to wait for him.'

The policeman stares at him curiously. 'Come along now,' he says, waving a hand to move him along.

'No, I cannot leave,' cries Duncan. 'And you cannot stop me from standing here.'

'Are you resisting me?' barks the policeman, his patience frayed.

At that moment, the workhouse gates open. They both turn to look, and through the fog Duncan sees a horse and cart heading out onto the street. He steps away from the policeman, and as the cart passes by, he catches sight of the driver and passenger. A grim-faced redhead holds the reins, and the young man who had spoken to the paupers at the workhouse gate sits beside her. There is a load on the back, covered with a jute sack, and although he cannot see what it is they are transporting, Duncan feels sick with foreboding.

He tears off down the street in pursuit of the cart as the policeman shouts something after him. But Duncan doesn't listen, doesn't care, for something feels very wrong, and he must see where they are headed.

Chapter 50

Duncan is running, further and faster than he has since he was a boy. Every muscle, every fibre of his body burns, but he will not stop. He cannot let them out of his sight. His eyes remain locked on the cart as it slips in and out of the murk like a spectre; on it trundles, the load on the back bouncing and shifting. Duncan pounds onwards, his boots skidding on the wet cobbles, as the cart enters the docks. Vast warehouses loom over row upon row of ships bobbing and jostling in the grey water. As the cart slows, he, too, slackens his pace, grateful to catch his breath and take in his surroundings. He sees, with a mounting alarm, that he has entered a pestilent underworld – a twisting labyrinth crammed with a multitude of brawling sailors and half-naked women, dock workers and merchants. He has witnessed the grinding poverty elsewhere in London, but here it oozes from the very pores of the place. Hunched figures lurk in every passage and doorway with hollow cheeks and that familiar despondent expression. The stench emanating from the Thames is utterly abhorrent; it catches the back of his throat and makes his eyes water, and Duncan wonders if he has entered Hell itself.

Wedged between the raucous taverns, ropemakers and chandlers sits an alehouse called the Prospect of Whitby, and it is here that he sees the cart has stopped. The woman talks urgently to a scrawny lad who takes hold of the horse's reins while they haul an enormous laundry basket from the back of the cart and then set off, arguing every step of the way.

It is now, as Duncan follows, with heavy trepidation, that he realises he has absolutely no plan. Perhaps there is merely laundry in that basket, and this is all a case of misunderstanding. As they walk deeper into the maze of warehouses, he is careful to hang back: too close, and he risks being seen. But to take his eye off them would be to lose them completely, such is the chaos surrounding them. Soon, they stop at a scruffy red door, the man fumbles with a key, the door opens, and they disappear inside.

Duncan moves to the other side of the street, to the doorway of a candlemaker.

'What is your business?' says a gruff male voice

behind him. 'I'm closing up for the night.'

'That door over there,' blurts Duncan, pointing, 'the people going in there ... I mean ... do you know who they might be?'

The man follows his line of vision to the ramshackle building with the red door. 'I think it unwise to ask questions round here,' he says. 'But I do often see a man and a woman enter that building. Another man comes, too, sometimes, in a black coat.'

'Do they usually bring a laundry basket?'

'Often,' the man says, closing the shop door and locking it.

Duncan thinks about Lucky Hare. And what he knows about her. Could it be something quite ordinary?

'I think they do something with dead animals,' says the man, about to walk away. 'Preparing them for some usage – maybe medicines?'

'Why would you say that?'

'The blood. The blood on the big fella's clothes.' He laughs as if this were the most normal thing in the world. 'Good night to you, young man.'

Duncan doesn't pause, doesn't think, doesn't plan. He strides across the street and pushes open the red door. Inside is a narrow staircase, which he climbs slowly, listening intently as he approaches the landing.

'He'll be here soon. Let's wait until then,' the woman says.

'Moth,' mutters the man. 'Always bloody late, he is.'

Duncan takes a step into a cramped room littered with rubbish and tools. The smell is powerful. Is it from the river? He isn't sure. But he senses he has stumbled into a house of perdition. There is a wide arched loading door, and outside on a platform, gazing out over the Thames, two figures stand silhouetted against the sunset. Duncan looks around for the laundry basket, but there is no need: its contents have already been deposited.

Joseph lies in the centre of the room.

Duncan moves quickly and silently over to him and kneels down. He takes his hand and squeezes it, and looks for signs of life in the ashen face.

'Joseph, Joseph,' he whispers urgently. He shakes his shoulders, but he doesn't wake up. Desperate, he grabs the coat lapels and begins to heave, as though this might spark him into life. But Joseph's body is a dead weight and slithers back to the floor.

'For God's sake, man, wake up!' He shouts and slaps his face, no longer caring about keeping quiet.

'Well, then,' says a woman's voice. 'Who do we have here?'

Two shadows blot out what little light of the day there is left.

Duncan begins to sob. 'What have you done to him? Burked him, have you? Like all the others, Lucky? Is that all you do in this dissolute life of yours?'

'Who the hell are you?' she replies. 'I've not been called that name in over twenty years.'

Jack doesn't wait for an answer. He hurls himself at Duncan, and with a strength that is both startling and terrifying he grabs his arms and yanks them back, locking them hard. Duncan feels himself being pulled upwards, away from Joseph's body.

Lucky approaches and puts her face close to Duncan's. He sees her clearly for the first time. She has removed her bonnet, and the red wig that clings to her scalp is threadbare. Her face is hard, with thin, shrivelled lips. It is difficult to imagine her as a young woman. She looks as though she has been a malevolent crone all her life.

'Is that Mary Paterson's hair?' he shouts. 'What madness is this that you wear the hair of a woman murdered?'

She smiles. 'You know all about me, do you? How charming.' Her dark eyes widen. 'I wear it as a reminder,' she says quietly. 'I want to remember how she died.'

Duncan can feel her breath hot on his cheek.

She steps back and regards him. 'Tell me, how do *you* know all this? How do *you* know who I am, boy?'

Jack snaps his arms together tighter. The pain is excruciating. Duncan cries out in pain.

'Tell her, or I'll break your arms,' bellows Jack.

'No, no,' Lucky barks at her son. 'No marks, no bruising.'

'Oh, of course!' Duncan laughs hysterically. 'My body must be pristine for the anatomists. Isn't that right? I wanted to find you, Lucky Hare, to find out where you were, if you'd buried that part of your life. But, no, I see you haven't changed.'

'Why would you do such a thing, I wonder?' She cocks her head. Then she reaches out and strokes his face, her fingernails sharp on his skin. He shudders at her touch.

'Give me one of his hands,' she says to Jack, who dutifully releases an arm. Lucky takes Duncan's hand in her own and looks closely at his palm, glancing up at him from time to time. She lifts the fingertips to the light and rubs them with her thumb.

'You're a nice boy, aren't you? With nice skin under that grime. And soft hands. Scottish, too, I wager. A long way from home. You're from a good family. With money.' She looks up and her eyes narrow. She is working it out. 'Ink stains on your fingers. A writer, I'd say. From a newspaper? Or maybe you want to write a book about me.'

She watches his reaction and smiles.

'You in these shabby clothes to fit in? Is that what you think I am? A dirty pauper? And you, just trying to make your way in the world, searching for the truth, eh? But your world is very different to mine, nice boy.' Her face hardens once more. 'And we've all got to find a way to survive. And what about this one?' She throws a look at Joseph. 'Why would you associate with a tramp like him? That *is* curious.'

'Never mind all this gabbing,' Jack interjects. 'How will we do him?'

'He's weak. We can Burke him,' she sneers. 'Look at him. No fight in this one. And worth a pretty penny, too, a fit young lad like him.'

Before Duncan knows what is happening, they have thrust him violently to the floor and Jack is on top of him, his solid weight crushing his ribs. Duncan kicks and struggles with every ounce of strength he can muster, but Jack is too strong, too heavy, and then he sees Lucky bending down.

'Night, night, pretty boy, give my regards to Mary Paterson, won't you?' She pinches his nostrils shut. Her grip is so hard, the pain radiates through his skull. Jack pushes his jaw upwards, clamping his mouth closed with his huge hand. Duncan jerks and writhes, the horror of his impending death giving him a wild strength. But it is no good. The room is spinning and fading, and he can feel a lightness in his head. A sensation washes over him that it will be over soon.

But there is an almighty bellow and a scream and then the crushing weight of Jack slides away from him.

Duncan is swallowing air once more, gulping and gasping. He can see Jack rolling on the floor, blood pouring from his neck, the handle of the awl, Joseph's cobbling tool, firmly embedded there. Above him, Joseph stands, panting and stooped, his eyes barely open.

Choking in agony, Jack claws at the awl handle and yanks it out of his neck. It rolls across the floor, and more blood gushes and spreads through his shirt. Jack tries to touch the wound and then gasps in anguish at the sight of his own blood.

Joseph staggers over to Duncan and pulls him up, but there is no time for words as Lucky is lunging towards Joseph, the bloody awl in her hand. Duncan lurches forward and grabs her before she reaches Joseph, wrestling her to the ground. In the struggle, Duncan pulls her hair, and it falls away in his hand, a repulsive mop of matted red. He drops it to the floor. Looking back at Lucky, he sees her transformed: her white hair shaved to the scalp, her head riddled with scabs and open sores. Scarlet with fury, Lucky spits and curses like a wild beast, hands grabbing, nails scratching and legs kicking until Joseph throws himself on top of her, trapping her arms. Duncan clamps his hands over her face, blocking her mouth and her nose, yet still she thrashes, eyes bulging with fury. They press on her skinny body with all their weight and strength until finally she relents. She stops fighting. When her body lies limp, the two men fall back exhausted.

Lucky Hare is dead.

Behind them, Jack staggers to his feet, still clutching the gash in his neck. He sees his dead mother, her eyes wide open, her face still contorted, and then, stupefied, he lurches out of the room and thunders down the stairs, his footsteps fading as he runs away into the London night.

'It's over,' says Joseph, his eyes closed.

They sit in silence for a while, allowing their breathing to return to normal. Duncan begins to shake, the cold and the aftershock overcoming him.

'I thought you were dead,' says Duncan. Tears are flowing down his face. He swipes them away with his sleeve.

'Me, too,' says Joseph.

'What happened to you in there?'

'They put something in my food. I only realised after I'd eaten some of it. Laudanum no doubt. It made me drowsy, and the next thing I knew, I was here and you were being attacked.'

'The awl – what were you going to do with it? It was missing from your pocket.'

'I thought I'd take it, just in case. Lucky I hid it in my sock. They made me empty my pockets at the door.'

'Lucky . . .' murmurs Duncan. He is about to ask if

his intuition is correct, that Joseph has some connection to Madgy Docherty, when they hear footsteps on the stairs. They look at each other in consternation.

'What now?' groans Duncan.

'I've no fight left in me,' sighs Joseph.

A man of huge bulk with an ankle-length black coat and battered top hat enters the warehouse. A jute sack is slung over one shoulder. He stoops a little under the timber ceiling beams and regards the scene in front of him.

'Well, now,' he says, pushing his hat back and scratching his chin. 'This is quite a to-do, is it not, gentlemen?'

'Who are you?' says Duncan. He feels himself shrinking at this fresh terror; this man has mischief in his beady eyes and wolfish grin.

The man strokes his ill-kempt beard. 'Meet me at nine o'clock sharp, Moth,' he says in a mimicking female voice. 'We'll have a nice fresh one for you. Just like the doctors asked for. All taken care of.' He sighs. 'You can't trust anyone these days, can you, gents? No one is true to their word any more.'

He notices Lucky and eyes her curiously. 'Forgive me for asking, but that is her, is it not?' He is evidently struck that she is dead. 'I can't be sure without that red mop she wears.' Duncan nods, and Moth smiles. 'Tell me, if you will, is her boy about?' Moth glances around as if Jack might be hiding somewhere.

Joseph shakes his head.

'Well, that is unexpected, but not entirely problematic,' growls Moth. He looks once more at Lucky Hare, and his expression brightens. 'You good gentlemen wouldn't mind if I were to dispose of her, would you? There's no use wasting a good body, is there? Unless, of course, you want to give her a proper burial, that is?' They stare at him. 'No, I thought not. Dumping her in the Thames would be too good for the likes of her! Are we right, gents?'

Without waiting for an answer, he bends down and hauls her up to a sitting position as though she weighed a few ounces. As she slumps forward, a grotesque marionette, he places the sack over her head, tugs it down and then tips her backwards and stuffs her in. He ties the ends with a piece of string pulled out of his pocket, then hoists the sack over his shoulder. He has done this before, thinks Duncan.

'You have a good evening now,' says Moth with a broad smile. He taps his hat and slips out of the room and down the stairs, whistling as he goes.

Chapter 51

Duncan and Joseph walk, dazed, through the docks, pushing past the unruly sailors and fallen women, then out and towards the city once more. Joseph leans on Duncan, still feeling the effects of the opiate. A heavy silence lies between them. In the moonlight, they see the outline of the great White Tower and then the silhouette of St Paul's spire.

'Did we mean to?' whispers Duncan. 'Kill her?'

'There was no other way,' says Joseph finally.

'Should we, do we need to, tell anyone?'

'You mean the police? To what end? I ask this sincerely, Duncan.'

The law didn't deal with Lucky Hare the first time. Worse than that, she was allowed to walk free. Look what she went on to become. How many more did she harm? There's nothing more to be said. I can live with my actions. It wasn't the first time they'd taken some poor soul there to be murdered. I believe justice has been served.'

'But is it justice, or is it revenge?'

Joseph stops. In the dim light he stares hard at Duncan. 'I have been carrying the weight of my father's grief and torment for my entire life. For–'

'For your grandmother?'

'Aye. So you know the truth?'

They start walking again.

'Madgy Docherty, also known as Campbell,' says Duncan.

'My father was broken by her murder – and her dissection. Perhaps more the latter,' says Joseph, 'if that's possible. It was what they did to criminals in days gone by, he used to tell me. Disembowelment. That was their punishment. He saw what happened to his mother as no different to that: punished for being poor. That the poor are considered as worthless as criminals, their bodies to be traded, broken, used and discarded. How could their mutilated bodies rise up again on the Day of Judgment? There had been no dignity, no respect, in the disposal of her remains. Nowhere for my father to go and reflect, no grave to weep beside. The emptiness of it all went against everything he believed in. He even made tiny wooden coffins with figurines to represent each person murdered by the Burkes and Hares in the hope that it would bring an ending to it all, that, somehow, their souls could finally rest.' He laughs bitterly.

Duncan looks at him with a dawning realisation of what he is describing.

'He had thought about finding a quiet corner in a graveyard so that they were laid to rest in consecrated ground, but he was too scared of being seen or, worse, assumed to be a resurrectionist. In the end, we buried them on Arthur's Seat one day in the pouring rain where we thought they wouldn't be disturbed. We hoped it would bring peace to them – and ultimately to him – but then they, too, were dug up a few years later by some lads and ended up being traded. Sold to that antiques shop to be gawped at as curiosities.'

Now, it truly makes sense to Duncan. 'I know the very ones, Joseph,' he says softly. And then remembers, horrified, that only days ago he had turned one over in his hands, delighting in its perfection, its childlike simplicity, unaware of its tragic history. He remembers, too, as though it were in another life, scribbling the notes for Mr Frazer's antiques sale.

'He just never forgave himself – for coming to Edinburgh from Ireland,' Joseph went on. 'She followed him there, this gentle woman who trusted strangers. That only one of them hanged and the rest walked free, the whole sordid business, haunted him until he could bear it no longer.'

Eventually, they find a boarding house that will take two dishevelled men at this hour. They must share a room with many others on straw beds on the floor, side by side, but they care not.

'What about Jack?' whispers Duncan as they lie facing each other in the dark.

'What about him? He's unlikely to survive that injury.'

'But what if he does? Then what?'

'London is crammed full of people, filled to the point of suffocation. There are countless streets where the police dare not venture. It should be easy to disappear. He is gone. Put him from your mind.'

'Perhaps he'll change his ways,' says Duncan.

'Have you learned nothing, Duncan? If anything, he'll be worse than his cursed mother. I'm just sorry he escaped,' he adds drowsily.

Duncan shudders at the memory. Lucky Hare, violent and sadistic until the very end, and Moth, that monstrous figure like the Grim Reaper himself, her body flung over his shoulder, vanishing into the night. 'Let this be over now,' he whispers, a prayer in the dark. 'I am ready to return to Edinburgh.' He can feel tears spilling from his eyes. 'Away from all this horror. Do you not agree, Joseph?'

But Joseph doesn't reply, for he has escaped his torment and fallen into a deep sleep. And there they lie, wordless, amidst the nocturnal sounds of a restless city.

Epilogue

Duncan feels the first warmth of spring sunshine on his face as he walks from the New Town to the Old, towards the Cowgate once more, a box tucked under his arm. For the first time since he returned from London several weeks ago, he feels a lightness in his step.

'Good morning, Joseph,' he says, opening the door into the tiny shop.

Joseph looks up from his work and gives Duncan a beaming smile. 'And a very good morning to you, too, Mr Fletcher. How may I help you? Do those shoes need attention?'

'No, they do not, Mr Campbell. That's not the purpose of my visit. I wonder if you might take some air with me?' he says cheerfully. 'Leave the shop for a stroll up to the Meadows? It's such a fine day.'

Joseph needs no persuasion. After locking the shop, they head up High School Wynd and along Infirmary Street with the great hospital beside them, then past the medical students and the university buildings, past the gloomy façade of the Edinburgh Poorhouse and out of the city centre towards the Meadows where the cherry trees bear a soft pink blossom. There, they take a seat overlooking the green fields. The air is sweet and healthy, and perched high above them, a blackbird sings its song.

'What a perfect day,' says Joseph, gazing up at the expanse of clear blue sky. 'Makes you glad to be alive, does it not?'

'Indeed, it does,' says Duncan.

'Have you written your report yet?'

Duncan smiles a little. 'No, not yet.'

'I'm teasing, of course,' says Joseph. 'I'm not sure it's something you would want to write any more. Come to think of it, would anyone in their right mind want to read it?' He says this with a twinkle in his eye.

'I will put words on paper at some point,' says Duncan. 'My aunt and uncle are keen to read the outcome of my adventures. But I'm not ready yet. Perhaps I need a little time. And it certainly won't be the piece I had hoped it would be when I started all this; that's just not possible. I cannot report the truth about Mrs Burke and Mrs Hare even if I wanted to. I was utterly naive.

Perhaps, instead, it will become a work of fiction, or maybe I should turn my attention to highlighting the plight of the poor. Though only for a brief spell, I have walked in your shoes, as you say, and there is much to be said.'

'Indeed.' Joseph nods. 'That is another truth that needs to be told. I think you're the very man for it.'

'However, to the here and now – I wanted to show you this . . .' Duncan reaches into his pocket and pulls out a newspaper cutting. 'I stumbled across it in *The London Times*.'

Joseph takes it and peers at the tiny print. '*A Most Curious Disappearance: Mayhem in Whitechapel!*' He reads the title, holding the paper close to his face. '*The Whitechapel and Spitalfields Workhouse has been thrown into chaos at the disappearance of its Master, Jack Feist, and his mother, the Matron, Mary Feist, who vanished some weeks ago. The guardians are now advertising for immediate replacements. Several witnesses including the Workhouse Clerk have come forward to report that the Feists had been involved in the dreadful crime of body trafficking for the anatomists, preying on tramps and vagrants. Violent and brutal mistreatment of inmates has also been cited against the Feists along with theft and embezzlement of workhouse funds. There have been unverified sightings of Jack Feist in the Whitechapel and Spitalfields area, but the whereabouts of his mother remain a mystery. It is thought she may have fled to France or Ireland.*'

Joseph shakes his head. 'I owe you my life, Duncan. What was I thinking walking into that workhouse? And now? It all feels as though it was something that happened to someone else, doesn't it? Like a terrible hallucination.'

Duncan nods. Two young lads are running and jumping on the grass, carefree and happy in the sunshine, as a woman, presumably their nanny, watches on. They laugh uproariously as one tries to catch the other, then they tumble onto the ground, rolling like puppies. The two men watch in silence, smiling at the innocence of childish play.

'It's as though there are many different worlds running in parallel at any given time,' says Duncan, remembering the oppressive London streets. 'Each oblivious of the other.'

'Thankfully, we are here,' says Joseph, 'in this moment.'

Duncan wants to ask him if he thinks that justice has now, finally, been served. If he felt relief that his quest for vengeance had succeeded. But he decides against it and continues to watch the boys playing.

'And now,' says Duncan, passing Joseph the box, 'a gift.'

The corners of Joseph's mouth curl into a smile and he looks quizzically at Duncan. 'I'm not sure I've ever been given a present.' He takes the box onto his lap as

Duncan watches his face closely.

Joseph lifts the lid and peers inside. Duncan hears a tiny, barely audible gasp as Joseph recognises the contents. He takes a moment before reaching in to lift out a tiny wooden coffin.

'Duncan . . . I . . .'

'The sale was yesterday. I couldn't let someone else get them, could I?'

Joseph turns to him, and Duncan realises that he is consumed with emotion. 'I thought I should never see them again,' he says softly. He lifts the tiny lid from one of the coffins and gazes at the dainty little body inside, dressed in scraps of fabric.

'They have so much meaning for me, too, now,' says Duncan. 'After everything that happened.'

'This is the one I helped my father to make,' says Joseph, tracing a finger over the face as if to stroke her staring eyes closed. 'It's my grandmother. I never knew her in life, but I feel a closeness to her in death. My father spoke so fondly of her, said I had her eyes and her joyous spirit.'

'I wondered if you might like to lay them to rest?' says Duncan. 'We could do it together. Somewhere they won't be found this time.'

Joseph wipes his wet cheeks with the back of his hand. 'I appreciate this more than you'll ever know, Duncan, but I think I might find a different way to honour them and bring peace to their souls. Perhaps they *should* be seen? Perhaps they ought to go in a museum again, when the time is right, that is. Somewhere everyone and anyone can see them. Not hidden away. Not buried underground. That way they can be remembered. And somehow that feels more hopeful, doesn't it?'

'It does,' says Duncan. 'It really does.'

'As my father used to say, *Never forget*,' murmurs Joseph. '*Remember always.*'

Acknowledgements

The National Museum of Scotland in Chambers Street, Edinburgh, houses the tiny coffins found on Arthur's Seat in 1836. They are astonishing objects and well worth a visit. You can read an article about them on the museum's website ('The mystery of the miniature coffins') here: https://www.nms.ac.uk/explore-our-collections/stories/scottish-history-and-archaeology/mystery-of-the-miniature-coffins/.

This is a work of fiction, inspired by true events. I have had a fascination with Burke and Hare since childhood but had never given any thought to the roles of their wives. After listening to the brilliant BBC podcast 'An Eye for a Killing', I began to investigate. As so often with women in history, their stories are often harder to find. But the involvement of Helen McDougal and Margaret 'Lucky' Hare was a tale I knew I wanted to tell.

If you are interested in reading more about the life and crimes of Burke and Hare, and their wives, there are many fascinating books. I recommend *Burke & Hare* by Owen Dudley Edwards (Birlinn), *The Anatomy Murders* by Lisa Rosner (University of Pennsylvania Press) and *Burke and Hare: The Year of the Ghouls* by Brian Bailey (Mainstream Publishing).

I could not have written this book without the generous help, advice, support and insights from a great many people. Thank you to Eric Melvin for taking me on a fascinating Old Town walk of the sites associated with Burke and Hare. Thanks also to Colin MacDonald whose wonderful podcast *An Eye for a Killing* on BBC Sounds inspired me with the idea in the first place. Colin's insights into the roles of the two women were invaluable, and he was a great support as the project progressed. Thanks to Robbie MacRae at the National Trust for Scotland and to Robert Shepherd of the Thistle Street Bar for additional thoughts and points to consider. Huge thanks to the staff of the National Library of Scotland for their help with maps, particularly Veronica Bell. Thanks to Emma Harper, Curator at the Charles Dickens Museum, and Peter Higginbotham for his help with my queries on Victorian workhouses. Thanks to Malcolm MacCallum, Anatomical Museum

Curator at the University of Edinburgh, and Cat Irving, Human Remains Conservator of Surgeons' Hall Museum, for patiently answering my many obscure questions.

Thank you to Polygon editor Alison Rae for believing in this book from the outset, and thanks also to my wonderful agent, Lindsey Fraser.

Huge thanks to Kay and Karen for reading the book through its early stages and to Jackie for so patiently talking (and walking) through the book with me over the last few months.

As always, thank you once again to my husband and family for their unfailing support.